PRAISE FOR *THE WATER RAT OF WANCHAI*
WINNER OF THE ARTHUR ELLIS AWARD FOR BEST FIRST NOVEL

"Ian Hamilton's *The Water Rat of Wanchai* is a smart, action-packed thriller of the first order, and Ava Lee, a gay Asian-Canadian forensics accountant with a razor-sharp mind and highly developed martial arts skills, is a protagonist to be reckoned with. We were impressed by Hamilton's tight plotting; his well-rendered settings, from the glitz of Bangkok to the grit of Guyana; and his ability to portray a wide range of sharply individualized characters in clean but sophisticated prose." —Judges' Citation, Arthur Ellis Award for Best First Novel

"Ava Lee is tough, fearless, quirky, and resourceful, and she has more—well, you know—than a dozen male detectives I can think of … Hamilton has created a true original in Ava Lee." —Linwood Barclay, author of *No Time for Goodbye*

"If the other novels [in the series] are half as good as this debut by Ian Hamilton, then readers are going to celebrate. Hamilton has created a marvellous character in Ava Lee … This is a terrific story that's certain to be on the Arthur Ellis Best First Novel list." —*Globe and Mail*

"[Ava Lee's] lethal knowledge … torques up her sex appeal to the approximate level of a female lead in a Quentin Tarantino film." —*National Post*

"The heroine in *The Water Rat of Wanchai* by Ian Hamilton sounds too good to be true, but the heroics work better that way … formidable … The story breezes along with something close to total clarity … Ava is unbeatable at just about everything. Just wait for her to roll out her bak mei against the bad guys. She's perfect. She's fast." —*Toronto Star*

"Seldom does one get a thriller about white-collar crime, with an intelligent, independent lesbian and Asian protagonist. It's also rare to find a book with such interesting and exotic settings ... Readers will find great amusement in Ava's unconventional ways and will certainly enjoy accompanying her on her travels." —*Literaturkurier*

PRAISE FOR *THE DISCIPLE OF LAS VEGAS*
FINALIST, BARRY AWARD FOR BEST ORIGINAL TRADE PAPERBACK

"I started to read *The Disciple of Las Vegas* at around ten at night. And I did something I have only done with two other books (Cormac McCarthy's *The Road* and Douglas Coupland's *Player One*): I read the novel in one sitting. Ava Lee is too cool. She wonderfully straddles two worlds and two identities. She does some dastardly things and still remains our hero thanks to the charm Ian Hamilton has given her on the printed page. It would take a female George Clooney to portray her in a film. The action and plot move quickly and with power. Wow. A punch to the ear, indeed." —J. J. Lee, author of *The Measure of a Man*

"I loved *The Water Rat of Wanchai*, the first novel featuring Ava Lee. Now, Ava and Uncle make a return that's even better ... Simply irresistible." —Margaret Cannon, *Globe and Mail*

"This is slick, fast-moving escapism reminiscent of Ian Fleming, with more to come in what shapes up as a high-energy, high-concept series." —*Booklist*

"Fast paced ... Enough personal depth to lift this thriller above solely action-oriented fare." —*Publishers Weekly*

"Lee is a hugely original creation, and Hamilton packs his adventure with interesting facts and plenty of action." —*Irish Independent*

"Hamilton makes each page crackle with the kind of energy that could easily jump to the movie screen ... This riveting read will keep you up late at night." —*Penthouse*

"Hamilton gives his reader plenty to think about ... Entertaining."
—*Kitchener-Waterloo Record*

PRAISE FOR *THE WILD BEASTS OF WUHAN*
LAMBDA LITERARY AWARD FINALIST: LESBIAN MYSTERY

"Smart and savvy Ava Lee returns in this slick mystery set in the rarefied world of high art ... [A] great caper tale. Hamilton has great fun chasing villains and tossing clues about. *The Wild Beasts of Wuhan* is the best Ava Lee novel yet, and promises more and better to come."
—Margaret Cannon, *Globe and Mail*

"One of my favourite new mystery series, perfect escapism."
—*National Post*

"As a mystery lover, I'm devouring each book as it comes out ... What I love in the novels: The constant travel, the high-stakes negotiation, and Ava's willingness to go into battle against formidable opponents, using only her martial arts skills to defend herself ... If you want a great read and an education in high-level business dealings, Ian Hamilton is an author to watch." —*Toronto Star*

"Fast-paced and very entertaining." —*Montreal Gazette*

"Ava Lee is definitely a winner." —*Saskatoon Star Phoenix*

"*The Wild Beasts of Wuhan* is an entertaining dip into potentially fatal worlds of artistic skulduggery." —*Sudbury Star*

"Hamilton uses Ava's investigations as comprehensive and intriguing mechanisms for plot and character development." —*Quill & Quire*

"You haven't seen cold and calculating until you've double-crossed this number cruncher. Another strong entry from Arthur Ellis Award–winner Hamilton." —*Booklist*

"Fast-paced ... The action unfolds like a well-oiled action-flick."
—*Kitchener-Waterloo Record*

"A change of pace for our girl [Ava Lee] ... Suspenseful." —*Toronto Star*

"Hamilton packs tremendous potential in his heroine ... A refreshingly relevant series. This reader will happily pay House of Anansi for the fifth installment." —*Canadian Literature*

PRAISE FOR *THE SCOTTISH BANKER OF SURABAYA*

"Hamilton deepens Ava's character, and imbues her with greater mettle and emotional fire, to the extent that book five is his best, most memorable, to date." —*National Post*

"In today's crowded mystery market, it's no easy feat coming up with a protagonist who stands out from the pack. But Ian Hamilton has made a great job of it with his Ava Lee books. Young, stylish, Chinese Canadian, lesbian, and a brilliant forensic accountant, Ava is as complex a character as you could want ... [A] highly addictive series ... Hamilton knows how to keep the pages turning. He eases us into the seemingly tame world of white-collar crime, then raises the stakes, bringing the action to its peak with an intensity and violence that's stomach-churning. His Ava Lee is a winner and a welcome addition to the world of strong female avengers." —*NOW Magazine*

"Most of the series' success rests in Hamilton's tight plotting, attention to detail, and complex powerhouse of a heroine: strong but vulnerable, capable but not impervious ... With their tight plotting and crackerjack heroine, Hamilton's novels are the sort of crowd-pleasing, narrative-focused fiction we find all too rarely in this country."
—*Quill & Quire*

"Ava is such a cool character, intelligent, Chinese Canadian, unconventional, and original ... Irresistible." —*Owen Sound Sun Times*

PRAISE FOR *THE TWO SISTERS OF BORNEO*
NATIONAL BESTSELLER

"There are plenty of surprises waiting for Ava, and for the reader, all uncovered with great satisfaction." —*National Post*

"Ian Hamilton's great new Ava Lee mystery has the same wow factor as its five predecessors. The plot is complex and fast-paced, the writing tight, and its protagonist is one of the most interesting female avengers to come along in a while." —*NOW Magazine* (NNNN)

"The appeal of the Ava Lee series owes much to her brand name lifestyle; it stirs pleasantly giddy emotions to encounter such a devotedly elegant heroine. But, better still, the detailing of financial shenanigans is done in such clear language that even readers who have trouble balancing their bank books can appreciate the way conmen set out to fleece unsuspecting victims." —*Toronto Star*

"Hamilton has a unique gift for concocting sizzling thrillers."
—*Edmonton Journal*

"Hamilton has this formula down to an art, but he manages to avoid cliché and his ability to evoke a place keeps the series fresh."
—*Globe and Mail*

"From her introduction in *The Water Rat of Wanchai*, Ava Lee has stood as a stylish, street-smart leading lady whose resourcefulness and creativity have helped her to uncover criminal activity in everything from illegal online gambling rings to international art heists. In Hamilton's newest installment to the series, readers accompany Ava on great adventures and to interesting locales, roaming from Hong Kong to the Netherlands to Borneo. The pulse-pounding, fast-paced narrative is chocked full of divergent plot twists and intriguing personalities that make it a popular escapist summer read. The captivating female sleuth does not disappoint as she circles the globe on a quest to uncover an unusually intriguing investment fiasco involving fraud, deception and violence." —*ExpressMilwaukee.com*

"Ava may be the most chic figure in crime fiction." —*Hamilton Spectator*

"The series as a whole is as good as the modern thriller genre gets." — *The Cord*

PRAISE FOR *THE KING OF SHANGHAI*

"The only thing scarier than being ripped off for a few million bucks is being the guy who took it and having Ava Lee on your tail. If Hamilton's kick-ass forensic accountant has your number, it's up." — Linwood Barclay

"One of Ian Hamilton's best." —*Globe and Mail*

"Brilliant, sexy, and formidably martial arts-trained forensic accountant Ava Lee is back in her seventh adventure (after *The Two Sisters of Borneo*) … Ever since his dazzling surprise debut with *The Water Rat of Wanchai*, Hamilton has propelled Ava along through the series with expanded storytelling and nuanced character development: there's always something new to discover about Ava. Fast-paced suspense, exotic locales, and a rich cast of characters (some, like Ava's driver, Sonny, are both dangerous and lovable) make for yet another hugely entertaining hit." —*Publishers Weekly*, *Starred review*

"A luxurious sense of place … Hamilton's knack for creating fascinating detail will keep readers hooked … Good fun for those who like to combine crime fiction with armchair travelling." —*Booklist*

"Ava would be a sure thing to whip everybody, Putin included, at the negotiating table." —*Toronto Star*

"After six novels starring Chinese Canadian Ava Lee and her perilously thrilling exploits, best-selling Canadian author Ian Hamilton has jolted his creation out of what wasn't even yet a rut and hurled her abruptly into a new circumstance, with fresh ambitions." —*London Free Press*

"It's a measure of Hamilton's quality as a thriller writer that he compels your attention even before he starts ratcheting up the suspense."
—*Regina Leader Post*

"An unputdownable book that I would highly recommend for all."
—*Words of Mystery*

"Ava is as powerful and brilliant as ever." —*Literary Treats*

PRAISE FOR *THE PRINCELING OF NANJING*
NATIONAL BESTSELLER
A KOBO BEST BOOK OF THE YEAR

"The reader is offered plenty of Ava in full flower as the Chinese Canadian glamour puss who happens to be gay, whip smart, and unafraid of whatever dangers come her way." —*Toronto Star*

"Hamilton's Chinese Canadian heroine is one of a kind ... [An] exotic thriller that also offers a fascinating inside look at fiscal misconduct in China ... As a unique series character, Ava Lee's become indispensable." —*Calgary Herald*

"Ava Lee has a new business, a new look, and, most important, a new triad boss to appreciate her particular financial talents ... We know that Ava will come up with a plan and Hamilton will come up with a twist." —*Globe and Mail*

"Like the best series writers—Ian Rankin and Peter Robinson come to mind—Hamilton manages to ... keep the Ava Lee books fresh ... A compulsive read, a page-turner of the old school ... *The Princeling of Nanjing* is a welcome return of an old favourite, and bodes well for future books." —*Quill & Quire*

"Hamilton uses his people and plot to examine Chinese class and power structures that open opportunities for massive depravities and corruptions." —*London Free Press*

"As usual with a Hamilton-Lee novel, matters take a decided twist as the plot unrolls." —*Owen Sound Times*

"One of those grip-tight novels that makes one read 'just one more chapter' and you discover it's 3 a.m. The novel is built on complicated webs artfully woven into clear, magnetic storytelling. Author Ian Hamilton delivers the intrigue within complex and relentless webs in high style and once again proves that everyone, once in their lives, needs an Ava Lee at their backs." —*Canadian Mystery Reviews*

"The best of the Ava Lee series to date … *Princeling* features several chapters of pure, unadulterated financial sleuthing, which both gave me some nerdy feels and tickled my puzzle-loving mind." —*Literary Treats*

"*The Princeling of Nanjing* was another addition to the Ava Lee series that did not disappoint." —*Words of Mystery*

PRAISE FOR *THE COUTURIER OF MILAN*
NATIONAL BESTSELLER

"The latest in the excellent series starring Ava Lee, businesswoman extraordinaire, *The Couturier of Milan* is another winner for Ian Hamilton … The novel is a hoot. At a point where most crime series start to run out of steam, Ava Lee just keeps rolling on." —*Globe and Mail*

"In Ava Lee, Ian Hamilton has created a crime fighter who breaks the mould with every new book (and, frankly, with every new chapter)." —CBC Books

"The pleasure in following Ava's clever plans for countering the bad guys remains as ever a persuasive attraction." —*Toronto Star*

"Fashionably fierce forensics … But Hamilton has built around Ava Lee an award-winning series that absorbs intriguing aspects of both Asian and Canadian cultures." —*London Free Press*

PRAISE FOR *THE IMAM OF TAWI-TAWI*

"The best of the series so far." —*Globe and Mail*

"One of his best … Tightly plotted and quick-moving, this is a spare yet terrifically suspenseful novel." —*Publishers Weekly*

"Combines lots of action with Ava's acute intelligence and ability to solve even the most complex problems." —*Literary Hub*

"Fast-paced, smoothly written, and fun." —*London Free Press*

"An engrossing novel." —*Reviewing the Evidence*

"Hamilton's rapid-fire storytelling moves the tale along at breakneck speed, as Ava globe-trots to put clues together. Hamilton has always had a knack for combing Fleming-style descriptors with modern storytelling devices and character beats, and this book is no different." —*The Mind Reels*

"An engaging and compelling mystery." —*Literary Treats*

PRAISE FOR *THE GODDESS OF YANTAI*
NATIONAL BESTSELLER

"Ava at her most intimate and vulnerable." —*Toronto Star*

"This time, [Ava's] crusade is personal, and so is her outrage." —*London Free Press*

"In *The Goddess of Yantai* … Ava's personal and professional lives collide in a manner that shakes the usually unflappable character." —*Quill & Quire*

"Told in his typical punchy and forthright style, Hamilton's latest thriller is a rapid-fire read that leaves the reader breathless and eagerly anticipating the next installment … This is a series of books that just seems to get better and better."—*The Mind Reels*

"I wanted to just rip through this book … If you love great writing, an intense pace, and a bit of a thrill, then [the Ava Lee novels] are perfect for you."—*Reading on the Run*

"Action packed and thrilling."—*Words of Mystery*

PRAISE FOR *THE MOUNTAIN MASTER OF SHA TIN*

"Whether it's the triad plot lines or the elegant detective skills of Lee, Ian Hamilton has managed to maintain a freshness to his stories. *The Mountain Master of Sha Tin* is as slick and smart as *The Water Rat of Wanchai*, the first Ava Lee novel … This is one of Canada's best series by one of our best writers."—*Globe and Mail*

"Propulsive."—*London Free Press*

"Hamilton's punchy, fast-paced style has woven a tapestry in over a dozen novels that have introduced us to a variety of characters … This novel, like the previous tales, rockets along."—*The Mind Reels*

"Hamilton provides a fascinating peek into a disturbingly glamorous world."—*Publishers Weekly*

"Another action-packed entry in a solid series."—*Booklist*

PRAISE FOR *THE DIAMOND QUEEN OF SINGAPORE*

"With crisp, taut storytelling, Hamilton whips us around the globe with his captivating prose that delivers like a phoenix strike … Hamilton's

Fleming-esque style of description elicits images and sensations that bring Ava's realm to colourful, glittering life … The perfect summer read, completely engaging, entertaining, and unputdownable."
—*The Mind Reels*

"Hamilton takes great care to make sure that the Ava Lee universe and the characters feel authentic, and it especially shows in this book … I'm looking forward to the next book and to seeing Ava take on an even bigger opponent." —*Words of Mystery*

"Another fantastic addition to Hamilton's box of jewels." —*The Bowed Bookshelf*

PRAISE FOR *THE SULTAN OF SARAWAK*

"Hamilton makes the intricate plot and his larger-than-life characters plausible. Fans of Lisbeth Salander will admire Ava."
—*Publishers Weekly*

"Another well-written addition to the Ava Lee series."
—*Words of Mystery*

PRAISE FOR *THE GENERAL OF TIANANMEN SQUARE*
NATIONAL BESTSELLER

"Smartly constructed, with plenty of action and intrigue (political and otherwise) … A worthy addition to a consistently strong series."
—*Booklist*

"Hamilton gives us a look into the darker, shadier side of the movie industry. He does so with a clever plot, vivid images, and international intrigue of a historical event." —*Miramichi Reader*

THE
FURY
OF
BEIJING

THE
FURY
OF
BEIJING

AN AVA LEE NOVEL
THE TRIAD YEARS

IAN HAMILTON

SPIDERLINE

Published in Canada in 2024 and the USA in 2024 by House of Anansi Press Inc.
houseofanansi.com

House of Anansi Press is committed to protecting our natural environment.
This book is made of material from well-managed FSC®-certified forests, recycled
materials, and other controlled sources.

House of Anansi Press is a Global Certified Accessible™ (GCA by Benetech)
publisher. The ebook version of this book meets stringent accessibility standards
and is available to readers with print disabilities.

28 27 26 25 24   1 2 3 4 5

Library and Archives Canada Cataloguing in Publication

Title: The fury of Beijing / Ian Hamilton.
Names: Hamilton, Ian, 1946- author.
Series: Hamilton, Ian, 1946- Ava Lee series ; 16.
Description: Series statement: An Ava Lee novel : the Triad years ; 16
Identifiers: Canadiana (print) 20230506410 | Canadiana (ebook) 20230506429 |
ISBN 9781487012359 (softcover) | ISBN 9781487012366 (EPUB)
Subjects: LCGFT: Thrillers (Fiction) | LCGFT: Detective and mystery fiction. |
LCGFT: Novels.
Classification: LCC PS8615.A4423 F87 2024 | DDC C813/.6—dc23

Book design: Lucia Kim
Text design: Alysia Shewchuk

*House of Anansi Press is grateful for the privilege to work on and create from the
Traditional Territory of many Nations, including the Anishinabeg, the Wendat, and
the Haudenosaunee, as well as the Treaty Lands of the Mississaugas of the Credit.*

 **Canada Council Conseil des Arts
for the Arts du Canada**

 ONTARIO ARTS COUNCIL
CONSEIL DES ARTS DE L'ONTARIO
an Ontario government agency
un organisme du gouvernement de l'Ontario

With the participation of the Government of Canada
Avec la participation du gouvernement du Canada | Canadä

*We acknowledge for their financial support of our publishing program the Canada
Council for the Arts, the Ontario Arts Council, and the Government of Canada.*

Printed and bound in Canada

MIX
Paper from
responsible sources
FSC® C103567

For Bruce Westwood and Kristine Wookey,
without whom there might never have been an Ava Lee.

AVA LEE SAT AT THE KITCHEN TABLE IN HER TORONTO condominium looking blankly outside at the swirling snow. From a nearby bedroom she could hear the sobs of her lover, Pang Fai. It was difficult for her to comprehend how, in the space of less than one hour, their moods could have swung so brutally from joy to total grief.

Ava could only remember a few other occasions when her life had been so abruptly turned upside down. One was when she had been drugged and raped in Surabaya, Indonesia. The pain from that emotional and physical violation may have eased over the years, but it had never gone away. Another was discovering that Uncle—her business partner, mentor, and grandfather figure—had cancer and had only a few months to live.

This time it was different, because the reason wasn't so directly personal, but its suddenness and awfulness had shocked and shaken her and left her immediately fearful that other friends, as well as Fai, could be in peril.

The cause of Ava and Fai's grief was the murder of Lau Lau, one of China's greatest film directors, and Chen Jie, who had produced Lau Lau's latest and maybe best film, *Tiananmen*. The two men had been gunned down outside the Palais de Chine hotel in Taipei while on their way to a dinner celebrating the Oscar nominations the film had received less than an hour before.

Ava and Fai were in Toronto but had been on speakerphone with the men and Chen's partner, Silvana Foo, when the nominations were announced. It had been a joyous occasion as Lau Lau was nominated for best director, *Tiananmen* for best picture, Silvana for best supporting actress, and Fai for best lead actress. Fifteen minutes after the shooting, Ava got a phone call from a friend of Silvana's telling her that both men had just been killed.

As shaken as Ava was, it paled in comparison to Fai's reaction. She was devastated, unable to stop crying, and could barely speak. Given the length and depth of her relationships with Lau Lau and Chen, Ava wasn't surprised. Chen had been Fai's agent and friend for close to twenty years. Lau Lau had discovered her, cast her in his early films, and eventually married her. The marriage provided cover for both of them because they were gay, and their careers in China would have been over if that had become public knowledge. But Lau Lau's drug abuse and behaviour eventually became too much for Fai to bear, and they divorced. He came back into her life after Ava met him in Beijing while helping Fai with a problem. He was a mess of a human being then, but remembering how brilliant his early films were, Ava convinced him to go to rehab and to try to write a script. He did both successfully, and when she read what he had written, she decided to find a way to finance making it into a film. *Tiananmen* was the result.

The financing and the shooting of the film had not been

easy to manage. For the Chinese government, the subject matter—the massacre of protestors in Tiananmen Square in June 1989—was the most sensitive subject in recent history. All references to the event had been deleted from the public record, and any attempts to discuss or memorialize it were forbidden. The government went to great lengths to ensure compliance, and the punishment for anyone who did raise the subject was immediate and harsh.

The fact that Ava's two business partners, May Ling Wong and Amanda Yee, lived respectively in Wuhan and Hong Kong—and that their company, Three Sisters, owned businesses in China that could be at risk—meant that the financing had to be done in secret. Ava had managed to find money that couldn't be traced, and set up a banking facility in the UK for a bogus company called BB Productions that also couldn't be connected to them.

As for the filming, Lau Lau had shot backdrop scenes in Beijing, but the vast majority of the filming had been done in Taipei—where the Taiwanese government were co-operative to the point of lending tanks to the production.

The finished product had been good enough to premiere at the Cannes Film Festival—and good enough, in fact, to win the Palme d'Or. But with the film's initial success came trouble.

It had begun even before the Cannes screening, when the China Movie Syndicate, a government organization that controlled every aspect of the film industry in China, went to senior officials of the festival in a futile attempt to stop *Tiananmen* being shown.

The trouble that came after Cannes, though, wasn't simply restricted to blocking distribution. The Chinese government had decided that the people who made the film needed to be punished, and Chen was their first target. On his way from his new home in Bangkok to Los Angeles he was waylaid at the Bangkok airport and put in a cell. The request to detain him had come from Chinese security officials, who wanted to deport him to China and were willing to pay the Thais to make that happen. Ava managed to free him by paying more than the Chinese had offered.

The tribulations surrounding *Tiananmen* didn't end there. In opposition to Top of The Road—the distribution company that had the rights to the film, and were being paid by the Chinese government not to release it—BB Productions went to court in Los Angeles and won the right to show it in a local cinema. It ran for seven days—the minimum requirement for Oscar eligibility—before the verdict was overturned.

When the week was over, the judge ruled in favour of Top of the Road, and the film's future was again in doubt. BB launched a yet-to-be-heard appeal against that decision, but Chen's hope had been that the Oscar nominations and perhaps a win would finally give them the leverage to re-acquire the distribution rights. In Ava's mind, the murders of Chen and Lau Lau changed everything. She was certain their deaths were linked to the film, and she saw no way forward if it meant putting Pang and Silvana at risk.

As she sat there remembering every torturous step of their journey since her first meeting with Lau Lau, she found herself swinging back and forth between guilt and anger.

The guilt came in the form of questions. What if she hadn't sent Lau Lau to rehab and had just left him to his own devices in the artists' commune in Beijing? What if she hadn't found a way to finance a film that everyone she spoke to considered controversial to the extreme? What if she hadn't asked Chen to sign on as producer?

Short of actually making the film, it had all been her doing. *Tiananmen* wouldn't exist without her active support, and Chen and Lau Lau wouldn't be dead. She had forged ahead, perhaps not believing that the Chinese government would react so strongly to a film. *It's only a film*, she thought, *and not an attempt to subvert the government. It's only a film, and making it wasn't illegal. It's only a film. It's only a film. Why would anyone take two lives because of a film?*

The anger was directed at the Chinese government, who she was convinced had hired the men in Taiwan—or had sent their own men from the mainland—to do the killings, and that was something she was determined to confirm.

But the government was a monolith—a mainly nameless, faceless collection of communist functionaries in suits. Someone inside that monolith, though, had given the order to kill Chen and Lau Lau. Ava wanted to know who it was, but realized it wasn't going to be easy to pinpoint someone specific in a system that was well practised in delegation and deniability.

There was one face that did have a name to it, though, and it belonged to Mo, the chairman of the China Movie Syndicate. Having failed in France and Los Angeles, he must have been under pressure from the people above him to make sure the film stayed buried. Instead, the Oscar nominations would keep it in the public eye, and the idea that Lau Lau and Chen might win must have made him and his superiors insanely angry. What Ava couldn't figure out was what they thought killing Chen and Lau Lau would achieve.

Surely all it was going to do was generate more publicity, perhaps create sympathy among the Oscar voters, and increase the pressure to properly distribute the film.

But that would be a short-term fallout, and Ava understood the Chinese government thought in the long term. Killing Lau Lau and Chen was a message to everyone that the subject of Tiananmen Square was as off limits as anything could be, and a message to every filmmaker in China—and every foreign filmmaker who wanted their work to be seen in China—that there were rules that could not be bent.

So what to do?

As she pondered that question, her phone rang and she saw it was an incoming call from Wuhan.

"May, I imagine you've heard what has happened?" Ava asked her business partner and friend.

"I just did, from a friend in Singapore, and I'm in total disbelief," May said in a hoarse voice. "I know the government feels strongly about the film, but this is going overboard, even for them."

"They don't care what anyone else thinks."

"I'm just grateful that they didn't harm Silvana as well."

"Speaking of whom, I need to talk to her. She was with them, and she must be hysterical. She was barely holding it together when she couldn't locate Chen after the Chinese had him detained in Thailand. This might have pushed her over the edge."

"How is Fai holding up?"

"Not well. She's in bed and hasn't stopped crying since we found out. I only hope she doesn't blame herself for bringing me, Lau Lau, and Chen together. I'll see her after I calm myself down a bit."

"And Ava, I hope you aren't blaming yourself either," May said.

"Why shouldn't I? Without me, there wouldn't have been a film."

"You had no way of knowing any of this would happen. You were trying to resurrect Lau Lau, and you did—and you also gave Chen a new lease on life. As I see it, the film was secondary, almost incidental."

Ava paused, then said, "Oh fuck, May, I haven't felt this sad since the day Uncle died. Except this time there's some guilt to go along with it."

"You can't heap all of the responsibility onto your shoulders. Even knowing it could be dangerous, everyone made their own decision to go ahead with this. And you know, when we won in Cannes, I was so happy for even having made a sliver of contribution to something so artistic and meaningful. It was the same kind of feeling I had when we launched PÖ in London. And if I was that happy, can you imagine how Lau Lau and Chen felt?"

Ava saw she had another incoming call, and this one was from Amanda. "Amanda is trying to reach me," she said. "I actually don't feel up to talking to anyone else right now. When we hang up could you call her for me and tell her I'll be in touch later?"

"Sure, but what are you going to do?"

"Console Fai."

"I mean what are you going to do about the killings? My first thought when I heard about them was that you would try to seek some kind of revenge, and my second thought was that I hoped you wouldn't. None of us who love you want you putting yourself in harm's way."

"It is way too soon to start thinking about doing anything. I need to get my emotions under control."

"Good, that's the right starting point."

After saying goodbye, Ava hung up, grateful yet again for May's friendship.

2

AVA AND FAI SPENT THE DAY CURLED UP IN BED, AND
it was late afternoon when the tears finally ebbed and hunger
kicked in. Neither of them felt like cooking, so Ava turned
on her cell—which had been off since May Ling's call—and
phoned Blu Ristorante, a local Italian restaurant that had
become a favourite. She thought comfort food was needed,
and ordered for delivery two tagliatelle bolognese, and a dish
of braised beef cheek ragù for them to share.

After freshening up in the bathroom, she checked her
phone for messages, saw that her voicemail was full, and that
she had received more than fifteen texts. Fai's phone, which
had also been off, had even more calls, and texts.

Ava opened a bottle of Chianti and they sat at the kitchen
table to respond to the texts. Most of the calls were from Asia
and it was too late to return them, but Ava's mother, Jennie,
had called in tears. Ava phoned her back.

"I'm sorry I didn't call sooner, but Fai and I didn't get out
of bed today after hearing the news," Ava said when her
mother answered her phone.

"All the girls are in shock," Jennie said, referring to the

mah-jong-playing group of single women and second wives who were her friends. "They met Fai when she came to my house, and knowing how close she must have been to Chen and Lau Lau makes it that much more personal."

"Did you speak to anyone in Hong Kong?"

"I spoke to your father. He is very worried about you and Fai—but of course, especially you. He said that Amanda was so upset that she left the office early. Michael doesn't want her to go back any time soon."

Ava's father, Marcus Lee, had taken Jennie as a second wife in the traditional Chinese sense, but when things didn't run smoothly, he had dispatched her, Ava, and Ava's older sister Marian to Canada. He had continued to support them financially, spoke to Jennie every day on the phone, and normally spent two weeks out of the year in Canada with them. Michael was Marcus's eldest son from his first marriage, and was married to Amanda Yee. Ava's *gweilo* friends were often taken aback by how complicated her family life seemed from the outside. They would have thought it even more so if she'd told them Marcus had taken a third wife, who lived in Australia with their two children. But she didn't get into that level of detail, and didn't find her family life that complicated at all. It was all she had known, and there was no lack of love or support.

"Michael is forever trying to get Amanda to quit our business. He doesn't understand her, and I can tell you that if he keeps nagging at her and pushing like that, she's more likely to leave him than us," said Ava. "It might be helpful if you could pass that opinion on to Daddy so he can talk to Michael."

"I'll do that," Jennie said. "But right now I don't care about

Michael or Amanda. I care about you and Fai. How are you holding up? Is there anything I can do?"

"We're doing the best we can under the circumstances, and the circumstances are horrible. We watched the Oscar nomination show with Chen, Silvana and Lau Lau on speakerphone, and then said goodbye as they went off to dinner. It was no more than half an hour later that I got the phone call telling me they'd been shot."

"My heart breaks for them, and for you and Fai."

"We weren't the ones who were shot," Ava said. "By the way, how did you find out?"

"The local Chinese news channel has been all over it. The fact they know Fai is living in Toronto has made it an even bigger story."

"Did they give any indication of who did the killing?"

"No, although they did mention that Lau Lau had a drug problem."

"Those sons of bitches. He's been clean for almost two years," Ava said. "I think the Chinese government was behind the shootings, and they're probably peddling that nonsense about Lau Lau."

"There was no mention of the government."

"Which isn't surprising given that the station was bought by a mainland company two years ago."

"You know I have no interest in politics," Jennie said. "I have friends in Hong Kong who won't talk about anything else these days. I find it very unpleasant."

"Mummy, it is reality. You can't shut it out."

"I can try. Now, back to you. I can drive into the city any time you want with some food. Would you like some barbecued pork and chicken from Johnny's?"

"Thank you, but I think we'll pass for now. We need to be alone. I'll call you in a few days. If we're feeling any better we'll arrange to meet," Ava said.

"Okay, but take care, and a big hug to both of you."

When Ava put down the phone, she picked up her wine glass. "My mother sends you her love," she said to Fai.

"There's a lot of love in these texts, but also a lot of worry. People are spooked. Several said I shouldn't go to the Oscar ceremony."

"How are you responding?"

"I'm telling them it's too soon to even think about that."

"Actually, it isn't that far away."

"I know," Fai said with a grimace. "And truthfully, I have thought about it."

"And ...?"

"I don't know if I want to be part of that circus. The sympathy votes will probably make us all winners, but if I go, I'll be the focal point. Whenever the film, Chen, or Lau Lau is mentioned, I can imagine a lot of eyes and cameras will automatically turn to me, to see how I'm handling it. If I cry every time, it will look overdramatic. If I don't cry, I could be accused of being unfeeling. I don't like being in a fishbowl at the best of times, and that would be the worst of times."

Ava's cellphone rang, and she checked the screen. "Our food is on its way," she said.

They ate slowly, finished the bottle of Chianti, and Ava opened another. When the last morsel of beef cheek was devoured, she said, "I've been thinking about the Oscars. I agree it would be uncomfortable and probably painful for you to be there. I don't think you should put yourself through something like that when you have the choice."

Fai nodded. "You're right. I'm not going to go. We'll have to find another venue to honour Chen and Lau Lau. We can't do it in China, but maybe there's a way to do something in Taipei. I wonder what Silvana will do, although I don't imagine it's something she's capable of thinking about yet."

"Which reminds me, I should call her. I know it's early in the morning there, but I don't imagine she slept much, if at all."

"I feel so sorry for her. She waits all this time to find the right man, and then boom, he's gone. I'm sure that adds to the misery," Fai said as Ava called Taipei.

"*Wei*," Silvana answered in a shaky voice.

"This is Ava. I hope I'm not disturbing you."

"No, I've been hoping you'd call. I'm sitting here with John Tam and some of our friends who were with us last night, before … you know, before. We've been talking about Chen and Lau Lau, trying to recall happier times."

"That was good of them to stay with you."

"People have been kind."

"Is there anything that Fai and I can do to help?"

Silvana hesitated, and Ava wondered if she was going to start crying. Instead, she said, "Are you going to go after the people who did this, like you said you would when we talked last night?"

The question caught Ava off guard, and then she remembered what she had said to Silvana. Given Silvana's state of mind at the time, Ava was surprised she remembered. "I'm going to do everything I can to find out who's responsible," she replied.

"Ava, you can't let them get away with this."

"Sils, I can't do anything unless I know who did it. Finding that out is a starting point."

"But if you do find out?" Silvana persisted.

"One thing at a time, Silvana, please ..." Ava said, not wanting to make a promise she might not be able to keep. "In the meantime, you need to get some rest. Will your friends stay with you for a few days?"

"They'll stay longer than that if I need them. I'm lucky to have friends like them, just as Chen and Lau Lau were lucky to have you."

3

SLEEP DID NOT COME EASILY, AND WHEN IT DID IT WAS fitful. By six a.m. Ava was sitting in the kitchen with a mug of instant coffee. She couldn't stop thinking about her conversation with Silvana, juxtaposed with the earlier one with May Ling. Both women had right on their side. Silvana was perfectly justified in wanting Chen's death avenged, while May was correct when she'd pointed out the dangers of trying to pursue that path. Was there a middle ground? Was there a way to identify the people responsible and impart some kind of justice without putting herself, her partners, their businesses, and Pang Fai in danger?

As those questions bounced around in her head, Ava went online to see what reaction the deaths had evoked. Not surprisingly, they were the subject of the main headline of nearly every newspaper and website she looked at. Equally not surprising, there wasn't a single mention in any mainland Chinese media outlet. The deaths were referred to as murders, and although some media had linked them to the Chinese government's animosity towards *Tiananmen*, only the *London Tribune*, in a banner headline, want as far as to say CHINESE GOVERNMENT OPERATIVES ASSASSI-NATE FAMED DIRECTOR LAU LAU. The story that followed was written by Harris Jones —a leading film critic, and the movie's most influential fan.

Shortly after seven, Fai joined Ava in the kitchen. "It's a wonder my phone didn't blow up. My voice mailbox is full, and I have too many texts to count."

"I was just looking at the news coverage. The story is everywhere, except of course in the Chinese media."

"In two or three days you won't see a mention anywhere else either. Interest will pick up again as we get close to Oscar night, but when it's over, thoughts about Lau Lau and Chen will fade with it," said Fai, as she sat down with her own cup of coffee. "I had trouble sleeping, and when I did sleep I had horrible dreams."

"So did I—I couldn't stop thinking about Silvana."

"And I couldn't stop thinking about you," said Fai. "I wish you hadn't told Sils that you would try to find out who killed Chen and Lau Lau. I believe you have taken this film and everyone associated with it as far as they can go. No one, including Silvana, would blame you for backing off now. Maybe it's time to let this go."

"We have a court date in July to appeal the judge's ruling about who is entitled to distribute the film."

"Can't you tell the lawyer to cancel it? Even if we won, without Chen we don't have anyone to put together a new distribution agreement. Besides, do you really think the Chinese government is going to pay any attention to a ruling from an American court?"

"I know what you're saying is correct, but ..."

"But?" Fai said, reaching for Ava's arm.

Ava shook her head. "Okay, I'll tell the lawyer to withdraw our appeal."

"Thank you."

"That doesn't mean I'm prepared to walk away from the rest of it," she continued. "I've been debating what—if anything—I can do. May Ling, like you, wants me to put it aside. The problem is that I don't think my conscience will let me. At the least I should make an effort—as I promised Sils—to find out who ordered the deaths of our friends. I may not be able to, but I don't think I could live with myself if I didn't try. The one thing I promise you is that I will be as careful as it is possible to be. Believe me, I don't want to end up in a Chinese prison, or facing a firing squad."

"How can you be careful enough?"

"You know I have friends I can call on for help. This is a time when I will probably have to depend on them more than I ever have," Ava said. "I'll use them and stay in the background as much as I can."

"Even so, I don't like the idea. Why does it have to be you?"

"Who else is there? Besides, Uncle trained me well, and I've had lots of practice working behind the scenes."

"You aren't going to change your mind, are you?"

"Not right away, although I'm prepared to if I think the situation is getting precarious."

"That's a small relief," said Fai.

"What you have to decide is how much you want to know. Would you prefer to stay in the dark, or do you want to be kept informed about what's going on?"

"I want to know."

"Good. I prefer that as well."

"So now what—how does this start?"

"With a phone call to Xu," said Ava.

Xu and Ava had a relationship that went beyond friendship; he often referred to her as *mei mei*, which meant little sister, and she called him *ge ge*, big brother. Xu was the son of one of Uncle's oldest friends, and Uncle had mentored him as he rose to become the Mountain Master of the Shanghai triads. Ava hadn't met Xu until Uncle's funeral, and he had only learned about her a few days earlier. It was Uncle's wish that they become friends and lend support to each other. During the years since, that support had been given in equal measure through difficult circumstances. Now, they shared absolute trust, and there wasn't anything Ava didn't think she could ask of him, and vice versa.

Xu lived in an early century English-county style home in the French Concession with his housekeeper, Auntie Grace, and it was her who answered the phone when Ava called.

"Auntie, is Xu available?" she asked.

"He's just pulling into the driveway. He'll be here in a minute. Are things still going well for you and Fai?"

"Very well. I've never been happier."

"When will you visit us again?"

"I don't know. There are things going on that may keep us here in Canada for quite some time."

"Bad things?"

"More like complicated things."

"Ah ... well, here's Xu now."

"Ava, what is going on? I just heard about Chen and Lau Lau," he blurted. "There's been nothing mentioned about it here. I was told by Zhao. He expressed concern for you. Evidently, he knows you were close to them."

Zhao was the Mountain Master in Kowloon, a good friend of Xu's, and someone who had been helpful to Ava.

"They were shot and killed outside a restaurant in Taipei," she said, still finding the words difficult to say. "They were going out to celebrate their Oscar nominations with friends."

"Who did it?"

"No one has taken credit or been blamed, but I think the road leads directly to the Chinese government."

"They do seem to have lost all sense of proportion when it comes to the subject of Tiananmen Square," Xu said. "But do you really think they would go to that extreme?"

"Yes, I do, don't you?"

He paused. "I think it's possible."

"Xu, I want to find out who killed them, and who ordered the killing. Can you give me some help?"

"You know the answer is yes, but can I act for a moment like a *ge ge*?"

"You're going to tell me to be careful."

"I want you to be so careful that you barely confide in yourself. You can't get too close to these people. Zhao was telling me about the arrests in Hong Kong, where simply speaking one's mind has become an offence that can land you in jail. It isn't much better here these days. Officials who aren't completely loyal to the premier have been disappearing on a regular basis. I know of three here in Shanghai who haven't been seen in months. All it takes is for someone to get paranoid to get you in trouble."

"Fai shares your view."

"Okay—with all of that said, what can I do to help?"

Ava felt a touch of relief. She had thought he would help, but had never taken it for granted. "Could you call Tsai, the

Mountain Master in Taipei, for me? I spoke to him once ages ago and I'm not sure he'll remember me—and even if he did, he might not be co-operative without a nudge from you."

"Sure, I can do that, but do you mind me asking why you want to talk to him?"

"If the Chinese government hired local killers, I figure he'll know who they are, or at least be able to find out."

"That is a logical assumption, but if it was his men who did the deed, do you really expect him to tell you?"

"Then maybe you could ask him the question for me. I don't think he'd lie to you," Ava said, knowing she was pushing her luck.

Xu hesitated before saying, "Yes, that might be a better idea."

"Thank you."

"Now, what else is there?"

"This will sound a bit strange, but I need a new identity," she said. "If I have to go to China, I don't want to go as Ava Lee, and my Jennie Kwong persona has been used a bit too often lately. Ideally, I'd like a Chinese passport, with maybe an ID card. I can make a business card with the same name here, but I'll need a phone number and address on it that are real. Is all of that doable?"

"What name do you want to use?" he asked, acting as if her request were normalcy itself.

"I thought I'd honour Uncle by using his family name, but I don't have a given name. Do you have any suggestions?"

"I've always liked Qi, and I think it's apt where you're concerned."

Ava smiled; *Qi* meant "wondrous." "Okay, so it will be Chow Qi."

"I'll need photos and a date for your birthday, for the passport and the TIN."

"TIN?"

"That will be your Tax Identification Number. It's used here as an ID card."

"I'll have photos taken today and couriered to you, and use May 24, 1985 for the birth date."

"Is that really your birthday?"

"Yes."

"I'll make a note of that. Send multiple copies of the photos, and after they get here it might still take a few days to get things done. The guy I use works slowly because he is so particular, but the finished product is worth the wait. If you can send one electronically, he might be able to use that for the TIN card," Xu said. "But, Ava, I still have to say I hope you never have to use them."

"I understand, but I have no idea what I'll be doing until I learn more about what happened."

"Speaking of which, I know you want me to talk to Tsai, but are you thinking of going to Taipei regardless of what he tells me?"

"I haven't actually thought about it. We've just been trying to cope with the day. I'll talk to Silvana again in a few hours to see if she knows what they're going to do with the bodies. I can't believe they'll be released right away, but if they are I can't imagine who will claim Lau Lau. I'll ask Fai if she has any idea."

"They are Chinese citizens in a foreign country. It could get complicated."

"I know, and I hope it's something we don't have to deal with in the next day or two. Our nerves and emotions need time to settle."

"Please take that time," Xu said.

"I will."

"Okay, let me go call Tsai. I'll get back to you right away with whatever he has to say."

4

FAI WAS IN THE BATHROOM DURING AVA'S CALL TO XU.
When she came out, her face looked freshly scrubbed, her
hair was slightly damp, and she was dressed in jeans and a
light blue sweater.

"You're dressed to go out," Ava said.

"I have an English language class that starts in about a
half hour, and I thought I'd go. It will be a distraction, and
I really need one. I can't stop thinking about them."

Fai had been taking classes for some months, and her
English had improved dramatically. In the past, her lack of
English had hindered her career opportunities. Her hope
now was to become proficient enough to get acting jobs in
places like the UK and the US.

"I think that's a great idea. Do you want to meet for lunch
at Dynasty?" Ava said, referring to a Chinese restaurant
within easy walking distance of the school and the condo.

"I'd like that," Fai said as she made a cup of coffee. "Did
you talk to Xu?"

"I did. He had just heard about Chen and Lau Lau from
Zhao in Kowloon. Evidently the Chinese media are ignoring it."

"That's to be expected," Fai said.

"Anyway, he's going to help me with a few things, and he asked a question I couldn't answer about Lau Lau. If his body is released, who will claim it? He must have relatives—a brother or sister, an aunt or uncle?"

Fai shook her head. "I don't think he did. The only member of his family he ever mentioned was his mother, and she died at least ten years ago."

"He must have a will?"

"If he does, I don't know when he did it. And if one exists, I would have no idea where to locate it. Why are you concerned about this?"

"I hate the thought of Lau Lau's body not being claimed and properly looked after."

"As his ex-wife, I might have some status to claim it."

"We need to find out how it works over there," Ava said. "I'll see if Silvana's friend John Tam can recommend a lawyer in Taipei."

"That's a good idea," Fai said, checking the time. "I should get going. I don't want to be late."

"So, twelve fifteen at Dynasty?"

"I'll see you there."

As soon as Fai left, Ava carried her phone to the bathroom and set it on the counter while she brushed her teeth. She had just finished rinsing when Xu called.

"Did you reach Tsai?" she asked.

"Yes, and it was a most interesting conversation. I have to say, my opinion of him improved substantially," Xu said. "He told me he was approached a few weeks ago by a local businessman named Song, who was looking for gunmen to get rid of two rivals who he claimed had been cheating him. Tsai didn't take his story at face value, and asked some questions, including who these rivals were. The businessman wouldn't say at first, but Tsai pressed him, and told him he wouldn't agree to do anything until he knew who the targets were. The man said they were named Chen and Lau Lau."

"Tsai's men provided security on the film set in Taipei. Tsai must have known immediately who they were," Ava said as a shiver went down her spine.

"He did, so he knew the story was bogus, turned down the contract, but decided to try to find out who Song really was, or who he was representing," said Xu. "Song had told Tsai he was an executive at the Green Dragon Import/Export Company, and that part of his story was true, but as Tsai dug into the company, he discovered the business's turnover was miniscule compared to the size of its offices and the number of people who seemed to be working there. He began to think it was a front for something, and contacted someone he knows in the Taiwanese National Security Bureau to ask if they knew anything about Green Dragon. He was told they suspected it was an operation set up by the Chinese Ministry of State Security."

"They suspected? They didn't know for certain?"

"They had been keeping an eye on the company for a few months but had no definite proof."

"And the guy who tried to hire Tsai's men—was he Chinese?"

"No, he was Taiwanese, but the idea that he would work for or with the MSS isn't odd. They commonly hire local people, and there are quite a few Taiwanese who want the island reunited with the mainland, so working for the MSS wouldn't bother them."

"From what I've heard, this MSS is quite powerful."

"It is difficult to overstate the kind of power it wields. It can arrest, jail, torture, and kill with virtually no oversight. There isn't an organization inside China that is more feared. What I didn't realize was that it operates outside of China as well."

Ava thought about Chen being arrested in Bangkok at the request of a Chinese security organization. Had that been the MSS? If so, there didn't seem to be anywhere in Asia they couldn't reach. "All this talk about the MSS aside, what I'd like to know is, if Tsai turned down the contract, who took it?"

"I asked him that. He didn't know, but he said he'd try to find out."

"He needs to talk to Song."

"That might not be so easy, so he'll start with Han—Taipei's other Mountain Master. He and Tsai each run half the city."

"I need a lead, any kind of lead. Just a foot in the door," said Ava.

"You'll get any information he passes to me as soon as I have it, but it's late in the evening in Taipei, so I don't expect to hear anything until tomorrow. Ava, I know your emotions are running high, but until we know more there's nothing to be done."

She sighed. "I apologize for being so impatient, but this is obviously eating at me."

"I understand, and I promise we'll do everything we can."

"I know you will, and thanks," she said, and hung up.

Ava had gravitated to the kitchen during the call. Now, she took a blank notebook and a pen from a drawer and sat at the kitchen table. She opened the book and wrote *Lau Lau/ Chen Murder* across the top of the first page, with the names *Song—Green Dragon—Ministry of State Security* underneath. When working with Uncle, she had kept a notebook for every job they took. It not only gave her a record—names, numbers, and contact information—of who she found, it also sometimes helped her organize her thought process. This wasn't a job, but it was something that could get complicated, and a written record would give her a sense of order. Her hope was that there would soon be enough information to fill the first page and then more.

There was now a definite possibility that she would be going to Taiwan. If she had to, what persona should she use? It would be ideal if she could go as Chow Qi, but it would take time to courier photos to Xu and for his forger to create the false documents and courier them back—she figured at least a few days. If she had a definite lead, there was no way she could wait that long. If it became necessary, she decided, Jennie Kwong would have to resurface. In the meantime, she needed to get the photos taken. She went online and found a shop on Bay Street that promised a one-hour service and was within walking distance.

Ava dressed quickly and was heading for the door when she remembered she hadn't phoned Amanda, and that she needed to talk to Silvana.

She tried Amanda's cell first, and when the call went directly to voicemail, she said, "Hey, I'm sorry I didn't get back to you sooner, but things have been hectic. I'll touch base with you tomorrow."

When she called Silvana, a man's voice answered. "This is John Tam."

"This is Ava. How is she doing?"

"She finally fell asleep. She had gone more than thirty-six hours without any."

"You are a very good friend to be staying with her like this."

"I'm not alone—my girlfriend Sara is helping, and some other friends have been dropping in. Silvana seems rather fragile, and we don't think she should be alone right now."

"When she wakes, tell her I called," Ava said. "But I'm glad you answered. I was going to ask her for your number."

"Why?"

"I wanted the name of a Taipei lawyer, and I thought you might recommend one. We know nothing about the law there with regard to what happens to the deceased's body in a case like this. Lau Lau had no family that we're aware of, and we're not sure he had a will, and we don't want his body left in limbo."

"My lawyer is in the entertainment business, but I'm sure he'll know someone who can provide the relevant information. I'll contact him in the morning and forward you his recommendations," Tam said. "But I have to say, you shouldn't feel rushed. The police were here today to speak to us and said it will be some time—maybe more than a week—before they will even consider releasing the bodies."

"That's good to know, and I'll thank you in advance for your help with the lawyer. How did it go with the police? Do they have any idea of who did it?"

"We asked the same question and got a vague reply. I'd say offhand that they don't, but they have some CCTV footage they said they're examining. They were hoping we recognized or could provide some kind of description of the shooters. We couldn't do either. It all happened so fast, and when it was over our entire concentration was on Chen and Lau Lau."

"But there is no doubt about the motive?"

"We all heard one of them shout 'congratulations on your Oscar nominations' before the firing started," Tam said. "The police seemed dubious about that as a motive, but what else could it be?"

"Nothing—I'm quite certain it was the motive. There are a lot of people who hate the film, hate them for making it, and would hate them for any success they get from it."

"Silvana told the police that she thought the Chinese government was responsible for the killings. I don't think they took her seriously."

"Well, as yet that's just speculation, but it isn't uninformed," Ava said.

5

THE ONE-HOUR SHOP TURNED OUT TO BE A FOUR-HOUR shop, and Ava didn't get her photos until after lunch with Fai. She walked Fai back to the Colonnade complex on Bloor Street that housed the language school, and sent the photos to Xu from the FedEx office on the main floor. When she got back to the condo, she emailed him an electronic version that she hoped he would be able to use for the TIN card.

She had turned her phone off during lunch and now switched it back on. There had been numerous texts and emails that she hadn't answered, and for the next hour she did. Some were from friends, none of whom knew about her involvement with the film, asking her to pass their condolences on to Fai and hoping that she was okay. Most of the others were business-related, and reminded Ava of how heavily invested Three Sisters—the investment company she owned with May Ling and Amanda—was in China. They owned warehouses, cold storage, and trucking operations in Shanghai and Beijing; the PÖ fashion company was headquartered in Shanghai; and they had a trading operation in Hong Kong that did business in many parts of China. Some of the emails she'd been cc'd on and they didn't require a response, but one that had been forwarded to her by Amanda caught her attention. It was from a valued trading partner in Guangzhou asking if Three Sisters still intended to get into the ginseng business.

Before the problems with the film in Los Angeles, Ava had been working on acquiring a controlling interest in a large ginseng farming operation near Waterford in south-western Ontario, only a short drive from Toronto. Then she had to put everything on hold, missed the fall harvest, and decided to wait until the following year. Ava knew Amanda was still keen to get into the ginseng business, and given that its base was in Canada, it now appealed to Ava more than it had, but with everything else going on, the timing was bad. She emailed Amanda:

I still want to do this, but it will have to wait until my mind is in the right place. I hope this doesn't cause a problem.

With that done and her other obligations met, Ava decided to go for a run. The sidewalks were snow- and ice-covered in places, but she was accustomed to those conditions and had learned how to navigate them—something you had to do if you wanted to run outdoors in Canada during the winter. She went into her bedroom, slipped on a long-sleeved T-shirt over her short-sleeved one, and put on an Adidas jacket and training pants. She pulled on her running shoes, and added gloves and a toque from a selection by the door. She was about to the leave the apartment when she decided to bring her phone with her.

When she left the condo building, she turned right and made her way to Avenue Road. Going north from there was less interesting but also less crowded than going south, and that's the way she chose. She had to stop at a light at Davenport Road, but the other lights co-operated, and she had a straight path all the way to Upper Canada College. As always, the physical stress she was feeling began to ebb, but her mind wouldn't let go of the events in Taipei, and the more she thought about them, the more she wondered if Fai could be in danger. It was true that the gunmen hadn't shot at Silvana—who was as prominent in the film and had also earned an Oscar nomination—but was that because she wasn't responsible for the film's production, or because she was a woman? As Ava weighed those possibilities, her phone rang. She glanced at the display and saw it was Xu. What was he doing calling her in the middle of the night in Shanghai?

"Xu, is everything okay? This is a strange hour to be calling me."

"Evidently my triad brothers in Taipei work late into the night, because Tsai phoned me five minutes ago," said Xu. "He managed to speak to Han and didn't want to wait until morning to fill me in. Han was offered the same contract the day after Tsai was, and he turned it down as well."

"Did he give a reason—beyond basic human decency?"

"Han's not stupid either. He wanted to know who he would be working for. Song told him he didn't need to know, but Han—like Tsai—persisted. When Song mentioned the Green Dragon Company, Han asked for twenty-four hours to consider the offer. He took the time to investigate Green Dragon."

"What did he find?" Ava asked.

"An import/export company that doesn't seem to do much of either. Given that Song is Taiwanese, Han told Tsai he figured Green Dragon might be part of the Taiwanese National Security Bureau, and that the contract offer could have been an attempt to sucker him into agreeing to commit a crime for which they could charge him."

"Did Tsai mention the MSS?"

"He didn't see the point after learning Han had turned down the contract."

"So if Tsai or Han's men didn't do it, who did?"

"In Taiwan there aren't many other options."

"Which leads to the logical conclusion that it was the MSS."

"Assuming, of course, that Song actually works for them."

"Even if he doesn't, he was the one offering contracts to kill my friends, and that means he was working for someone. Xu, there is no doubt in my mind that if Song is still in Taipei, I'll be going there to talk to him. He's the first link in the chain that led to Chen and Lau Lau's deaths."

"If it does come to that, I don't want you operating there alone," Xu said sharply. "And I don't think you can depend on Tsai or Han to give you the kind of support you might need."

"If I do go, I'll ask Sonny to join me," Ava said, referring to Sonny Kwok, a Hong Kong triad who had been Uncle's bodyguard and driver, and was now employed by Ava. He was at her service twenty-four hours a day when she was in Hong Kong, and no job was too much for him to handle. When she wasn't there, he drove for Ava's father and her half-brother Michael.

Xu paused. "As much as I admire Sonny, I think that Lop would be even more useful. He knows people inside the MSS, and he's got his military contacts. And you know he can look after himself."

Ava had worked with Lop three times, and on each occasion he had been indispensable. A former captain in the

Special Forces branch of the People's Liberation Army, he was now a key member of Xu's team, and brought a level of discipline to everything he did that was almost robotic. "I would love to have Lop alongside me," she said.

"If it comes to that, you'll have him," Xu said.

"Thanks, and by the way, I couriered passport photos to you today, and emailed an electronic version."

"I got the latter. I'll send it to my guy in a few hours so he can start to work on the TIN. In the morning I'll phone Lop and explain the situation. He might be able to confirm that Green Dragon is attached to the MSS."

"Will you call me back when you find out—positive or negative?"

"Sure—and now I'm going back to bed for a few hours. I'm not accustomed to working in the middle of the night."

Ava resumed her run north for another kilometre, then turned and headed back. She started to focus her attention on Song, the MSS, and the Chinese government. She was certain she would find Mo somewhere in the mix. As much as she disliked him, though, it was hard to believe he had the power to order the murders. Someone else had done that, but had it been on his orders? Had he become frustrated at his inability to completely derail *Tiananmen* and turned the problem over to others? Or had others become impatient with his handling of the matter and taken control? Either way, Mo could be a step towards an answer, and she already had some leverage where he was concerned.

(6)

HALF AN HOUR LATER, AVA STEPPED INTO THE CONDO
with her mind still full of Song and Mo, and feeling an
uncommon mix of emotions that the run had heightened
rather than quelled. There was anger exacerbated by the
sense of personal loss, and a growing sense of fear that Fai
might be in danger. And overlying all of it was a lingering
sense of guilt for having built the foundation for the film and
everything that followed. When she heard of the deaths, her
first reaction had been numb shock. But as the numbness
had faded, she realized guilt had filled the gap. She had been
too smart, too confident for her own good, and others had
paid the price. How to rectify that? Was it even rectifiable?

She went into the bathroom, stripped, and stepped into
the shower. She turned the water pressure to the maximum
level and let the water batter her for several minutes. As it
did, she tried to get her emotions under control. There was
no value in overreacting, she thought, and nothing concrete
could come from blaming herself for what had happened.
When she finished, she put on a sports bra, a clean Giordano
T-shirt, and a pair of jeans, and went into the kitchen where

she opened a bottle of Pinot Grigio, poured a glass, and sat at her laptop with the cellphone alongside. She picked up her notebook and began to write

Is Song employed by the MSS? *What is the address and other contact information for Green Dragon Import/Export? Where does Song live? How did he know Chen was going to dinner at Le Palais? Is he still in Taipei?*

She had questions but no answers. The last question could be addressed by a call to his office. As for the others, she hoped that Lop could help. With that in mind, she opened her computer and sent a quick email to Xu with her questions, and a note that read:

Could you forward this to Lop. Maybe by the time I talk to him he will have found some answers for me.

Ava sat back, the jumble of emotions she'd felt earlier now partially replaced by a feeling of determination. It was always easier when she had a clear target, and in this case his name was Song. She had no idea who he would lead to, although she was sure that Mo—even if he wasn't the last piece of the puzzle—would be encountered along the way. And the thought of Mo made her reach for the phone to call Derek Liang.

Derek was married to Ava's best friend in Canada, Mimi, but Ava had known him for many years. Like her, he was adept enough at martial arts to have graduated to bak mei— perhaps the deadliest of the arts, and one historically taught one-on-one. They had shared the same teacher, Grandmaster Tang, and met as they came and went from his studio. When Ava got into the debt collection business, she had called upon Derek from time to time to help in situations she thought might turn physical. He had never failed her. But aside from bak mei, Derek—the only child of wealthy Hong Kong parents—had lived an idle, playboy life, and when he and Mimi had started dating, Ava was fearful it wouldn't turn out well for her. She was wrong. They had married, had a child, and now Derek was a devoted stay-at-home dad who had developed computer skills that Ava used often.

"This is Derek," he answered.

"And this is Ava—how are things?"

"I should be asking you that. How is Fai? We were going to call when we heard the news about Lau Lau and Chen, but we thought she would be bombarded and decided to wait."

Ava had kept her involvement with the film a closely guarded secret, and apart from her business partners, Fai, Silvana, Chen, Lau Lau, and her lawyers in Hong Kong, no one knew. "She was obviously shocked, as we all were. It will take some time for her to get over it."

"Is she going to the Oscars?"

"No, she's already decided that wouldn't be a good thing to do for a whole bunch of reasons."

"That's what Mimi thought," Derek said, and paused. "Ava, do you have any idea who killed them?"

"I have an opinion, but that's all it is."

"Are you going to test that opinion?"

"What do you think?"

"I've known you long enough and worked with you often enough to be quite certain that you will."

"Speaking of work, are you very busy right now? Could you take on a project for me?"

"Does it have to do with what happened in Taiwan?"

"Indirectly," she said.

"Then I'll find the time to do whatever you want."

"Do you remember researching a young man named David Mo for me? He's the gay son of Mo Ming, the head of the China Movie Syndicate."

"Of course I do."

"Could you revisit him for me? I'd like to know what he's up to and who he's with these days."

"Sure, I can do that. What else do you want—updated phone numbers, email address, home address?"

"All of it—and anything else you find the least bit interesting."

"As I recall, he was attending UCLA. If he hasn't graduated it shouldn't be that difficult."

"Even if he has, I'm sure he'd still be in the LA area. Given his sexual orientation and history, I can't imagine he'd go back to China."

"I'll get on this right away."

"Thank you again."

"Momentai," Derek said. "And I'll tell Mimi you called. She was going to invite you and Fai to dinner before this happened, but I think we should put that off—don't you?"

"Yes, it would be better to wait."

Another thought came to Ava just as she was about to put down the phone. "Derek, there's something else I'd like to ask of you. I may decide to leave Toronto for a few days, and if I do, Fai won't be going with me. Could you stay in touch with her, and keep an eye on her? I can't believe she's in any danger, but it would be comforting to know that you are there for her if she needs you."

"It would be my pleasure—and hell, she could move in with us if she wants. We have a spare bedroom."

"Thanks, I'll mention that to her," Ava said.

7

AVA AND FAI ATE DINNER AT THE CONDO, RAIDING THE fridge for Chinese food left over from a trip to Richmond Hill two nights before the Oscar nominations were announced. To Ava, it seemed like a lifetime ago.

They drank Pinot Grigio as they worked their way through beef noodles with XO sauce, chicken feet, and a large portion of Fukien fried rice. The rice—covered in a thick, rich sauce and laden with shrimp, scallops, and squid—had held up particularly well, and to Ava's surprise they were able to finish it. They chatted as they ate, with Fai quizzing Ava about her conversations with Xu and Derek.

"So if this guy Song is in Taipei, you'll be going there?" Fai asked.

"Yes, but first I have to confirm that he's there. I'll call his office in a few hours. It should be open by then."

"If you do go, I'm glad Xu offered to send Lop," said Fai, who had met him in Beijing when he helped Ava stop Mo's attempts to ruin her career. "I've never known anyone scarier than him."

Ava smiled. At first glance, Lop—who was of medium

height and a slight, wiry build—looked harmless, but when you were with him you soon noticed the tension in his body, and the eyes that were perpetually penetrating and questioning. This almost manic exterior, though, was complemented by an interior that was cold and controlled. Like Sonny, he didn't seem to know what fear was, and his commitment to the job at hand was always total to the point of potentially sacrificing his own life. Those traits, combined with his Special Forces training, made him extraordinary. "If it is not Lop, it will be Sonny," Ava said. "I meant it when I said I was going to be careful."

"And what about David Mo—how does he fit into the grand scheme of things?"

"He doesn't, at least not yet. But I want to know where he is and what he's up to in case the need arises."

"I do wish he weren't gay. I hate the idea of using that against him, even if the target is his father."

"I feel the same," Ava said, reaching for Fai's hand. "But we're at war, and we didn't start it. I hope as much as you do that David Mo doesn't become collateral damage. If he does, the fault will lie with his father and not with us."

"But how is it possible that Mo wasn't involved?"

"I don't know, but it is possible this went further than even he wanted. I don't think he has the power to order the deaths of Lau Lau and Chen, and it's even possible he wouldn't condone it. The point is that I need to find out who is responsible."

"What if it's someone in Beijing?"

"Then I might choose to go to Beijing."

"Ava …! After what happened to Chen when he was in Bangkok, how can you risk going to China? They could arrest you at the airport and I might never hear from you again."

"If I do go, it won't be as Ava Lee—or Jennie Kwong for that matter. Xu is getting me a Chinese passport in the name of Chow Qi. But listen, there's no point in getting worried about something that might never happen. Let me gather the facts first."

Fai drained her glass. "If you do go to Taipei—or, god forbid, Beijing—I can't stay at Derek and Mimi's. It was kind of them to offer, but I want to be surrounded by familiar things, by things that remind me of you."

Ava raised Fai's hand and kissed it gently.

"Do you know what I'd like to do right now?" Fai asked.

"Go to bed and cuddle."

Eventually they did cuddle, and then lay wrapped in each other's arms, their breath intermingling. Ava may have had times in her love life when she was as happy, but this was different. Before, when the exuberance of the early days of an affair ebbed, so did the desire to continue it. With Fai, Ava couldn't bear the thought of not being with her, and it was a feeling that had nothing to do with sex. May Ling was a Taoist, and often spoke about yin and yang—not as a man and a woman and not as two opposites, but as two people who filled the gap each had in their life. May contended that every yin had a yang waiting to be discovered. In Fai, Ava thought she had found hers.

At nine o'clock Ava got out of bed, went into the kitchen, drank a glass of water, and took a plastic bag from a drawer. The bag contained a number of SIM cards, including one she had bought when staying in Taipei while *Tiananmen* was being filmed. She swapped out her Toronto one, sat at the table, and found the phone number for Green Dragon

Import/Export in her notebook. Taipei was twelve hours ahead of Toronto so she assumed their offices would be open.

"Good morning, Green Dragon Import and Export," a woman answered.

"Good morning, can I speak to Mr. Song please," Ava said.

"He hasn't arrived yet, but we're expecting him soon. Do you want to leave a message?"

"No, I would rather call back," said Ava and hung up.

"Well?" Fai said from the kitchen entrance.

"He's in Taipei."

"Shit," Fai said softly.

"I'll leave tomorrow. There's no point in putting it off."

"Well, the sooner you go, the sooner you'll be back," said Fai.

Ava nodded, opened her laptop and found the website for EVA Air. There was a direct flight to Taipei scheduled to leave Pearson International at nine the next morning. Ava did a quick calculation, taking into account the time difference and a sixteen-hour flight, and figured that would get her into Taipei early afternoon the day after the next. To her mind it couldn't be much better, and she booked a seat in the first-class Royal Laurel. With that done, she switched to the Mandarin Oriental hotel site and reserved a suite for two nights.

"Could you pass me that plastic bag on the counter," she then said to Fai. When she got it, she replaced the Taipei SIM with her own and phoned Xu.

"*Wei*," Auntie Grace answered.

"Hi, it's Ava, is Xu available?"

"He's out by the fish pond having his morning smoke. I'll tell him you're on the line."

A moment later Ava heard Xu say, "Have you located Song?"

"Yes, he's still in Taipei. I've booked a flight that will get me there mid-afternoon Taipei time, the day after tomorrow."

"I'll make sure Lop arrives there that morning."

"And I'm staying at the Mandarin Oriental."

"We'll put him there as well," said Xu. "He should be able to bring your TIN card with him."

"That would be terrific, but in the meantime I'm using the Jennie Kwong name."

"I'll let him know."

"*Ge ge*, one more thing. Did you get the chance to read the email I sent with questions for Lop?"

"I forwarded it to him an hour ago. He's already working on coming up with some answers. He told me he has some former Special Forces colleagues who work for the MSS now. He's sure they'll be helpful."

"That sounds promising."

"It could be; those Special Forces ties run very deep. It's a real brotherhood, which extends beyond a man's actual length of service."

"Like the triads," Ava pointed out. "So Lop is doubly blessed with brothers."

8

THE EVA FLIGHT LEFT PEARSON AND LANDED AT
Taoyuan International Airport almost exactly on schedule.
An hour later, Ava had cleared customs, claimed her bag, and
was in a taxi for the forty-kilometre trip to the city centre. She
turned on her phone to check her messages as soon as the cab
left the arrivals level curb. Fai, Derek, and Lop had all called.

It was the middle of the night in Toronto, but Fai always
wanted to know she had landed safely regardless of the time,
so Ava phoned her.

"Is everything okay there?" she asked when Fai answered.

"Just fine, but I wanted to hear your voice," Fai said sleepily.

"Well, I'm here. All is well, so you go back to sleep. I'll
call you later."

It was definitely too late to call Derek, but there wasn't any
urgency to his message, which was simply that he'd located
David Mo. That fact alone was enough to please Ava.

Lop had phoned to say he was at the hotel waiting for
her, and to call his room when she arrived. There was no
mention of Green Dragon or the MSS, and she couldn't help
wondering what he'd found out.

The traffic on the highway was heavy but moving well, and it wasn't quite four o'clock when the taxi came to a stop at the entrance to the Mandarin Oriental. Ava paid the fare, then waved off the valet and carried her Shanghai Tang Double Happiness and Louis Vuitton bags into the lobby. Check-in was typically quick, and within a few minutes she entered a suite similar to the one she'd shared with Fai during the filming of *Tiananmen*. She thought about calling Lop before deciding that a shower and a change of clothes was in order.

Half an hour later, feeling refreshed, and dressed in black slacks and a crisply ironed white Brooks Brothers button-down shirt, she phoned Lop's room.

"I've arrived, I'm here in my suite, and I'm ready to meet," she said when he answered.

"Me too."

"Do you want to come to me, or shall I come to you?"

"Truthfully, I haven't eaten since leaving Shanghai. What are the restaurants like in the hotel?"

"What do you feel like?"

"A bit of a snack, nothing too heavy, just something to carry me through until dinner," he said.

"The café on the ground floor has an all-day dim sum selection that is of good quality."

"That sounds perfect."

"Then I'll see you there in about five minutes," she said, finding his remark about a later dinner slightly curious.

Ava put her phone into the LV bag, checked her appearance in a mirror, and left the suite. When she exited the elevator in the lobby and started towards the café, she saw Lop standing at the entrance wearing grey slacks that had a sharp crease, and a snug-fitting blue Lacoste polo shirt. As always, he was clean-shaven, and his hair was buzz-cut. *You can take the man out of the military, but you can't take the military out of the man*, she thought.

Lop's eyes turned in her direction. She smiled. He lowered his head slightly, and said, "*Xiao lao ban*, it's good to see you again, although from what I've been told I wish the circumstances were different."

Xiao lao ban meant "little boss," and it was a term that many of Xu's men used when they spoke of Ava. She had resisted acknowledging it at first, but gradually gave way. It was a compliment, and she knew she should be graceful enough to accept it.

"Yes, Lop, difficult times bring us together again."

"Hopefully with equally successful results."

She offered her hand, and he took it gently. They shook. "Let's go inside," she said.

One of the idiosyncrasies of the café was the rhino head mounted on a wall. Ava insisted on sitting at a table where it couldn't be seen. "I've had the har gow, the siu mai, and the vegetable-mushroom dumplings, and can recommend them all," she said as they sat.

A server came to the table almost immediately. Lop ordered everything Ava had mentioned, and a Tsingtao beer. She asked for a glass of Chardonnay. "You'll share the food with me?" he asked.

"I will try a little, but my body clock is working against me. It's about five in the morning in Toronto," she said. "You mentioned dinner when I spoke to you just now. Is that something I'm expected to attend?"

"Only if you want to, but I don't think it's necessary. I'm

meeting Tsai and one of his men. They're bringing me a gun and a knife. Obviously I couldn't carry them with me on a commercial flight."

"Does Tsai know why you're here?"

"Yes, Xu and then I spoke to him, and supplying me with the gun and knife seems to be as directly involved as he wants to get," Lop said, and then he reached into a pocket, took out a plastic card, and passed it to her. "This is for you. Your TIN card, and Xu said to tell you the passport will be ready by tomorrow."

"That's great, thanks," she said, looking at the TIN. Her picture wasn't the least bit flattering, but she thought the name Chow Qi had a nice ring to it. "In a way, I hope I don't need to use this, just as I hope you don't have to use the gun or the knife."

"I agree, but you can't be over-prepared when you're dealing with the MSS."

"Xu said you know quite a lot about them."

Lop shrugged. "I thought I did, but after talking to a few friends last night and this morning I know a hell of a lot more now."

"Like what?"

Their conversation stopped as their drinks were placed on the table. Lop picked up his glass after the beer was poured and held it in the air. "*Wan shou wu jiang*," he said, wishing her good health and a long life.

"And the same to you," Ava replied.

After his initial sip, Lop said, "I always knew that the MSS was running intelligence operations domestically, but what I didn't realize was how widespread their activities are worldwide, and not just in terms of gathering intelligence. Their mandate is to ensure China's security by any means they deem necessary—and there are no limits to those means, at least not that anyone is aware of."

"Lau Lau and Chen were hardly threatening the security of the Chinese government. I mean, the Syndicate had already blocked the film's distribution. What could the government possibly gain by having MSS kill those two gentle souls?"

Lop leaned towards her and lowered his voice. "Ava, everyone in Beijing is hypersensitive these days. I'm told the film generated a great deal of anger, and now you have the Oscar nominations on top of that. Some people would see those as a deliberate slap in the face from the West—a way to insult the Chinese government by honouring a film that everyone knows they think is loathsome."

"Are you suggesting the order to kill Lau Lau and Chen came from the top?"

"Not necessarily—it could have been ordered by someone deep down in the MSS or in the Communist Party who thought it was something their bosses would appreciate."

"Is the MSS part of the government or the Communist Party?"

"Truthfully, these days there isn't much obvious difference, although there was once, and the MSS is an example of that. Technically it is a government department, but in reality it's a political entity, beholden first and foremost to the preservation of the Communist Party. If you need proof of that, you need look no further than its emblem. Unlike every other government body, which display the national emblem—oddly enough, a representation of Tiananmen Gate with five stars above it—the emblem of the MSS is the hammer and sickle of the Communist Party."

"So the MSS functions as an extension of the party—as its spy network?"

"Not just spying, they have a security division and operate a secret police force," Lop said. "It wouldn't surprise me if the men who killed your friends are part of that force."

"But your friends don't know if they are or not?"

He smiled grimly. "It is an enormous organization, and there's as much secrecy practised internally as externally. My friends knew about the deaths, but nothing about who did it or authorized it."

"Were you able to confirm that Green Dragon Import/ Export is a front for the MSS?"

"I was. There are five staff from the mainland assigned to it, and a local staff of six. Aside from spying, their job is to sow as much political discord as they can. The ultimate objective is get enough pro-unification politicians elected that they can win a legislative vote to get the island returned to China. They've been heavily financing a group of hand-picked potential candidates, and offering very large bribes to people who already hold office. My sources think this will all pay off sooner rather than later."

Their food arrived, and conversation dwindled as chopsticks plucked dumplings from the plates. Lop was originally from Sichuan province and liked his food spicy, and so slathered a thick layer of chili sauce on his. Ava's intention was to eat sparingly, but found herself keeping up with Lop.

"Would you like to order more?" she asked when the last morsel was gone.

"I'd better not. Tsai is taking me to a Korean barbecue restaurant he swears by."

"That sounds good," she said. "Tell me, despite his

reluctance, if we need indirect help from Tsai, other than supplying weapons, is he up for it?"

"Such as?"

"Could he supply us with a car and driver? Renting a car or taking taxis raises our profile. I'd prefer to be as invisible as possible."

"I'll ask him tonight."

The server arrived to clear away the dishes. When she left, Ava said, "I'd like to back up a bit. You mentioned how secretive the MSS is, yet they approached two triad gangs to do the killing. Why do you think that was? It sounds as if they have enough people here who could have done the deed."

"There is no one assigned here who is attached to the secret police division—that's where the government assassins are headquartered. They could have brought men over from the mainland, but maybe they thought their best first option was to get it done locally by people who know how to keep their mouths shut."

"Except they didn't keep their mouths shut. Both Tsai and Han were willing to finger Song as the guy offering them the job."

"Only because they were talking to Xu. It was still kept inside the triad family."

"What did you find out about Song?"

"His full name is Song Pin-Lin. He's forty-four and he has been working for the MSS for some time," Lop said. "Green Dragon is the third front the MSS has used over the past five years. The first two were travel agencies and Song worked at both of them. They were shut down when they attracted too much attention from the Taiwanese National Security Bureau. That bureau, by the way, is quite competent, so I'm guessing it will only be a matter of time before they force the Green Dragon operation to shut down."

"Does it actually import or export anything?"

"It imports some sauces and frozen vegetables, and exports rice, but hardly enough to justify a staff even a quarter of that size."

"What is Song's job there supposed to be?"

"He's the sales director."

"We need to get our hands on him," Ava said quietly.

"I assumed that would be the case."

"And we need some place to take him when we do."

"I thought about that as well. The easiest way is probably to get him where he lives. I have the address. I was told he isn't married, and so I assume he lives there alone."

"Is it an apartment?" Ava asked.

"Yes, and I have its number."

"We could tail him from his work, or wait outside his building for him to arrive. Waiting would be easiest, but we need to be able to identify him."

Lop smiled and reached into his pocket. "It isn't a sharp image, but his looks are so distinctive that I don't think we'd miss him," he said as he passed her a photo.

Ava stared at it. Lop wasn't wrong about Song's looks, she thought, as she eyed the large fleshy face, totally bald head, and thick moustache that ran from his lips down both sides of his mouth. "How did you get this?" she asked.

"Through one of my friends inside the MSS, and he assured me it was quite recent."

"Did he ask you why you wanted it, or why you were asking about Song?"

"No—the fact that I asked was enough."

"I have that kind of relationship with several people. I value them tremendously," Ava said, and then stared at the photo again. "He looks like a large man."

"Does that matter?"

"No."

"I didn't think it would," Lop said. "But, Ava, I have to ask, what is the endgame with Song?"

"Are you asking if I intend to kill him?"

"I am."

Ava stared into his eyes. "I don't know. That might depend on how co-operative he is or how secure we feel about letting him live. What I want more than anything is to identify the person who actually authorized and ordered the killings. I strongly suspect that Song is no more than a step in that direction."

Lop looked grim. "Speaking strictly for myself, I don't believe in loose ends."

"Me neither, but let's not pre-judge how Song is going to react."

"Okay, we'll play it by ear, but I wanted you to know how I normally like to operate in situations like this," he said. "Dead men don't talk."

"Your position is clear, and I'm not unsympathetic to it."

Lop nodded but looked doubtful.

Ava began to say something else when a yawn caught her by surprise. "Excuse me," she said. "I think the time difference is beginning to catch up to me."

"Why don't you get a good night's rest? We can talk again in the morning. How early can I call?"

"I'll be up by seven, so any time after that," she said. "Enjoy your meal with Tsai."

9

AFTER LEAVING LOP, AVA WENT TO HER ROOM. THEIR conversation had gone as well as she could have hoped, although she found his question about Song's eventual fate disquieting. It wasn't something she had thought through, perhaps because she wasn't ready to reach the conclusion that Lop had intimated. She knew that they might end up there, but didn't want to accept it as inevitable. In fact, she hoped that Song would make it possible for them not to have to kill him.

Of greater interest to her was Lop's description of the workings of the Ministry of State Security. She had known a little about the MSS—mainly about its efforts to keep the lid on any possible internal dissent—but she'd had no idea it operated as an overseas spy agency and had a secret police force attached. It suddenly made the job ahead of her seem all that more formidable. But what the hell, she thought— they needed to take one step at a time, and the first was Song Pin-Lin.

She took her notebook from her LV bag, sat at the desk in the suite, and opened it. She recorded the key points Lop had made about the MSS, and then about Green Dragon Import/Export. She had begun to underline some of them when her phone rang, and she saw Derek's name on the screen. She checked the time, and saw it was just past six in the morning in Toronto.

"You're up early," she said when she answered.

"The baby calls the shots around here, and she's an early bird."

"Anyway, I'm glad to hear from you, and I did get your message about David Mo."

"He was easy enough to locate. He's all over Instagram, TikTok, and Twitter, and writes a monthly column for a gay online publication. He's still attending the UCLA film school, and is still living with Mark Simmons. I have the contact information for both of them."

"Can you email all of that to me?"

"Yeah, but there's one more thing you should know," said Derek. "In some of the Instagram photos and in two of the TikTok videos, he's heavily made up and dressed like a drag queen."

"Goodness me."

"I'm not sure that's what his father would say."

"That's very true, but I doubt there's much he can do to change his son. When you send me the information, make sure you include a couple of those photos."

"I'm doing it now," he said. "Okay, everything is on its way."

"Thanks, Derek, and big hugs to Mimi and the baby."

She waited for a moment before going to her email. Derek's was there: David Mo's address and his and Mark Simmons's cellphone numbers were included, and there were four attachments. She opened them one by one and saw that—if anything—David Mo had become more willing to share his sexual identity with the world. It was something she had difficulty understanding. Ava had never hidden or lied about her sexuality, but for her it was something private, not something to be paraded. Maybe that was her Chinese gene, but maybe also it was a reflection of a Canadian attitude typified by Justice Minister Pierre Trudeau introducing a bill in 1967 that decriminalized homosexual activities conducted in private and saying, "The nation has no business in the bedrooms of the nation." Ava couldn't have agreed more—what went on in her bedroom was going to stay in the bedroom.

Ava copied David Mo's address and cell number into her notebook, and then unleashed a massive yawn, a sure sign that she wasn't going to stay awake much longer. She didn't want to wake Fai, but if she didn't call her now she thought she might miss the chance.

"Hey babe," Fai answered on the second ring.

"I wasn't sure you'd be up, but I'm fading fast here and wanted to talk to you before crashing."

"I had trouble sleeping after your earlier call. I'm not used to an empty bed anymore."

"I'll try to call at better hours from now on," Ava said, smiling at the empty-bed reference.

"Did you meet with Lop?" Fai asked.

"I did, and he was as capable as ever. He's found the home address of the guy who tried to hire the triads to kill Chen and Lau Lau. He's our target tomorrow, but after that—who knows?"

"What I hope is that he's the end of the road."

"I only wish that was the case."

"But you don't think so."

Ava hesitated. "I have no idea what to expect, I really don't. Whatever it is, though, we'll deal with it."

An hour later she could no longer fight off the need to sleep, and got into bed. But as she lay there, her mind took its time to calm. The last few days had been a blur, and the reality of being in Taipei again was only beginning to sink in. She tried to clear her head by concentrating on her breathing. She took in as much air as she could, and then slowly emptied her lungs. She rarely got past ten breaths before falling asleep; tonight she stopped at eight.

She slept dreamless and soundly until two a.m., when the need to go to the bathroom woke her. When she got back into bed, sleep came easily, but this time it was accompanied by a dream. She had arrived at Chek Lap Kok, Hong Kong's international airport, and was walking through the arrivals hall when she heard her name being called. She looked to one side and saw Uncle sitting at a table in the Kit Kat Koffee House. He smiled and waved to her. He had an unlit cigarette dangling from his lips, and a cup of coffee sat on the table next to the racing form.

"You are as beautiful as ever," he said as she approached.

She leaned over and kissed him on the forehead. "What a nice surprise to find you here," she said.

"Join me for a coffee."

She sat, and a minute later a server put a cup of black coffee in front of her.

"How do you always know when I need to see you?" she asked after taking a sip.

"You are the one who tells me, who calls on me, and I would never say no."

"Did you hear about Lau Lau and Chen?"

"Who hasn't?"

"I'm trying to find out who ordered their deaths."

"I know, but there are some things you're better off not knowing," he said. "This may be one of them."

"I feel an obligation."

"To the dead men, or are you trying to forestall an attack on Fai—or against May Ling, Amanda, and your businesses?"

"May, Amanda, and the businesses are well insulated. There is absolutely nothing connecting them to the film."

Uncle stared across the table at her. "There is one thing, and that's you," he said. "I know you've been cautious, but you're living with Fai, and Mo knows you had a relationship with Chen. And don't forget that you were front and centre at Cannes. All it will take is for some imaginative officer in the MSS to start connecting dots."

"That thought scares me."

"And so it should. Mo knows your real identity, doesn't he?"

"He does, but in all of my interactions with film people since Cannes I've been using the name Jennie Kwong. And I do have some leverage where Mo is concerned."

"That gives him all the more reason to get rid of you."

"I didn't think of it that way," Ava said, suddenly feeling foolish.

Uncle reached for her hand, took it, and held it gently. "I'm not trying to alarm you. I just want you to think this through properly," he said. "What is the end result you're after, and what are you prepared to do to get there? Those are the questions you need to answer before you start down a path so fraught with danger."

"I told you—I want to find out who ordered their deaths."

"And then?"

She shook her head in frustration. "I don't know."

"That causes me to worry."

"Everyone seems to be worried."

"For good reason, wouldn't you agree? I had my own experience with the MSS, and it wasn't pleasant. They are a law unto themselves, and it took an intervention from Deng Xiaoping himself to save me. You don't have Deng or any senior government official in your corner."

"I have Lop and his contacts," Ava replied. "And I have my wits."

Uncle squeezed her hand, and his voice dropped a tone. "Would you please do something for me?"

"You know I'd do anything."

"Don't start down the path you seem to have chosen without having decided what you'll do each stop of the way—starting with that man Song."

Ava hesitated, and then said, "Lop asked me about Song, and I wasn't clear in my answer."

"What is his opinion?"

"He doesn't want any loose ends."

Uncle nodded. "I agree with his approach. Do you remember what we did when we stumbled into the 'Ndrangheta mess in Surabaya? We did everything humanly possible to cover our tracks. It was exactly the thing to do, and as vengeful and determined as the 'Ndrangheta is, the Chinese government is that tenfold."

"You know that after killing the Red Pole Lok in Macau I've had nightmares, and I'm not sure I'm capable of doing something like that again."

"That's why you have Lop. He won't hesitate. He won't

regret it. It's all business with him, as it is with the MSS. I know you don't like having someone do a job on your behalf, but this is one time when you shouldn't feel guilty about having that kind of help. Let him do what has to be done."

"I think you're right, but I still need to think about it more carefully," she said.

"Trust Lop," Uncle said, taking his black-crackle Zippo from his pocket and lighting his cigarette.

Ava saw the server point to the sign that read NO SMOKING and then start walking towards them. She turned to say something to Uncle, but he was gone, and she found herself sitting upright in bed with the smell of cigarette smoke in the air.

10

AVA WOKE AT SIX THIRTY FEELING WELL RESTED, IF slightly troubled. Uncle's nighttime visits usually helped her navigate her way through whatever situation she was in, but this dream had left a large question she couldn't yet answer.

She slipped out of bed, made a coffee, and sat at the desk. She checked her phone and then her laptop for texts, emails, and messages. When she couldn't see anything that required her immediate attention, she opened her notebook and wrote SHOULD SONG LIVE? Under that she created two columns, for pros and cons. Five minutes later she sighed, gave up trying to list any pros, and made another coffee.

The suite overlooked the street below. Ava took her phone and coffee and pushed a red leather easy chair closer to the window. She sat and absent-mindedly watched the traffic and pedestrians below. Taipei was a busy city even at this time of the morning and scooters were everywhere, but everything was orderly and purposeful—though not in the sense of being directed or controlled, in the style of Singapore. It was more like Hong Kong, she thought, where things could be busy without the chaos of cities such as Manila or Bangkok.

She finished her coffee and was thinking about making a third when her phone rang.

"Good morning, Lop, how was the dinner?" she said.

"I got what I was promised, and he agreed to provide us with a car and driver, although he stressed again that he doesn't want the driver directly involved in whatever goes on with Song. He is quite paranoid about the MSS."

"He's not the only one," Ava said, thinking about Uncle.

"Tsai also asked me when I thought we might go after Song. I asked him why he wanted to know, and he said he had no real reason other than passing on some advice."

"Which was?"

"Well, he said that many Taiwanese businessmen start work late, end late, and go out to eat and drink after. He thought it might be easier—and would draw less attention to us—if we went after him earlier, like this morning before he left for work."

"What do you think?"

"I'm not that good at waiting. We drove over there last night to have a look at the building, and I managed to get inside. It is an older one with CCTV in the lobby but none on the individual floors, and there's no security officer. You need a code to get through the doors, but with lots of people coming and going in the morning, we shouldn't have any problem accessing the building."

"How do you suggest we get into his apartment?"

"I thought you could knock on his door. You're hardly a threatening figure. I'm sure he'll open it for you."

"And if he doesn't?"

"Then we'll wait for him to step outside and take him back inside."

Ava tried to think of any downsides to what Lop was proposing, and came up with one. "You don't think they'll notice when he doesn't show up for work? They could come looking for him."

"We could have him call in to say he has an outside meeting and doesn't know when it will be done. I would have the gun pressed against his temple when he did, of course."

"Of course," Ava said, deciding Lop was making sense. "Okay, let's do it that way. You're right that there's no point in wasting a day just hanging around without any idea of when he's going to show up."

"When could you be ready to leave here?"

"How far is Song's apartment building from the hotel?"

"Tsai said it's about a half-hour drive."

Ava checked the time. "Then give me half an hour. That should get us there by eight o'clock."

"Great, I'll phone the driver and tell him when to pick us up."

"Could you ask him to bring some duct tape with him? If he can't then he'll have to stop somewhere on the way."

"I'll tell him," Lop said matter-of-factly, as if it were a normal request.

"All right, we have a plan."

"It appears that way. I'll see you in the lobby in half an hour," he said.

Ava shivered slightly as she put down the phone. Things were moving faster than she had anticipated, and she had a disquieting thought that maybe they were moving too fast. But she did trust Lop's judgement and wasn't prepared to argue with him.

She got up from the chair and went to the bathroom. Ava

THE FURY OF BEIJING   63

showered quickly, brushed her teeth, pulled her hair back and fixed it with her lucky ivory chignon pin. She applied some mascara and a touch of pale red lipstick, and then went into the bedroom to dress. She wanted to look as low-key and professional as possible, and so put on a white cotton button-down shirt, a pair of black cotton slacks, and black flats. She stood in front of the mirror. Would she open the door for a stranger who looked like her? *Why not*, she thought.

Before leaving the suite, she picked up the phone and made a call.

"Hi babe," Fai answered.

"I'm going to be leaving the hotel soon with Lop. I'll probably be out of touch for a few hours. If you don't hear from me or can't reach me I don't want you to worry. Things are moving ahead very nicely."

"Telling me not to worry doesn't mean I won't," Fai said. "You have to call me whenever you and Lop have finished whatever you're doing. I don't care what the time is."

"I will call. I promise," Ava said. "Love you."

"Love you too."

Ava left the suite with her LV bag. When she exited the elevator in the lobby, she found Lop standing off to one side. He was wearing the same pair of grey slacks as the previous day, but had traded the blue Lacoste polo shirt for a black one. He was holding a plastic shopping bag in his right hand. Ava assumed it had the gun and the knife in it.

"Good morning," he said. "The car is here already."

They began to walk to the exit. "Did the driver manage to find some duct tape?" she asked.

"He brought a very large roll," Lop said, raising the bag. "It's in here, along with my gun and knife."

"Good, should I pay him for it or tip him?"

"Just saying thanks should be enough. His name is Liu."

Outside, Ava saw a stocky man wearing jeans and a black T-shirt, with heavily tattooed arms, leaning against a car in front of the hotel doors. Lop went directly to him. "We're ready to leave," he said.

Liu nodded and opened the back door for them.

"Thanks for driving us, and for the tape," Ava said.

The man looked at her as if he was trying to remember something.

"Is there a problem?" she asked.

"No, I'm just wondering if you're the woman who took down Wang on that movie set about a year ago."

"Is Wang completely bald?"

"Yeah."

"Then yes, I think I remember him."

Liu smiled. "The guys still talk about it, and Wang can't live it down. It is an honour to be driving for you."

Ava slid into the back seat and was quickly joined by Lop. "What was that about?" he asked.

"Some of Tsai's men tried to strong-arm money from friends of mine who were making a film. I negotiated a settlement that satisfied both sides."

"It sounds like the negotiations happened after you put down Wang."

"That is how it went."

Lop shook his head. "You never fail to surprise."

"How is traffic?" Ava asked Liu, wanting to change the topic. "I was told it was a half-hour drive."

"Traffic is fine, so maybe a bit less than that," Liu said as he pointed the car in the direction of the street.

There was a lot of traffic but it moved steadily. As they left the downtown core Ava thought about what she was going to say to Song when he answered the door. She knew something specific would work best, and considered several options. One seemed the most compelling and practical, but until she got to the building she wouldn't know if it was workable.

There wasn't any conversation in the car until twenty-five minutes later, when they reached a street lined with identical ten-storey, brown brick apartment buildings. Ava always found this kind of uniformity depressing.

"That's his building over there," Lop said, pointing to the right.

Liu drove past it and parked a hundred metres away. "I'll be waiting here," he said. "Do you have any idea how long you might be?"

"Not a clue," said Lop. "You can go to a restaurant or do something else if you want—just don't go too far away. I'll phone you when we're ready to leave."

Ava and Lop exited the car and walked to Song's building. There were two glass doors at the entrance that led inside to a vestibule, and then two more doors with a keypad to the right. On the wall behind a glass panel to their left was a list of occupants and their apartment numbers. Ava went to it, found the information she had been hoping would be there, and then scanned the index for Song.

"There are four Songs," she said to Lop.

"He's in number 1008," he said.

They stood off to one side, trying not to look conspicuous while they waited for someone to open the entrance doors. It took about a minute, but it felt longer. Finally, a middle-aged woman exited one of the building's two elevators and walked across the white tiled lobby towards them. She opened one of the doors without giving them a glance. Lop held it for her, and then he and Ava slipped into the lobby. She saw CCTV cameras above the elevator doors and on two walls. She also noticed lights above each elevator that reported which floor it was on.

"Can we use the stairs?" she asked Lop.

"You want to walk up nine flights?"

"No, but if we're the only people in the elevator, security footage could show it stopping on the tenth. Why take even that small risk? We can get off on the eighth and walk from there."

"Good thinking," Lop said. "And have you decided what approach you're going to take at the door?"

"The sign in the vestibule said the building is managed by the Opal Building Management Company. I'm now a representative."

They were the only two people in the elevator, exited on the eighth floor, and walked up two flights of stairs. Ava felt a flutter in her stomach when they reached the tenth. It was a sign of nervousness—a common feeling back when she was in the debt collection business, but something she had experienced less often since.

"Please wait for a minute before opening the door," she said to Lop, then took several deep breaths and forced herself to calm.

"Are you okay?" he asked.

"I'm fine. I'm just gathering myself," she said. "Let's go."

The floor had eight units, each with an identical red door and peephole. The doors looked sturdy enough to prevent an easy break-in and were thick enough to be soundproof.

Some were festooned with metal and cardboard characters intended to bring good fortune or protect the residents. Song's unit was at the far end, on the right.

When they reached his door, Lop stood off to one side so he wouldn't be visible through the peephole. Ava stood directly in front and pressed the buzzer. There was no immediate answer, and she couldn't hear anyone moving around inside. *He's not here*, she thought with a sense of panic, and then pressed the buzzer again. She stared into the peephole and finally saw it change colour as someone looked out.

The door opened a crack, and a man she recognized as Song stared back at her. Any thoughts she'd had about rushing him vanished when she saw a metal chain stretching across the gap.

"Good morning, Mr. Song. My name is Jennie Kwong. I work for the Opal Building Management Company and we are responsible for the management and upkeep of this apartment complex. There are some renovations that are in the planning process and we are here today to consult about them with as many residents as we can. Would it be possible to have five minutes of your time to review them with you?"

"I'm not interested," he said.

"Perhaps you aren't, but you live in a corner unit, and the renovations are going to impact you quite severely. If you have any objections to what's being planned, this is your opportunity to voice them. Otherwise, the work will go ahead without your input. I promise, it will only take a few minutes."

He looked hesitant, and then said, "Tell me what's planned."

"I'd rather show you. I have a chart that explains it all, but

I need a table to spread it out," Ava said, and smiled. "Really, it will be easier, quicker, and more informative that way."

Song was wearing black sweatpants and a white T-shirt that stretched across his chest and looked one size too small. He tugged at the bottom of the shirt to cover a sliver of exposed belly. Then he shook his head, but Ava wasn't sure if it was in resignation or a prelude to a no. "Okay, you can come in. But for five minutes, that's it."

"That's all I need," she said.

He unhooked the chain and stepped back. Ava walked through the door, and then moved to one side as Lop came in right behind her with the gun in his hand.

"What the hell!" Song shouted.

Lop pointed the gun at his head. "Not another word out of you."

11

SONG'S HEAD SWIVELLED BETWEEN AVA AND LOP AS he tried to make sense of the situation.

Ava looked around the apartment. It consisted of a bedroom, bathroom, and a combination kitchen/living room. There was a small round table with two wooden chairs in the kitchen. She went in there, picked up a chair, and carried it to the middle of the living room. "Take a seat," she said to Song.

He hesitated. "What do you want?"

"You'll find out after you sit."

"Do you know who I am? Do you know who I work for?" he asked.

"We have a good idea, but you're going to confirm it," Ava said. "Now sit, and don't make me ask again."

Song scowled, and then made a deliberate show of reluctance as he sat.

Ava walked into the kitchen again and opened drawers until she found a pair of scissors. "Pass me the tape," she said to Lop when she came back into the room. "I'm going to tape you to the chair by the ankles, and then I'm going to tape your wrists together behind your back," she said to Song. "It's as much for your protection as anything. My partner doesn't react well to sudden moves, and this way you'll be locked down."

"What the fuck do you think you're doing?" Song asked.

"I'll tell you in a minute," she said as she taped first one ankle, and then the second. "When you're secured, we want you to make a phone call to your office. Where's your phone?"

"By my bed."

"I'll get it," Lop said.

A moment later he returned with a Samsung Galaxy. "Is there a passcode?" he asked Song.

"Yes."

Lop handed him the phone. "Enter it, and then call your office. Tell them you have a meeting with an importer and won't be there until about noon. Put the phone on speaker mode."

Song stared at it and didn't move. Lop stood next to him and pressed the gun against his temple. "You have fifteen seconds to make the call."

"You won't shoot me," said Song.

Lop sighed. "Toss me one of the cushions on the couch," he said to Ava.

She did, and watched Lop place it against the side of Song's left thigh and then press the barrel of the gun into it.

"I'll start with that thigh, and then I'll do the next, and then maybe your forearms, or even your testicles. You won't die, at least not right away, but you sure as hell are going to be in a world of pain," said Lop.

Song looked up at him and seemed to see nothing that suggested Lop wasn't serious. He lowered his head, entered the passcode, and when the phone came to life, he hit a contact number. Seconds later he said, "Kimmy, this is Pin-Lin. I have a meeting downtown so I won't be in the office until around noon. I'll call if there are any other changes."

Ava detected some stress in his voice, but not so much that it should have alarmed Kimmy—whoever she was.

"Okay, I'll let everyone know," Kimmy said, and then hung up.

"See, that was easy," Lop said.

"Now, put your arms behind your back," Ava said to Song.

He did, and she duct-taped them together at the wrists.

"When are you going to tell me what this is about?" Song asked.

"You have things backwards," said Ava. "*You* are going to be doing the telling."

Ava went back to the kitchen and returned with the second chair. She put it down directly facing him, about a metre away. Lop took a seat on the couch. Song furrowed his brow and glanced at Lop, as if confused by Ava taking the dominant position.

"Mr. Song, you can make this easy on us and yourself, or you can make it hard. If you choose to make it hard, you will pay the price because we are patient, persistent, and confident of eventually getting the information we're after," she said.

"I have no clue what you're after."

"You'll know soon enough, but to start, will you please confirm that you are employed by the Chinese Ministry of State Security."

Song blinked, and his tongue licked his upper lip, wetting his moustache. "I work for the Green Dragon Import/Export Company."

"Which we know is a front for the Chinese Ministry of State Security."

"That's more than I know."

Ava groaned. "Mr. Song, let's not start this way. We are not employed by the Taiwanese National Security Bureau, and we're not here to arrest you for engaging in what some would regard as traitorous behaviour. Our interests lie elsewhere. So please, answer my question."

Song looked at Lop again. "Who are you working for? What do you want with me?"

"Hey, she's the boss here, not me," Lop said. "Pay attention to her, and don't be stupid—answer her questions."

Song hesitated, and then stuttered. "I have heard that some Chinese investors may have a financial interest in our company."

"Are any of the employees from the mainland?" she asked.

"A couple of them are."

"But you don't know if they're attached to the MSS?"

"That's right."

Ava nodded and said, "Mr. Song, I have to tell you that we're not getting off to a good start here. I don't want to ask my friend to put his gun to your thigh again, but that's where we're heading if you aren't more forthcoming."

She saw sweat begin to bead on Song's forehead.

"I'm doing the best I can," he said.

"No, you aren't," Ava said, and turned to Lop. "Shoot him in whichever thigh you want."

Lop started to rise from the couch, but before he had got fully to his feet, Song shouted, "Wait a minute. Let me rethink your questions. I may have misheard them."

"Okay. To help you, I'll restate my last one more clearly:

are any of the mainland Chinese working at Green Dragon actually employed by the MSS?"

"Yes. I know at least two of them are."

"What is their objective?"

"Obviously to represent the interests of the People's Republic."

"Yes, obviously it would be, but how in specific terms?"

"The People's Republic believes that Taiwan should regain its status as a Chinese province. There are a great many people in Taiwan who believe that as well. The MSS guys provide them with money and support."

"Are you one of those people who believe Taiwan should be returned to China?"

"You could say that, but it isn't something I feel that strongly about."

"Is that your roundabout way of saying yes?"

"Yes."

"So officially, while you are employed by Green Dragon, you are also working with the MSS to help them reach their goals?"

"I deal in sauces and rice."

"And when you aren't doing that, you're trying to undermine the Taiwanese government, and perhaps arranging to have people killed?"

"What are you talking about? That's nonsense," Song blurted.

"Which part?"

"All of it."

"Okay, I'll forego the remark about the Taiwanese government, but I can't let you lie to me about trying to arrange the deaths of certain people."

"I have no idea what you're trying to get at."

"Their names were Chen Jie and Lau Lau. Does that ring a bell?"

"No."

"I was told by someone I trust that you tried to hire local people to kill them."

"That's not true."

"And I believe that when that didn't work, the mss sent assassins from the mainland to do the job," Ava continued. "They gunned down Chen and Lau Lau in front of the Palais de Chine hotel earlier this week. Surely you heard or read about that. I was told it was on the front pages of all the local newspapers."

"I don't bother with newspapers."

"And you didn't try to arrange a contract on their lives?"

"No."

Ava shrugged. "I'm trying to be patient, but I'm starting to lose it," she said as she got up from the chair. She looked at Lop. "I have to go to the bathroom. Shoot him in the right thigh while I'm gone. I'll bring a towel to wrap around his leg."

She did have to go to the bathroom, and was sitting on the toilet when she heard the muffled gun shot. When she returned to the living room minutes later, Song's head was slumped against his chest and he was uttering a litany of groans. She gave the towel to Lop. When he had tied it as best he could around the leg, Ava resumed sitting across from Song. "Please, no more nonsense. I don't like having to do this. If you are just honest, there's no reason for us to hurt you."

"Who are you?" he asked, tears trickling down his cheeks.

"We're friends of the people who were killed. We don't

represent anyone but their memories and ourselves," she said. "What we want to know quite simply is who ordered them to be killed. I don't think it was you, was it?"

Song shook his head.

"So, who was it?"

"Pan," he moaned.

"And who is Pan?"

"The boss at Green Dragon."

"Is he with the MSS?"

Song nodded.

"And it was Pan who instructed you to find some local killers to take out Chen and Lau Lau?"

"It was," Song said.

"Was he disappointed when you couldn't?"

"He was furious. He told me I was making them all look bad. He said Beijing would be angry that they had to send people from China to Taiwan."

"Is that what happened—did they send people?"

"Yes."

"Did you meet them?"

"No, but I saw them in the office with Pan."

"Were you ever told why the MSS wanted to kill Chen and Lau Lau?"

"Pan said they were traitors of the worst kind. He said they were telling lies and smearing the reputation of the People's Republic around the world."

"And that is all you needed to know?"

"I am a loyal person," Song said, his voice breaking.

"I'm sure you are, and I think that's admirable," Ava said. "Now tell me, how did Pan and the killers know where Chen and Lau Lau were going to be that night?"

"We'd been tracking Chen's phone ever since he arrived in Taiwan a month ago. We listened to every call and heard him make the dinner reservation."

"How did you know he was coming to Taiwan?"

"Beijing told us. They said they'd had him under surveillance for even longer."

Ava paused, then asked, "But even knowing he was here, they waited until the Oscar nominations were announced before killing him. Was that deliberate?"

"I don't know if it was or wasn't."

"What if he and Lau Lau hadn't been nominated?"

"I don't think that would have made any difference. The men from the secret police were already here. They wouldn't have left without finishing the job."

"Did you ever deal with Beijing yourself?"

"No, Pan runs the show. He was the one in contact with them. The rest of us just did what Pan told us to do."

Ava frowned, glanced at Lop, and rose from the chair. "I'll be back," she said to Song. She walked to the couch and sat next to Lop. "We need to get Pan here. Do you have any suggestions?"

"Song will have to ask him, and he'll need a reasonable excuse and to be able to communicate it properly. Beyond that, I don't know what else might work."

"It will be challenging for him."

"Yes, but I'm sure he wants to live. That should be motivation enough," Lop said.

"I hope you're right." Ava got up from the couch and went over to sit opposite Song. His eyes were squeezed shut. She touched him lightly on the knee of the leg that hadn't been shot. "Mr. Song, we need you to do something for us. It won't be easy, but I think you can do it if you concentrate. I want you to call Pan and ask him to come here."

"Why?"

"I want him to tell us who in Beijing decided that Chen and Lau Lau had to die."

Song looked doubtful.

"Would you like a glass of water?" Ava asked, deciding that it might be the right time for persuasion rather than duress.

He nodded.

She brought a glass of water from the kitchen and held it lightly against Song's lips. It took several minutes, but he drank it all.

"I don't have any more questions for you, if that's what you're worried about," she said. "I think you've told us everything you know. Now we need to talk to Pan, and we'll be very grateful if you could make that phone call."

"What would I tell him?"

"You should know that better than us. Is there some business or personal issue that would get him to leave the office?"

Song shook his head. "I'm not thinking so clearly."

"Lop, can you come up with something?" Ava asked, struggling to find a reason that made sense.

"Better to keep it simple, don't you think? Can't he just say he's got a serious problem that he can't discuss over the phone?"

"That could be little bit too simple, but if he thought there were some guys who were after him, that might get Pan's attention."

"Yes, I think that might work," said Lop.

"Although it might sound so suspicious that he won't come here alone."

"That is a risk."

"Well, I can't think of anything else, so risk or not, let's give it a go," Ava said, and she smiled at Song. "The important thing is not to get dragged into details. Some guys you don't know are after you. Don't tell Pan any more than that, and if he pushes, keep repeating it. The one question you might not be able to duck is why does he have to come to you? The answer is that you're afraid to leave the building."

"And if he won't come?" Song asked.

"Then we'll find another way to get to him."

"What about me? What happens to me?"

"Let's not get ahead of ourselves," Ava said as lightly as she could, and then turned to Lop. "Could you bring Mr. Song's phone to me please?"

Ava found the office number in his contacts, hit it, put the phone on speaker mode, and held it near Song's mouth. His voice wavered as he asked Kimmy to transfer him to Mr. Pan.

"What the hell is going on with you today?" Pan barked when he came on the line.

"I have to talk to you. I need you to come to my apartment. I'm afraid to leave. A guy phoned me and told me to come outside to meet him. He wouldn't say who he was, and when I looked out I saw four guys I don't know."

"What do they want?"

"I've never seen them before. You need to come. You have to help."

"Calm down."

"I can't. You have to come," Song said.

This wasn't going to go any better, Ava thought suddenly, and ended the call.

"That was a good effort, but I'm not sure it's going to work.

We should probably start thinking about a Plan B," she said to Lop.

"How far is your office from here?" Lop asked Song.

"In good traffic it's a forty-five-minute drive."

"Then let's wait it out here for at least an hour," Lop said to Ava.

She nodded, and walked over to the window in the living room. She opened the blinds and looked outside. "You can see the building entrance from here. We should move him so he can see it. If Pan comes, he can identify him."

12

IT TOOK LESS THAN HALF AN HOUR AFTER TAKING Song to the window to realize he wasn't doing well. He had obviously lost a lot of blood, and the shock of being shot was beginning to wear off, replaced by pain.

"I'm not sure he's going to be alert enough to identify Pan when he arrives," she said to Lop.

"I could take him to the bathroom, clean him up a bit, and look for some painkillers."

"Yes, that's a good idea."

Lop removed the tape from Song's ankles while Ava undid it behind his back.

"Put your arm around my neck. I'll help you get to the bathroom. Do you have any painkillers in there?" Lop said.

"Lots," Song mumbled.

Once they had left the room, Ava collapsed onto the couch. *So far, so good*, she thought, but Pan was going to be the main catch in Taiwan. But where else might he lead them? She stared at the closed bathroom door. She couldn't help feeling a bit sorry for Song. He was just a little man caught up in a big system, obeying orders. Unfortunately for him, one of those orders had been to find someone willing to take on a contract to kill Chen and Lau Lau.

Fifteen minutes later, Ava was beginning to think that Lop was taking an inordinate amount of time, and wondered if he needed help in the bathroom. Before she could follow through on that thought, the door opened and the two men appeared. Lop helped Song hobble back to the chair.

"Do we tape him again?" he asked Ava.

"Just his arms."

While Lop secured Song, Ava went to the window and looked down. There was a steady stream of traffic, and no parking in front of the building—in fact, there were hardly any parking spots in sight.

As they settled in to wait, Song said, "Can I ask you something?"

"Sure," Ava replied.

"What are you going to do with me if Pan doesn't come?"

"Do you think that's possible?"

"He's a really suspicious guy."

"We'll cross that bridge when we come to it," she said, hating to use that cliché to fudge the truth.

Song lapsed into silence, and Ava could only imagine what ugly scenarios were running through his mind.

Lop motioned for her to come to the other side of the room. "What if Pan doesn't come?"

"Then we'll have to locate him. Can your friends at the MSS supply us with another address?"

"I'm not sure. If Pan is actually running operations here, that could be a big ask."

"Then let's hope he shows."

Lop went to stand by Song while Ava occupied the couch.

She watched the two men at the window, but her mind was elsewhere. Every death in which she had been involved—and there were several—had been a matter of self-defence, and never revenge. But this was different, on so many levels. Two men had been murdered for no valid reason, and no one was going to be arrested or held accountable unless it was by Lop and her. And in the back of her mind, holding those behind the killings accountable was also an indirect way of trying to protect Fai.

"Song says they've arrived," Lop blurted, breaking into her thoughts.

"*They've* arrived?" Ava said, walking to the window. She looked down and saw three men on the sidewalk approaching the building.

"The small one with the grey suit and scraggly beard is Pan," Song said with difficulty. "The other two are some of his MSS guys from China."

"I was afraid this might happen," she murmured.

"We can't stay," Lop said. "This apartment is so small that if we're here when they arrive it will be bedlam. We'll have no control."

"Yes, we need to go," Ava agreed. "We'll take the stairs down to the eighth floor and catch the elevator there."

"You go ahead, I'll catch up," Lop said.

On her way out of the apartment, Ava paused just outside the door. When she heard the dull thud of a muffled shot, she closed her eyes. *It had to be done*, she told herself.

Lop emerged carrying his bag. They hurried to the stairway and went down two flights, then had to wait a few minutes for an elevator. When they reached the ground floor and the elevator doors opened, they found themselves face to face with the small man in the grey suit and his two cohorts.

"Good morning," Ava said as she and Lop stepped out.

The three men brushed past them without a glance or a word.

Ava and Lop made their way out to the street, and stood on the sidewalk gathering their thoughts.

"Thank you for taking care of Song," she said.

"No loose ends."

"What do you think they'll do?" Ava asked. "Will they call for an ambulance, call for the police, or just leave Song there and get out as fast as they can?"

"I don't think they'll be calling anyone," said Lop.

"Then let's wait in the car for them to come back down. We'll trail them. They'll probably head for the Green Dragon offices—but you never know, we could get lucky and Pan gets dropped off along the way."

Lop hesitated, and then said, "I don't see our car. I'll call Liu."

Two minutes later the car emerged at the far end of the street. When it stopped in front of them, Lop opened the door. "We're waiting for some guys to leave the building. When they do, we want you to follow them."

"Will they be heading for the city?"

"I think so."

"Then I should park on the other side of the street," Liu said.

Once Ava and Lop were in the car, Liu drove for about a hundred metres, until he found a parking spot on the other side of the road, did a U-turn, and slid into it.

"Well done," said Ava. "I just hope we don't have to wait here too long."

"It makes no difference to me," Liu said.

In the end, the wait couldn't have been much shorter, because almost as soon as Liu spoke, the three men hurried from the building, looked around, and then quickly walked away in the other direction.

"I guess Song is on his own," Lop said dryly.

At one point Ava lost sight of them. "Can either of you see them?" she asked.

"If they're going to the city, this is the only direction they can take," Liu said. "Parking is hard to come by and they probably couldn't find a spot that was close."

Ava eased back into the seat, realizing there was nothing she could do.

As cars went past them, Ava and Lop stared at the drivers and passengers. After seeing about twenty vehicles without Pan or his men in them, she began to worry they had gone in another direction. Then a large black Kia suv rumbled past with Pan sitting in the back seat.

"That's them," she told Liu.

He waited for a few seconds before leaving the parking spot, and then sped up until he was fifty metres behind the Kia. "There are a lot of stop signs and traffic lights in this area," he said. "It's hard to stay close without making it too obvious we're following them. If they are going to the city, they'll use the highway. Are you okay if I let them get quite a bit ahead here, knowing I can catch up to them on the highway?"

"Do what you think is best," said Ava.

They lost the Kia in local traffic a few minutes later. Ava tried not to be anxious as they made their way to the highway, but as they climbed the on-ramp into a wall of cars she was sure they'd never catch up to Pan.

"This looks tough," Lop said to Liu, echoing her thoughts.

"It will thin out," Liu replied.

It took some time, but eventually he was able to get directly behind the Kia. He only stayed there long enough to confirm Pan and two other men were in the car before slowing down and letting another car get in between them. They remained like that until they exited, with Liu staying a conservative distance behind.

It turned out the Green Dragon offices and warehouse were less than a kilometre from the highway, and to Ava's chagrin the Kia turned left and drove to the warehouse's triple doors. As Liu drove past them, one door raised, and the Kia went inside.

"I guess we shouldn't have expected anything else," Ava said. "Now what do we do?"

Lop sighed. "I'm going to call my MSS contact in Beijing. If he won't help, then our only option is to wait for Pan to leave."

"Call him now, could you?" she asked.

"Yeah, but it's a conversation I would like to have in private."

"Do you want us to get out of the car or take you somewhere?" she said, understanding there were some things he wouldn't want to share.

"No, I'll get out. I like to walk when I talk, and here's as good a place as any," Lop said as he opened the car door.

Ava watched as he tapped a contact on his phone, listened, and turned to her with a thumbs up. He then got out and started to walk. He must have gone fifty metres away from them and the warehouse before turning back, continuing past them, and continuing for at least another fifty metres. He repeated this route three times, his pace varying, and twice he even stopped for a short period. At one point he waved an arm in the air, and became more animated than Ava could ever remember seeing him. She had no idea if that meant it was going well or badly. Finally, she watched him end the call, shake his head, and walk back to the car.

"Well?" she said as he opened the door, expecting the worst.

"That was harder than I thought it would be, but I have the information we need," he said. "On top of the favour I'm going to owe, he wanted something from Xu as well. I promised to get it for him."

"Did you clear that with Xu?"

"I didn't have to. Xu told me before I left to do whatever was necessary to help you. And in this case it's only money, and a paid weekend vacation in Shanghai."

"I'll reimburse Xu," Ava said.

"Please don't even try. You know he'll say no."

"And what favour did you have to give him?" she asked.

"I don't want to discuss it—and besides, it has nothing to do with what we're trying to do."

Ava nodded. "Is the information worth the price?"

"Oh yes. Mr. Pan, it turns out, is really Mr. Bai. The MSS created a Taiwanese identity for him, and that's the name attached to a house he has in the Danshui district," Lop said, and turned to Liu. "Do you know that area of the city?"

"Yeah, it's about thirty kilometres from here, near the northernmost station of the MRT. It's a family neighbourhood, close to some beaches. My father used to take us there on Sundays to swim."

"Our man owns a house at 18 Willow Street. I think we should go now and have a look at it," said Lop.

Liu put the address into his GPS. "It will be a forty-five-minute drive," he said a moment later.

"Let's go," said Lop.

13

MUCH OF THE DRIVE TO DANSHUI WAS ON A HIGHWAY, but stop-and-go traffic ate up time, and it took forty minutes before they exited into an area filled with shops, apartment buildings, and streets containing mainly single-family dwellings. The entrance to Willow Street was anchored by medium-sized apartment buildings, but the rest of the street—all the way to a dead end—were modest one-storey houses. They reminded Ava of the housing built in many parts of Toronto after the Second World War, with small lots and box-like, twelve-hundred-square-foot homes. Number 18 Willow was almost exactly that. There was a neatly trimmed lawn in front with an asphalt driveway to the left. Three concrete steps with iron railings led to a front door, flanked by large windows with lace curtains that weren't drawn.

"This couldn't be more non-descript," Lop said. "It's a good cover."

"Yes, he's your average Joe, just fitting in," Ava replied, starting to plan how and when they should get inside.

"There's someone in there," Lop said suddenly.

Ava had turned away from the house, and now looked back to see a woman walking past the window. "Did your contact mention a wife or girlfriend?" she asked.

"No."

"I don't like it, but it's a complication we're going to have to manage."

"What are you thinking?"

Ava paused. "Do you think the house has a security system?"

"Given the job he's doing, I would be very surprised if it didn't."

"If it does, then I'm thinking that the only way not to trigger it is to be invited in through the front door," she said, staring at the house.

"That could be true."

"So, in a way, having that woman in the house might be an unexpected advantage."

"That could also be true. Are you considering finding that out right now?"

"Why not? We're here."

"How do you want to do it?"

"Well, she shouldn't panic if I'm the one knocking on the door. You can stay in the car until I take care of her."

"She'll see you," said Lop.

"She'll see *a* woman for a few brief seconds."

"Are you going to knock her out?"

"Yes," Ava said. "And hand me two strips of tape."

Lop cut them from the roll and handed them to Ava. She put them, sticky side up, in her bag.

"Okay, let's get on with this," Ava said, getting out of the car.

There was a small fence and gate at the entrance to the property, but they were decorative rather than providing any form of security. Ava opened the gate and walked up the pathway to a wooden green front door that had a pane of glass set almost level with the top of her head. A small brass knocker was set beneath the glass, and Ava rapped it twice. There was no immediate response, and no noise from inside that she could hear. She waited, counted slowly to ten, and rapped again. The door opened and a young woman in a pink sweatsuit stood there with one hand gripping the side of the door. Her hair was tousled, and her eyes were bleary.

"Good morning, I hope this isn't too early," Ava said. "I represent the Danshui Committee for Safety and Cleanliness and I'm taking a survey in the neighbourhood. Can I have a few minutes of your time to answer some questions?"

The woman frowned and gave her head a little shake, but before she could speak, Ava pointed over her left shoulder. "What is that?" she asked.

When the woman turned to look, Ava pounced. She slid behind the woman, one hand pulling one of her arms behind her back to immobilize her, while the other searched for and quickly found the carotid artery. She pressed down. There was barely a struggle, and in a matter of seconds she sagged in Ava's arms. Ava picked her up, carried her inside, laid her on a couch, and took the tape from her bag. One strip went across the woman's eyes; the second secured her arms behind her back. When that was done, she went to the door and waved for Lop to join her.

"That was quick," he said when he entered the house.

"She wasn't that alert. She seemed tired or hungover," said Ava.

Lop looked at the woman on the couch, which—like two chairs nearby—was covered in plastic. "When will she come to?" he asked.

"In a couple of minutes. I took it easy on her. Stay with her while I take a look around."

Ava walked towards the front door to examine the alarm system on the wall beside it. It didn't look armed, but that didn't mean it wasn't preprogrammed. From there she went to a kitchen that was basic to the extreme—just a simple wooden table with two folding chairs, and on the counter a rice cooker and water thermos. She opened the fridge and saw plates of fried rice and chicken feet covered in plastic wrap, four bottles of beer, and half a loaf of bread. The house had one small bathroom with a sink, toilet, and walk-in shower, and two bedrooms, only one of which was furnished—and that was with an unmade double bed. There was a large suitcase on the floor near the closet. She opened it and saw an array of women's clothing. She peered into the closet and saw no women's clothing, only two men's suits and five shirts.

"I don't think the girl is here permanently," Ava said to Lop when she returned to the living room. "There's nothing of hers in the closet."

As if on cue, the woman stirred, drew several deep breaths, and then gasped in fear.

"Don't panic," Ava said loudly. "We're not going to hurt you."

"Who are you?"

"That doesn't matter. We're here to see your friend Bai or Pan—and by the way, which name does he use with you?"

"Bai."

"Are you his wife or girlfriend?"

The woman hesitated. "I'm not his wife," she said finally.

"When did you meet him?"

"Last week."

"In a bar?" Lop asked.

"No, I work in a club, a high-class club."

"I'm sure it is a high-class club," Ava said. "Now, are you up to answering a few questions about Mr. Bai?"

"What do you want with him?"

"That's not really your concern, and actually, it's better if you don't know," Ava said. "What is important is for you to realize that the more you co-operate, the easier it will be for you."

"Is that a threat?"

"No, it's a simple statement of fact."

The woman nodded. "The truth is that I hardly know anything about him."

"We'll keep it simple. For example, what time did he leave for work?"

"It was early this morning, around seven. Usually it has been closer to nine."

"And does he call you during the day?"

"No."

"What time does he normally get home?"

"Seven thirty or a bit later."

"Does he come home alone or does he bring friends with him?"

"He has a driver who drops him off."

"Does the driver come into the house?"

"Not since I've been here."

"Does he ever discuss his work with you?"

"He told me he exports rice and imports sauces."

"Did he tell you he's originally from mainland China?"

"He didn't have to. I noticed he had an accent," the woman said. "Is that what this is about?"

"My friend and I are members of an organization committed to keeping Taiwan independent. Bai works for the Chinese Ministry of State Security and wants the opposite."

"I know nothing about any of that."

"I didn't think you did."

"Then can you take the tape from my eyes?"

"I'm afraid that isn't going to happen," Ava said. "What I will do is give you a choice of where you want to be—here or in the bedroom."

"Are you going to be waiting for him to come home?"

"We are."

The woman shook her head. "I knew this was too good to be true.'

"What do you mean?"

"He's a decent guy. Most of them just want a fast one-night fuck or blow job, or usually both in a hotel and then they're gone," she said. "We started in a hotel, but then he brought me here. I was hoping for something long-term."

"Don't give up hope," Ava said.

"I'm not a fool."

"Of course you aren't, so you'll understand why it's important for you to be co-operative. Now, I can't take the tape off, but we can let you lie on the bed where you'll be more comfortable."

"It sounds like Bai has gotten himself into a jam of some kind."

"You could say that."

"If he has, I have nothing to do with it."

"That's understood."

"Good, then in that case I would prefer to be lying on the bed," the woman said. "But I'm parched and would like something to drink, and at some point I'll have to use the bathroom."

"We'll get you some water now, and let me know when you need the bathroom and we'll make arrangements," said Ava.

14

AFTER SECURING THE WOMAN IN THE BEDROOM, LOP went outside to tell Liu that they would be staying in the house for at least the day, and that as long as he was available by phone he could leave. But first, Lop went with him to a 7-Eleven and stocked up on snacks and drinks. When he returned with a full bag, Ava said with a smile, "We're here for the day, not a week."

"I wasn't sure what you'd like so I got a bit of everything," he said. "Besides, it's going to be a long day."

Lop couldn't have been more correct about how long the day would be; Ava couldn't remember when one had gone by so slowly. The house had no television or computer; she and Lop eventually ran out of small talk; and after saying goodnight to Fai after half an hour of chit-chat, Ava put her phone to one side. She helped the woman go to the bathroom twice and sat on the bed next to her to ask the same kinds of questions she had before. As boring as that was, the answers remained the same, which provided a level of certainty.

The house, she figured, was used for sleeping and not much else. She and Lop searched every room for anything that might give them some insight into Bai's professional and private life. But aside from his clothes and basic toiletries, there was nothing—not even a shred of paper.

Ava fed the woman fried rice early in the afternoon, and then again as dusk made its appearance. After the second meal and another bathroom run, she said, "Bai should be here soon, so we have to take some extra precautions."

"What?" the woman blurted in panic.

"We can't have you yelling or screaming, so I'm going to tape your mouth, and we don't want you to hear our conversation in the living room so I'm going to put some toilet paper in your ears and then wrap them with tape. When we're finished with Bai, I'll come back."

"You'll come back to do what?"

"Relax, we know you aren't involved in his work."

After taping the woman up, Ava returned to the living room to find that Lop had turned on a lamp and moved one of the kitchen chairs in front of a window that looked out onto the street.

"Things need to look normal, so we'll have to leave lights on," he said as he sat. "At this angle I can see the entire area but I don't think he'll be able to see me. Still, could you go outside and check?"

Ava walked out of the house and went to the sidewalk. She stood in various spots and couldn't see Lop until she was far off to one side and almost in front of a neighbour's home.

"He won't be able to see you from outside," she said when she returned.

"How do you want to get him? I was thinking of waiting by the door and sticking the gun into his back when he came in. I don't imagine he'll be armed."

"That sounds fine," she said. "Then we'll tape him to the chair like we did Song."

"He might be a tougher nut to crack."

"There's no imminent deadline. We have all night."

The night began ten minutes later, when a blue Toyota sedan stopped in front of the house. Ava stood behind Lop so she had a clear view. She saw Bai sitting in the front passenger seat, and expected him to exit. Instead it was the driver—who was twice Bai's size—who got out of the car. He stood on the sidewalk looking in all directions, and then opened the passenger door.

"I hope casing the neighbourhood is the only precaution he's going to take, but I have a feeling the driver's going to come into the house," Ava said softly. "Song's death has to have alarmed Bai."

"If he does, I'll take care of him while you look after Bai," Lop said.

Now both men stood on the sidewalk looking around. She saw Bai say something and the driver nod. They began to walk towards the house, then stopped, turned, and looked around for a third time. Before they reached the steps that led to the front door, Lop stood up from the chair and took position by the door. Ava slipped in behind him.

The door opened. Ava braced herself and saw Lop tense.

The driver took three steps into the living room with Bai hard on his heels. When they were fully inside and before Bai could close the door, Lop leapt from behind it and smashed the butt of the gun into the back of the driver's head. Ava saw a stunned look on Bai's face as the driver fell to the ground, but before he could react it was her turn to leap. She drove the knuckle of her right hand's middle finger into his ear. It was the Phoenix Eye Fist, a classic bak mei strike, with all the power her body could muster concentrated in the knuckle. Bai groaned, and then crumpled. She knew he would be incapacitated for at least several minutes, but the driver wasn't completely out and began to struggle to get to his feet.

Lop pressed the gun against the side of his head. "Stay down," he said, and then turned to Ava. "Tape him."

She taped the driver's wrists behind his back, then his ankles, his eyes, mouth, and ears. When she'd finished, Lop grabbed him under the arms and dragged him into the vacant bedroom.

While he was gone, Ava sat Bai in the chair and started to secure his ankles and wrists. He mumbled something she didn't understand, and she began to worry she had hit him so hard that he would be incoherent for a while.

"That went well, but we've filled every room in the house. Let's hope no one else shows up," Lop said when he returned.

"Did you go through the driver's clothes?" she asked.

"Yes, I have his gun, wallet, car keys, and phone."

Ava searched Bai, but all she found was his wallet and what looked like office and house keys on a small ring. She opened the wallet. All of his identification was in the name of Pan Yong, and according to his business card his official title at Green Dragon was executive vice president.

"I think we should move the car to another street," she said.

"There's a public parking lot next to the 7-Eleven. I'll leave it there."

"Perfect."

By the time Lop came back, Bai was less incoherent, but

still wasn't making complete sense and seemed temporarily incapable of stringing sentences together.

"Give him some water, that might help," Ava said to Lop.

Bai shook his head when Lop held the glass to his lips, and it wasn't until Lop grabbed his jaw that he finally sipped.

Ava retrieved the second chair from the kitchen and set it down about a metre in front of Bai. Lop now stood behind him and slightly to one side, in what was clearly a menacing position.

"Can you understand what I'm saying?" Ava asked.

Bai glared, tried to spit at her, and only wet his own shirt as the spit turned into drool.

He was a small man—maybe five foot four inches, she guessed—and couldn't weigh much more than one hundred and thirty pounds. His grey suit jacket hung loosely over his shoulders, and its arms extended halfway down the backs of his hands. His hair was buzz-cut, and his clean-shaven face was bony and gaunt. If she hadn't known what he did for a living, she might have assumed he was harmless. But she did know, and that fact was quickly emphasized as he seemed to regain his senses and his dark brown eyes bored into her. This wasn't a man, she thought, who was going to be easily intimidated. So what approach to take, and where to start?

"What did you do with the girl?" he asked before Ava could speak.

"She's in the bedroom," she said, pleased to see he seemed to be partially recovered.

"Did you hurt her?"

"Not yet."

Bai took a deep breath. "I assume you're with the

Taiwanese National Security Bureau—and if you are, you're making a mistake." It appeared he was thinking more clearly.

"How so?"

"I'm a naturalized Taiwanese citizen and a businessman. I have rights."

"Those rights exist outside of this room. Right now, what my associate and I decide are the only rights that count."

Bai stared defiantly at her, and she could see his mind was turning. "You aren't with the Bureau, are you," he finally said.

"We never said we were."

"Then who are you, you crazy fucks?"

"You can think of us as avenging angels."

"What the fuck do you mean by that? What do you want?"

"We want answers to some questions, but before we get into the heavier stuff, why don't you start by telling me what your real name is? It seems you use Pan for business purposes and Bai otherwise. Why do you need two names? You have to admit it's a bit odd."

"I like to keep my professional and private lives separate. What difference does it make to you?"

"And by 'professional' do you mean your job at Green Dragon or your position as the head of Chinese Ministry of State Security operations in Taiwan?"

"For the record, I'm the executive vice president of Green Dragon Import/Export. That's the only job I have."

"We've been told otherwise," Ava said.

Bai's eyes flicked in her direction, turned away, and then looked at her as if he was seeing her for the first time. "By whom?" he asked.

"Why don't you guess?"

"I'm not going to play your fucking games."

"Except this isn't a game, and it isn't something you're going to find the slightest bit entertaining. This is serious stuff—deadly serious stuff."

"Fuck you, you bitch."

Despite his situation, Bai exuded the arrogance of someone accustomed to being in control. It annoyed Ava, even more so when she thought about Chen and Lau Lau. She decided the time was ripe to rattle him. She looked up at Lop. "Can you do me a favour? There's a meat cleaver in the kitchen. Could you bring it to me?"

"Gladly," Lop said, without any hesitation.

"It's been a few years since I used a meat cleaver, but it's the kind of thing that doesn't require a lot of practice," she said to Bai.

"Who the fuck are you?" he said in a tone that was angry, but also now tinged with doubt.

"I told you, we're avenging angels."

"That's bullshit, and you aren't going to scare me by threatening me with a meat cleaver."

"Let's keep this simple. You have information we want. If you give it to us freely then there will be no reason to use the cleaver. If you decide not to co-operate then I'm going to carve you into little pieces until you have a change of mind."

"I don't believe you," Bai spat.

"Mr. Bai, I mean every word I say."

Bai lowered his head and she saw his teeth biting into his lower lip. When he looked up she sensed his confidence was continuing to ebb.

"You're the fuckers who killed Song," he said.

"Yes, we are," said Ava.

15

LOP PUT THE CLEAVER ON THE FLOOR NEAR AVA'S chair. She glanced at it, and then looked at Bai. "I sincerely hope I don't have to use it," she said.

"Is that what you told Song before you shot him?"

"He was most uncooperative. You don't have to be."

Bai shook his head. "Go fuck yourself."

"Before you continue down that path, let me give you a bit of background," Ava began. "We've been hired by friends of Chen Jie and Lau Lau to find out who ordered them killed. We know you instructed Song to hire some local gangsters to do it, and he failed. We also know that you then spoke to Beijing and they sent two of their assassins to Taiwan. What we don't know, and the reason you are here, is who in Beijing gave you your orders. We would appreciate having that name or names."

"I have no idea what you're talking about."

"That's what Song said before giving us your name and some other tidbits."

"And you still killed him."

"As I said, he was most uncooperative," said Ava. "What

you have to decide is how much pain you are prepared to endure before you decide it isn't worth it."

Bai looked startled, and Ava knew her bluntness had hit home.

Lop had been listening to their conversation, and now he moved next to Bai. "I was in the Special Forces division of the PLA, so I know a thing or two about pain. Let me assure you that what she has in mind will hurt beyond anything you can imagine. I promise you that you won't be able to withstand it. You'll talk eventually. The question is, why go through all that hurt when the end result is a foregone conclusion?" he said sympathetically. "One more thing—I was an officer and was responsible for many men. You have the woman and one of your men in those bedrooms, and I'm sure you feel some sense of responsibility towards them. Tell us what we want to know and they won't be touched."

"Why should I believe that?"

"We are truth-tellers."

"I know this is a lot to absorb," Ava said. "My friend and I will go outside for a few minutes. Take that time to think this through."

Ava and Lop left the front door open, and stood against the wall to the left of it.

"Do you really think he cares enough about the woman and his guy to rat out his superiors to save them?" she asked.

"No, I suspect he's more concerned about avoiding pain, but he can tell himself he's making a sacrifice for them. In situations like this, people can be even more self-delusional than usual. So, if he references them, don't be afraid to go overboard complimenting his integrity."

"And Lop, I have to ask, how do you view the two of them? Are they loose ends?"

"Do you think they saw our faces? Do you think they could identify us?"

"No."

"Neither do I."

"So we'll leave them here alive?"

"Yes."

"Good, I think that's the right decision."

"Now let's go back inside and see if Mr. Bai has decided to co-operate."

Bai stared at them when they went back into the house, and Ava thought she detected defiance—and perhaps a return of his arrogance. Without hesitation she reached down for the cleaver.

"Let me tell you how this is going to work," she said. "We are going to tape your mouth so you can't scream. Then I'm going to chop off a thumb. When that's done, we'll take you into the kitchen, turn on an oven element, and cauterize it. Then I'll wait fifteen minutes, chop off the other thumb, and we'll revisit the kitchen. After that, I will cut off a finger every fifteen minutes until you have none left, and then I'll switch to toes."

"You should believe her," Lop said. "It isn't something she enjoys, but it is something she's good at."

"Actually, this is one time I might enjoy it," Ava said.

Bai paled, and Ava began to think they were making progress.

"You have one minute to decide how this is going to play out. In case you choose the hard way, do you have a prefer-ence to which thumb you lose first?"

Bai's tongue flickered over his lips. "If I decide to co-operate ...?"

"We want names," said Ava.

"I get that."

"And my associate will have to verify they're believable."

"How can he do that?"

"He has his contacts."

"And if he verifies the names?"

"Your co-operation will be acknowledged."

"By doing to me what you did to Song?"

"I told you, he wasn't co-operative."

Bai looked doubtful, but Ava now sensed he was leaning in their direction.

"You need to understand that killing people is not part of my job, and it isn't something I condone," Bai said.

"I understand—you were simply following orders."

"I was."

"Who gave the orders?"

Bai grimaced, and then said, "His name is Lin. I'm not sure about his specific title, but I've heard the name, and I do know he's many levels above me. In fact, he's near the top of the MSS."

"Did he speak to you directly?"

"He called my director, and my director brought me into the call. That surprised me. Usually, my instructions come straight from the director. Never, ever, had I dealt with some-one as senior as Mr. Lin."

"So Mr. Lin told both of you what he wanted done?"

"Yes."

"How specific were his directions?"

"Very."

"Could you expand on that?"

Bai looked away from Ava in obvious discomfort.

"I want to know what he said and how he said it," she pressed. "We won't hold his words against you."

"He told me there was a job in Taiwan," Bai said hesitantly. "There were two traitors, two enemies of China, who would be there, and they were to be eliminated. Then he asked me to find some local gunmen to take it on."

"Why use local men?"

"He said it would provide us with cover."

"Did he tell you who the two targets were?"

"Yes, and he said Lau Lau and Chen were already on the island. They had hacked Chen's phone and had been tracking his movements for months."

"Did you know why they wanted to kill Chen and Lau Lau?"

"Not at first, but my director was curious and made some phone calls."

"What did he find out?"

"He was told that the China Movie Syndicate had been pushing for something to be done about Chen and Lau Lau. They had made a film about Tiananmen Square that had upset a lot of people in the syndicate and government. They thought it was a disgrace to Chinese culture and a perversion of Chinese history."

"When you say they were pushing for something to be done, are you implying they wanted them killed?"

"That is obviously how it was interpreted, and that was our order."

"Was the name Mo mentioned at any time during your conversation with Mr. Lin?"

"Yes. When he told us he wanted them eliminated, he said that a Mr. Mo had provided us with the date it should be done."

"He was specific about that?"

"Yes."

"Did he tell you who Mo was?"

"No, but my director found out later."

"So you had the names, and the date, and all you needed was someone to do the deed. Finding that someone was the task you passed on to Song."

"That's right. I thought he knew more about the local gangster scene than me. But, of course, he failed, and I had to tell my director the bad news."

"And your director then told Mr. Lin?"

"He did, and my director told me he was livid, and hung up on him," Bai said. "An hour later my director phoned me back to tell me that Lin had authorized the sending of two men from an MSS special unit to Taiwan. I was to provide them with weapons, and any other assistance they needed— no matter what it was. When I told him he could count on me, he said that I had better not fail because Mr. Lin was already deeply disappointed in our unit, and that one more mistake could mean demotions or worse."

"When did the men arrive?"

"Three days before the shootings."

"What assistance did you give them?"

"The weapons, of course, and we provided a car and driver, and hotel rooms. They were quite self-sufficient and close-mouthed. I met with them several times, but they never talked about why they were here."

"How did they find out where Chen and Lau Lau were going to be that night?"

"I told you, the MSS had hacked Chen's phone. They tracked every text and heard every conversation. He had phoned the restaurant to make the reservation the day they arrived."

"And if he hadn't made a reservation?"

"They knew which hotel he was staying in, and they had Lau Lau's address. In one place or another, it was going to happen that night."

"What were the plans after the fact?"

"One of my men drove the special unit guys back to their hotel, and then he disposed of the weapons. I phoned my director to tell him the job was done."

"How did he react?"

"He was relieved."

"Did you ever hear from or speak to Mr. Lin again?"

"No."

Ava glanced at Lop, who had been listening intently to the conversation. "Do you have any questions for him?" she asked.

"No."

"Have you heard of Lin?"

"No, but that doesn't mean anything. The MSS is a large and secretive organization."

"We still need to confirm Lin's existence."

"I'll go outside to make my calls."

"Thanks."

Ava waited until Lop left before speaking to Bai again. "Are you certain that the idea of killing Chen and Lau Lau on that specific date came from the China Movie Syndicate, from Mr. Mo?"

"That's what Mr. Lin said. Besides, I don't think it could

have come from anyone in the MSS. It isn't the Ministry's style. They prefer to do things quietly, without a fuss, and without publicity. If they had targeted those guys on their own, the first objective would have been to get them into a Chinese jail. They might have been killed after that, but like I said, it would have been done quietly, and not in front of a hotel in plain sight."

LOP WAS GONE FOR ABOUT TWENTY MINUTES. AVA HAD nothing more to ask or say to Bai, so she took advantage of the time to check on the woman and the driver. Both were where they'd left them. She unpeeled the tape from the woman's ears, and said, "We'll be leaving soon. I'm going to put the tape back on, but don't let that worry you. We'll call the police after we're in a safe place to let them know where you are. You should also know that Bai's driver is in the other bedroom. We'll leave him taped up as well."

Ava saw the woman's body tense and she began moving her head from side to side as if she had something to say. Ava removed the tape from her mouth. "Don't make too much noise," she warned.

"What about Bai? Where will he be?"

"Where he is now, sitting on a chair in the living room."

"Okay," the woman said.

Ava re-applied the tape to her ears and mouth and returned to the living room. She sat on the sofa, took out her phone, and checked for messages. There was a text from

Fai that read: I can't stop worrying about you. Let me know you're alright. Love you.

Ava responded: I'm fine. *Lop* and I are just about finished in Taiwan, and I suspect we'll be going to Beijing as soon as tomorrow. I'll phone as soon as our schedule is finalized. Love you too.

She locked her phone and looked at Bai. His head was slumped forward and his chin rested on his upper chest. The threat of the cleaver had turned him from a profane lion to a lamb, and now he was going to be a sacrificial one. She almost wished there was another option, but he knew they had ties to Chen and Lau Lau, and Lop had mentioned his own past in the Special Forces. That was too much for Bai to know.

Lop came back into the living room with a grim look on his face.

"What happened?" she asked.

"We now know who Lin is."

"Why is that a problem?"

"Our friend there," Lop said, pointing to Bai, "actually understated who he thought he was talking to—by quite a bit."

"Is Lin that senior?"

"Well, there's the Secretary of Public Security, who is one of seven members of the Standing Politburo, and the Deputy Secretary, and then there's Lin," Lop said.

"Are you saying, outside of the politicians, that Lin is the top man at the MSS?"

"He is indeed."

"Good god," Ava said. "Why wouldn't Bai have been certain about that?"

"According to my contact, Lin and some of his other senior colleagues are secretive to the point of being paranoid. Only a handful of people within the MSS and the upper levels of the Communist Party know who does what within the senior group that actually runs the MSS."

"How does your contact know?"

Lop stared at her so hard that she wondered if she had offended him.

"I'm sorry if you found my question impolite," she said.

"No, it's justified. But all I can say is that he's with the PLA and has a working relationship with the MSS."

Ava hesitated before saying, "So, our trail leads us to a very big fish; in fact, given that Mo was involved, two very big fish."

"Perhaps too big," Lop said.

"We got to Mo before. I don't see why we can't do it again."

"I doubt we'll be able to lure him with the promise of sex to another meeting at a hotel."

"No, but we know where he works. And as I remember, the place isn't heavy on security."

"Okay, I'll buy that it's possible for us to get to Mo, but Lin is another challenge altogether."

"I agree that on the surface it seems much tougher, but we don't have enough information to entirely write off the possibility."

"Ava, I don't want to sound negative, but there are only so many times I can ask for favours, and there is only so much information people will be prepared to share."

"I appreciate that, and I know I have already asked for more than I have any right to expect."

Lop shook his head and smiled. "All right, I'll make more phone calls, but I can't promise any meaningful results."

"Thank you."

"And now we have to deal with the situation here."

"I told the woman that we'd call the police to come for her and the driver after we left."

Lop pointed to the driver's phone, which was sitting on the kitchen table. "It's unlocked. We can use it to call the cops from the car. I'll phone Liu and tell him to meet us at the 7-Eleven."

"That leaves Bai."

"Yeah," he said, reaching for a cushion from the sofa. "Do you want to wait outside?"

"I think I do."

She left the house and walked down to the sidewalk. There were no street lamps, and the lights from the houses did little to illuminate the street, so she was confident she couldn't be clearly seen. Three or four houses down she heard a dog bark, but otherwise the street was quiet. Ava began to count under her breath, and was just past sixty when the front door opened and Lop stepped outside.

"Did you hear anything?" he asked when he drew near.

"No."

"Good. Now let's head to the 7-Eleven."

They walked for several minutes in silence, and then it was Lop who spoke first.

"I assume you're going to go to Beijing. Do you have a schedule in mind?"

"I can't go until I have my new passport," Ava said.

"It was supposed to be delivered to the hotel sometime today."

"If it was, then I'll leave tomorrow."

"You mean *we'll* leave tomorrow."

"Lop, seriously, you don't have to come. I can't help feeling that I've imposed enough."

"What would be worse is trying to explain to Xu why I let you go alone," said Lop, and he paused before continuing. "But seriously, we've come this far together. I would like to see it through to a logical end. We may not get the result you want, but I owe it to you to give it my best effort."

"In that case, I'll be both pleased and grateful to have you alongside me."

Liu was waiting for them when they reached the 7-Eleven ten minutes later. He looked at them curiously but the only question he asked was "Am I taking you back to the hotel?"

"Please," said Ava.

As they climbed the ramp onto the highway that would take them back to the city, Lop took out Bai's driver's phone. "What number do I dial for a police emergency?" he asked Liu.

"One-one-zero."

Lop hit those buttons, and seconds later said, "I would like to report suspicious behaviour at 18 Willow Street in Danshui. I heard a great deal of yelling and screaming, and then I swear I heard a gunshot." There was a pause before he continued. "No, I don't want to leave my name. I'm convinced something bad happened in that house, and I don't want to get involved."

"Will they send someone to investigate?" Ava asked as Lop lowered his window and threw the phone out of the car.

"So the woman said."

Ava saw Liu glancing at them in the rear-view mirror. She imagined he'd have quite the story to tell Tsai when they met up.

They rode in silence the rest of the way to the hotel. When they reached the entrance, Ava took out two US hundred-dollar bills from her bag and passed them to Liu. "I don't think we'll need you tomorrow, so that's to thank you for your help."

"Tsai won't be pleased if I take it."

"I won't tell him, so he won't know unless you do."

"Thanks," Liu said.

When they entered the hotel, Ava went directly to the reception desk and asked if they had anything for her. A minute later she headed for the elevator with a small bulky envelope clutched in her hand. She waited until she and Lop were in the elevator alone before opening it.

"It's my new passport," she said.

"So tomorrow we are off to Beijing."

"I'll book afternoon flights and a hotel. Do you have any suggestions about where we should stay?"

"No, I trust your judgement."

"There's a Grand Hyatt within easy walking distance of Tiananmen Square. The proximity appeals to my sense of irony."

"That sounds fine to me."

The elevator stopped at Lop's floor first. "Do you want to meet later for dinner?" he asked.

"I don't think so. I ate so much of the stuff you bought at 7-Eleven that I'm not the least bit hungry."

"Then I'll order room service. That will also give me more time to make some phone calls. I'll let you know if I find out anything of interest."

"Yes, please do, and I'll forward you our flight information."

On opening the envelope, Ava had only glanced at the

maroon passport. After entering her suite, she sat at the desk and examined it in more detail. It was, she thought, a masterful piece of work. According to Xu's forger, Chow Qi—female, single, and in business—had been born in Shanghai on May 24, 1985. The passport had been issued there as well, two years prior, and had eight years left before it expired. It all looked genuine to her eyes, but there was a surprise when Ava leafed through to what she had assumed would be blank pages. According to the stamps inside, Chow Qi had travelled out of the country during those two years. She had been to Thailand, the Philippines, and Vietnam for short visits, and of course been welcomed back to China. Ava had no idea how Xu's man could create something so authentic. She reached for her phone and called Shanghai.

"*Wei*," Auntie Grace answered.

"It's Ava. Is Xu available?"

"He's sitting next to me here in the kitchen. I'll pass him the phone."

"Ava, I've been thinking about you," he said. "How are things going in Taipei?"

"They went well. Lop was his usual efficient, professional self. But there's nothing more to be done here. We're heading for Beijing tomorrow, and I was just calling to thank you for the passport. It arrived today, and I have to say it is a work of art."

"I'm pleased you're happy with it, but I am less pleased to hear that you're going to use it so soon, and that you intend to go to Beijing. I was hoping when you said things went well that you had resolved all of your issues."

"We resolved Taipei, but we found out that the decision to kill Chen and Lau Lau was definitely made in Beijing.

My old adversary Mo evidently had a hand in promoting it, but it appears likely that a man named Lin authorized it. According to one of Lop's contacts, Lin is the top bureaucrat in the MSS."

"Which makes him untouchable," Xu said quickly.

"That might be the case, and if he is, I'll have to settle for Mo."

"How did you settle things in Taipei?"

"The MSS now has two fewer men here."

"Do you plan on landing with Mo in the same way?"

"I do."

"You might be able to get to him, although given your history with him, you can't discount that it might attract attention that you don't want," Xu said. "But, Ava, if Lin is who you think he is, I can't imagine you'll even get within a kilometre of him. He'll have layer upon layer of security."

"Lop is still trying to gather information on him, so it's too early to make assumptions. But regardless of what he finds, you needn't worry. We aren't about to do anything silly or suicidal."

17

AFTER SPEAKING TO XU, AVA RESERVED TWO BUSINESS-
class seats on a non-stop EVA Air flight from Taipei to Beijing,
and then booked two suites at the Grand Hyatt. It wasn't
until that was done that the reality that she was actually
going to Beijing began to sink in.

It was a city that triggered mixed emotions. Until she met
Fai, it had been a place she passed through on her way to
somewhere else, or a place she spent a day or two pursuing
a deadbeat. But it had been Fai's home for many years, and
during the early days of their relationship Ava had stayed
with Fai in her small house located in a hutong that was several hundred years old. Through Fai, Ava got to experience
Beijing through a local's eyes and developed an apprecia-
tion for its everyday subtleties—such as tiny neighbourhood
tea rooms, and the plainest of restaurants where the food
rivalled the best that any five-star hotel could offer, at a quarter of the price.

It was also in Beijing that she had met Chen and Lau Lau
for the first time. Neither relationship had started smoothly,
partially because of circumstances that threatened Fai's

career, and Ava's focus had been entirely on saving her lover. But her first impressions of the two men had softened when it became clear that Fai's well-being was of concern to them as well. And when, with their help, Ava managed to thwart Mo's attempts to blackmail and blackball Fai, friendships had developed. And now she was going back to Beijing because of them.

Those memories stung, and the anger she'd felt when she learned they were killed swelled again.

"Calm yourself," she muttered, and then thought about phoning Fai. She checked the time. It was almost ten o'clock, and she assumed Fai would be at her English class. She called her anyway, and was disappointed when she was sent to voicemail.

"Hey, it's me. I guess you're at school. We've finished what we set out to do in Taipei, and tomorrow we'll be heading for Beijing. I was just sitting here thinking about spending time with you in the hutong and meeting Chen and Lau Lau. It will be strange being there without any of you, especially you of course. I'll call again in the morning. Love you."

Ava went to the mini-bar and took out a bottle of Chardonnay. She turned on the television, and without any real purpose started to watch a local news program. It hadn't run for more than a minute before the announcer said there was breaking news. The police had discovered the dead body of an adult male in a house in the Danshui district. The cause of death seemed to be a gunshot to the man's head. The police said two other adults were found in the house, both unhurt. The announcer said the man's name was not being released until the police concluded their investigation.

Two things about the news report interested Ava. The

first was that the woman and driver had been found. The second was that there had been no mention of Song. Had Bai and his people really just left his body there in the apartment to rot, or had they found a way to discreetly remove it? But how did one remove a body from such a public building? It certainly seemed they hadn't informed any authority because—considering he had also died from a shot to the head from the same gun—there was a link that was too obvious not to go reported. Given the silence, Ava's guess was that Song had been left in the apartment.

Thoughts about Bai and Song started to fade, and she found herself thinking about Beijing again. Whatever Lop was able to find out about Lin would determine what—if anything—they could do. How to get to Mo, she reasoned, was her responsibility, and that was a job made tougher by the fact that he knew both her and Lop, and the staff around him knew her too. She had to find an angle that wouldn't expose her and Lop but would isolate Mo. His son, David, was the only leverage she could think of, but even then she wasn't sure how he could be used. During their previous encounter, threatening to expose David's sexuality had been enough to win Mo's co-operation. But the stakes were higher—much higher—this time, and she couldn't imagine that gambit would work again.

Ava finished the small bottle of wine and took another from the mini-bar. She opened it, sat at the desk, and took out her Moleskine notebook. She wrote the name *MO* across the top of a new page, and then underneath: *How? Where? When? How? How?* But nothing came to her. Frustrated, she sipped the wine faster than she should have and started to feel light-headed. It had been a long, eventful day, and it was already late enough to go to bed. She considered showering before deciding to wait until the morning. She went into the bathroom, brushed her teeth, changed into a black Giordano T-shirt, and headed for bed. Halfway across the suite she realized she hadn't touched base with Lop. She phoned him while she sat on the side of the bed.

"We're on an EVA flight that leaves here at one o'clock. I suggest we meet in the lobby at ten," she said when he answered.

"Okay," he said, sounding less than enthused.

"You don't sound like you're up for it. Has something happened?"

"Nothing specific, but I have been getting an education in how the upper echelons of the Communist Party work and live."

"And what have you learned?"

"The MSS's official address is on Dong Chang'an Jie, near Tiananmen, and close to the Grand Hyatt, but the office is a front," he said. "The real decisions are made in offices located in a compound in Xiyuan, close to the Summer Palace. The compound also includes living quarters for senior personnel. The entire area is closely guarded by armed police. Getting in without an invitation is almost impossible. And if we somehow managed to get in, we probably wouldn't get out."

"That is discouraging," Ava said slowly.

"But not unexpected," Lop replied.

"Do those senior officials ever leave the compound?"

"I'm sure they must, but how would we know if Lin does? We don't even know what he looks like yet, although I think a friend will supply me with a recent photo."

"That would be helpful."

"Anything would be helpful," Lop said.

"So what to do? Are you suggesting that we postpone or cancel the idea of going to Beijing?"

"No, but I think our expectations have to be realistic, and I'll keep trying to gather as much personal information about Lin as I can. Who knows, we might find something we can use."

"Thank you, I appreciate it," she said. "By the way, there was a story on the local news tonight about Bai's body being found. There was no mention of Song."

"He's probably still sitting in that chair at his apartment."

"That's what I think too."

"Getting back to Beijing, have you come up with any ideas on how to get to Mo?" Lop asked.

"Not yet, but I'm working on it."

Lop didn't respond at once, and Ava imagined his second thoughts about going to Beijing were becoming more entrenched.

"Don't worry, I'll come up with something," she said.

"Xu says that you always do. I'll see you in the lobby at ten."

Ava put her phone down on the bedside table, turned off the lights, and slid into bed. She lay on her back with her arms across her chest. She wasn't accustomed to not having a plan, but as hard as she tried she couldn't get her mind to fix on one. Finally she gave up and focused on falling asleep. She was halfway through a bak mei mental workout with Grandmaster Tang when she finally succumbed.

Then she dreamt—except it was unlike any dream she'd ever had.

There was no visit from Uncle; and she wasn't chasing and never catching up to her father. Instead, she was standing on the sidewalk in front of an art deco hotel that was surrounded by fountains and palm trees. But despite its pleasant appearance, she approached the front door with a sense of foreboding, and that grew deeper when she walked through the door into an empty lobby.

For some reason she knew she was supposed to go to a penthouse suite, and without thinking about the logic of it, she decided to climb eight flights of stairs rather than take an elevator. There were two suites on the floor, and the door to one of them was ajar. She was drawn to the open door, entered the suite, but found no one. Ava then heard a moan that was loud enough to penetrate what she thought must be the closed bedroom door. She shivered, hesitated, but forced herself to go towards it. She opened the door, took three steps inside the room, and then stood frozen on the spot.

Fai lay naked on the bed with her wrists tied to a brass bedpost. Standing over her was Mo, and several feet behind him were Song and Bai. Mo had a knife in his hand. He smiled at Ava.

"We were waiting for you. Now we can start," he said, placing the tip of the knife high on Fai's chest.

"Ava, help me," Fai gasped.

Ava tried to move her feet, but it was as if they were nailed to the floor. She opened her mouth to speak and couldn't utter a sound.

She watched Mo apply pressure to the knife and then start to pull it down Fai's chest.

"Help," Fai cried.

Mo turned his head to smile at Ava again.

The knife tracked slowly down, leaving a line that was only as thick as a strand of red silk.

Move, speak, do something, Ava thought, but she was immobile, and her lips felt like they were glued together. She closed her eyes, hoping she was only imagining the scene. When she opened them, nothing had changed except that the knife was on Fai's stomach and inching towards her crotch.

Fai was crying now, her head turned away from Ava as if she accepted that she had been forsaken.

When the knife reached between Fai's legs, Ava felt a pain in her chest as if her lungs were filled with gas. She began to breathe as quickly as she could, and as she did she felt the gas begin to dislodge and move up her throat. It arrived in her mouth like a thick, wet mist, and when it did, Ava's lips parted and she yelled, "NO!"

She woke in a cold sweat, the front and back of her T-shirt damp and clinging to her skin. Still disoriented, she turned on the bedside light to verify where she was. The dream was still with her. The image of Fai lying on the bed fixed in her mind.

Ava climbed out of bed, went to the bathroom, and drank a glass of water. She stared in the mirror and saw a face that was filled with worry. What had that dream meant? The most obvious interpretation was that Fai was still in danger, and Ava wasn't in a position—or hadn't done enough—to protect her.

In the bedroom, she changed into a clean T-shirt, and then went to the living area and sat at the desk. She opened the notebook, saw the name "Mo," and realized that her focus might have been too narrow. She was so intent on avenging Chen and Lau Lau that she had done very little in terms of protecting Fai and Silvana. The fact that no attempt had been made on their lives didn't mean they weren't in peril and it wasn't being planned. Maybe the MSS were waiting for a time closer to the Oscars. Maybe they wanted the deaths to appear accidental. And if something was in the works, then going after Mo might accelerate such a plan rather than prevent it. It was all maybe maybe maybe, she thought, frustrated at having nothing definite to grab on to. What to do?

Ava didn't believe that her dreams represented the truth or were foretelling the future, but she did think that they tapped into her subconscious—into facts she might have ignored or downplayed. In this case, the dream was telling her to find a way to protect Fai. But how? The MSS would have to be told that she was off limits, and who was best positioned to tell them that? The only person she could think of was Mo. But why would he agree to do that?

There was only one reason that came to mind, and when it did, she realized it opened up another opportunity.

She checked the time. It was four a.m., which meant it was one p.m. in Los Angeles. She picked up her phone, found the number she wanted, and made the call.

"The law offices of Hines and Ford," a woman answered.

"My name is Ava Lee. I'm a client of Mr. Hines. I'm calling from Taipei and I really need to speak to him."

"Just one moment, Ms. Lee," she said.

Am I going too far with this? she wondered while she waited.

"Ava, what a nice surprise to hear from you," said Harold Hines. "But I was told you are in Taipei. What time is it there?"

"Four in the morning."

"This must be important."

"I'm sure you heard that Chen and Lau Lau were murdered here."

"I did, and I sent you a text with my condolences."

"I'm sorry, I didn't see it."

"Well, I was shocked and appalled."

"As we all were," said Ava.

"Do you have any idea who might have committed such a heinous crime?"

"Yes, but that isn't why I'm calling," she said. "Is our court appeal on the ruling about Top of the Road's withholding of *Tiananmen's* release still scheduled to be held this summer?"

"It is."

Ava felt a sense of relief. Despite telling Fai she would cancel the appeal, she hadn't, and for once her procrastination hadn't backfired. "Our team has decided not to pursue it if the Chinese government will provide some guarantees about the safety of the other people involved in making the film."

"I'm not sure where you're going with this," Hines said.

"The Chinese Ministry of State Security orchestrated the deaths of Chen and Lau Lau—perhaps at the behest of the China Move Syndicate. We don't want anyone else associated with the film to be hurt," she said. "We are prepared to drop the appeal and basically consign the film to history if they'll agree to leave everyone else alone."

"You seem very sure about who was responsible for the deaths."

"Mr. Hines, please believe me, we have proof."

"I don't doubt that you do," he said carefully. "But what do you want me to do with that information?"

"Nothing, I just wanted you to know who we're dealing with, but what I would like you to do is call Eli Brand," she

said, referring to the lawyer for Top of the Road Distribution.
"I want you tell him we're prepared to do a deal that should
please the Syndicate—and indirectly the MSS as well,
although you shouldn't mention them."

"I don't mean to question your judgement, but after everything everyone has gone through, do you think all of your
people are prepared to walk away from the film?"

"Chen and Lau Lau were the most committed and
invested, and they are gone. BB Productions will be dis-
solved. That basically leaves Pang Fai and Silvana Lau. They
need to be protected and I don't believe they will argue with
me about that," she said. "Besides, the film won the Palme
d'Or, and there are the Oscar nominations, so it has been
recognized as the work of art it is. And isn't it possible that
by withholding it from general distribution it will become
even more notorious? It could become sort of the forbidden
fruit of filmdom."

"That is entirely possible."

"So please reach out to Brand."

"I will—but to be clear, you want me to offer to withdraw
the appeal, and guarantee it will be our last legal manoeuvre?
In other words, we are giving Top of the Road total control
in deciding if *Tiananmen* is ever to be seen again."

"Yes, and in exchange, we get a guarantee that Fai and
Silvana will be free to come and go to China and Hong Kong,
where they will have immunity from prosecution and their
well-being ensured."

"Top of the Road can't give you any of that."

"I know. The Chinese government is going to have to be a
signatory to the agreement. I would love it if someone from
the MSS would be a party to it, but that may be a stretch. Mo

from the Syndicate needs to sign, and I'd accept someone like Wang Ping, the Chinese Consul General in LA."

"Ava, I'm not sure this is the least bit doable," Hines said carefully.

"Which part—crafting an agreement, or getting the Chinese to sign off on it?"

"Both."

"Well, we won't know until we try."

"I'm not saying we won't give it our best effort, because we will," said Hines. "But let's say we get an agreement of sorts and the Chinese government violates it. What's the penalty?"

"All rights to *Tiananmen* are returned to us—and if they are, we'll spend whatever it takes to make sure the film is seen in every corner of the world."

"Okay, you've given me enough to start a dialogue with Brand."

"Could you start that process today?"

"Yes, we'll do what we can," Hines said, sounding slightly annoyed with her impatience. "I can reach you at the phone number on the screen?"

"You can, and I apologize for being pushy, but I really believe that lives may be at stake."

18

AVA'S MIND WAS RACING AFTER HER CONVERSATION with Hines, and she knew sleep was going to be impossible. She made coffee, sat at the desk, and made notes about the conversation. Hines was an excellent lawyer, and the doubts he'd expressed about the viability of her proposal was an example of that. His reactions were never knee-jerk, and he wasn't reluctant to tell clients things they didn't want to hear. Still, despite his reservations, she was hopeful their offer of a deal would get a positive response.

Her attitude was based on emotions—and logic. Regardless of how sensitive the Chinese government was on the subject of Tiananmen Square, their visceral reaction to the film had been shocking. It had been a steadily escalating stream of challenges and threats, but they still hadn't succeeded in derailing *Tiananmen*, and Ava's hope was that by giving them what they wanted, they would call off their dogs.

She checked the time, and guessing that Fai would have left school, she phoned her.

"Ava, I just listened to your message," Fai answered. "But why are you calling back so early? Is everything okay?"

"I'm fine, I just miss you. Where are you right now?"

"Two blocks from the condo."

"I wish I was there."

"Me too, especially since I hate the idea of you going to Beijing."

"I don't think I have a choice."

"That's what I've been told several times today about going to Los Angeles for the Oscars."

"I don't understand," said Ava. "Who has been telling you that?"

"I've been getting calls, texts, and emails from people in the business, including quite a few members of the Academy, telling me I have to attend the Oscar ceremony—and not just because of my nomination. They say I have to represent the film and Lau Lau's memory."

"How do you feel about that? Has it changed your mind about going?"

"No," Fai said loudly. "If anything, it has made me more determined not to go. I have played drama queens in several movies, but I have no intention of playing one in real life, and that's what would be expected of me if I went."

"You know I totally support any decision you make," said Ava. "The movie and everything connected to it has taken its toll. I don't want to see anything added to that."

"What else can they do to us?"

Ava hesitated, but knew she had opened the door to the subject she had been discussing with Hines. "I am afraid for you and Silvana. I know nothing has happened beyond Chen and Lau Lau, but that doesn't mean it isn't possible. You going to the Oscars would only increase the anger on the other side, and I want to see it subside rather than get worse."

"How can we make it do that?"

"I've been thinking that maybe there's a deal—a trade to be done," Ava said.

"Like what?"

"Well, if we dropped our appeal—like you wanted—and gave total control of the film to Top of the Road, we might be able to get the Chinese government to back off. I mean the film has already made its mark, what more is there to prove?"

Fai didn't respond right away, and Ava wondered if she had offended or upset her.

"Truthfully, I like that idea," Fai said finally. "I'm not as brave as you, and I'd like our lives to be as normal as possible. I don't like the thought of always having to look over my shoulder to see if something is coming at me from behind."

"I'm really glad to hear that. I'll talk to Harold Hines and ask him to explore it with Top of the Road's lawyers."

"Oops," Fai said suddenly.

"What happened?"

"I slipped on a patch of black ice on the sidewalk."

"Please be careful," Ava said. "Put your phone away and concentrate on walking. I'll call you again before Lop and I leave for the airport."

Ava ended the call realizing she should have spoken to Fai before Hines, and made a mental note not to take for granted that Fai would always agree with her. Then she yawned and felt the tension she'd been experiencing start to ebb. Without any further thought she went back to bed and quickly fell asleep.

She slept soundly, didn't dream, and might have slept for several more hours if the phone ringing hadn't woken her. She saw it was just past seven and wondered who could be calling at this hour.

"Yes," she answered.

"Ava, this is Harold Hines."

She sat up. "Did you manage to speak to Eli Brand?"

"I spoke to him right after we talked, and he immediately patched Larry Christensen into the conversation," he said, referring to the CEO of Top of the Road. "And a few minutes ago I finished a second call with the two of them."

"Did they mention Chen and Lau Lau?"

"Of course, during the first call—and to quote Christensen, 'their deaths were tragic, and a devastating loss to the international film community.'"

"Such bullshit."

"What else would you expect?" Hines said. "They were also quick to ask who was making the decisions at BB Productions with Chen gone. I told them I wasn't at liberty to give them a name, although I could tell them the company was registered in the UK and had British shareholders. I then said that the deaths of Chen and Lau Lau had caused the shareholders to re-evaluate their foray into filmmaking and their ties to *Tiananmen*. That captured their interest enough that I felt comfortable outlining your proposal."

"How did they react to it?"

"Favourably, but Christensen said that it obviously wasn't his decision to make and that he would have to discuss it with his clients—and he did. In fact, he spoke to someone in Beijing immediately after our first call."

"So soon—it's the middle of the night there."

"Evidently he thought it warranted waking someone up."

"And what did that someone say?"

"They have a strong interest in the proposal."

"I can't believe it appears this easy."

"Good, because it isn't," Hines said. "They are obviously pleased we're prepared to drop our appeal and walk away from the film, but it isn't enough to get what you want in return. Their attitude is that they would have won the appeal anyway and been able to keep the film from being shown for at least a few years. So they want more."

"What more do we have to give?"

"The Oscar nominations."

"What?"

"That was my reaction as well, although I didn't voice it," Hines said. "Simply put—they want Pang Fai and Silvana to decline their nominations, and they want whoever controls BB Productions now that Chen is gone to refuse the best film and best director nominations. They want the refusals to take the form of a public statement that is in essence an apology for having distorted the truth about what happened in Tiananmen Square."

"That's …" Ava said, and then struggled to find the words.

"I think 'unreasonable' describes it best."

"Nevertheless, what did they offer us in return?"

"The guarantees you wanted."

"In writing?"

"I told them we would insist on that, and no one said no. Do I sense from what you're saying that you are considering accepting their conditions?"

"I will have to consult with Fai, and I should speak to Silvana. They're the ones who would be most affected."

"When could that be done?"

"Immediately after I get off the line with you."

"Ava, I suspect the quicker we move this along, the happier the other side will be. They want to bury the film, and the fact Fai and BB would help them do it publicly has to have enormous appeal. All of a sudden they won't look so much like the villains."

"It's a shame, though, that we would have to disparage the film."

"We'll work on the wording so it isn't that severe, and I also suspect that many people will view Fai's decision as an accommodation to secure her safety, and not as a genuine reflection of how she feels."

"Harold, that may be true, but she hasn't agreed to do it yet."

"What about BB? I've never been told who actually controls it."

Ava took a deep breath. "This is never to be shared, but my partners and I set up and financed BB. With Chen gone, the decision will be ours."

"I thought as much, but I didn't want to speculate."

"Now you don't have to."

"Okay, I think the situation is clear enough. I'm going to keep my phone on. You can call me whenever a decision is made. Christensen told me he and Brand will be available all evening."

"You'll hear from me one way or another."

19

DESPITE WHAT SHE SAID TO HINES, AVA DID NOT CALL
Fai immediately. Instead, she brewed a fresh cup of coffee
and sat by the window that looked down onto Dunhua Road
to think about the offer from Beijing. If nothing else, it laid
bare their intentions of not just preventing the film from
being seen, but also discrediting anyone involved in making it, and using their own words to do it. She could imagine what they would want in the public statement from BB
Productions and Fai, and it wouldn't be even-handed. Words
like *humiliating* and *grovelling* came to mind. Maybe Hines
could negotiate something that wasn't totally degrading, but
she had no doubt the Chinese would want their pound of
flesh.

And in return, what could they realistically expect to get?
Or put another way: could they really depend on the Chinese
government to keep their word when it came to the freedom
and safety of Fai and the others? If the deal was made public,
Ava thought, that would bring some pressure to bear on the
Chinese government. But would the Chinese accede to that?
Well, even if they didn't, with the help of people like Harris

Jones, it would find its way into the open. And, she reasoned, if the agreement was reached in the US and registered in a US court, any breach would offer the possibility of BB regaining control of *Tiananmen*.

The main question was what mattered most to the Chinese government—ensuring that the film would never be seen again, or continuing to punish people like Fai? Ava's fear was that they would still try to accomplish both. Still, there was going to be no gain without taking the risk ... and there was a potential added benefit, she realized, that hadn't entered into her initial calculations. Or was she being cynical to believe that, and had she subconsciously factored in the idea of using the deal to get Mo to come to Los Angeles?

Now that thought was in her head, she realized the plan could be viable. But how could it be structured? Maybe by making the deal too good for Mo to pass up, and then insisting it would only happen if the main parties to it met and signed in person. Ideally, two people from each side. Mo and whomever Beijing designated for the Chinese, and Fai and someone representing BB. But who could represent BB? Ava knew it would be unfair to introduce someone neutral into that situation, but she and her partners had to stay behind the scenes, and the lawyers who had incorporated BB lived and practised in Hong Kong, which made them vulnerable. *Why not Silvana?* she suddenly thought. She was part of the *Tiananmen* team and had been living with Chen. A credible claim could be made that he had left his shares in BB to her. Yes, she thought, as she rose from the chair to call Fai. It might work.

Fai answered on the second ring. "I thought you would have gone back to bed," she said.

"I did, but then Harold Hines phoned. He had been going back and forth with the Top of the Road guys in LA, and they had been talking to Beijing—to Mo most probably. It appears we have a chance to get a deal, although it's a bit more complicated than the one you and I discussed earlier."

"In what way?"

Ava took her time to explain what Christensen had counter-proposed, and what she believed were the ramifications in terms of risk and reward. Fai listened without interrupting. Then her first question was "Have you discussed this with anyone else?"

"Only Harold Hines. I thought I'd run the idea past you first."

"May Ling and Amanda may not be pleased to walk away from the investment."

"We can worry about that later," said Ava, realizing that was another call she would have to make. "Right now I'm more interested in what you think about you and Silvana rejecting your Oscar nominations, and BB turning down the best picture nomination."

"Before I answer that, there's something I need to know, and you have to be honest with me."

"I promise I will be."

"In the grand scheme of things, winning an Oscar for me or the film doesn't matter that much, but being safe, and us being able to live a normal life, does matter—it matters a great deal. How sure are you that if we give the Chinese what they want, they'll honour their side of the agreement?"

"I'm not certain they will, but Harold Hines will do everything he can to make sure it's in their best interests to honour it. And Fai, any kind of an agreement is a far better option than doing nothing, because, as Uncle used to say, doing nothing lets other people dictate how your life is lived."

"Then I'm prepared to do whatever it takes to give us a chance to take control of ours," Fai said. "I'll reject my nomination, and as Lau Lau's ex-wife I'll do the same for him. But obviously I can't speak for Silvana or the film's nomination."

"Will you talk to her about her nomination?"

"Okay."

"And I thought she could also make the decision on behalf of the film. She was Chen's partner after all, and we could make the case that his financial interests in BB Productions were going to be passed to her."

"That does make sense. I'll go over both issues with her. It might be easier for her to agree to it if the request comes from me, and she knows that I'm already onside."

"I think you're right," Ava said. "But if she does agree, there's one more thing you need to do, and that is to ask her to come to LA to sign the agreement. I want to have all of the parties in the same room for the signing."

"All of the parties?"

"Yes, you, Silvana, Hines, Brand, Christensen, and two representatives of the People's Republic of China—one of whom we would insist is Mo."

Fai lowered her voice to a whisper. "Ava, I know why having Mo there is logical, but is anything you learned in Taipei part of the reason?"

"Yes."

"And if he comes to Los Angeles?"

"Fai, you need to understand that Mo was very much involved in what happened to Lau Lau and Chen."

"So if he comes to Los Angeles?"

Ava paused. "He won't leave unless it's in a coffin or an urn," she said, with no idea of how Fai would react.

"You don't think that would be too dangerous, and be too obvious a connection to you?" Fai asked calmly.

"It would have to be carefully managed, just as the meeting will. Remember, Brand and Christensen only know me as Jennie Kwong, while Mo knows who I really am. That's why I won't be at the meeting," Ava said. "Thus far the only thing connecting me to the film is my personal relationship with you. If Mo has an accident, there should be nothing of substance to connect me to it, just as there is nothing to connect Lop and me to events in Taipei."

"What about going to Beijing? If Mo comes to LA, is that still necessary?"

"I don't know. There is one other man who has our friends' blood on his hands, and that's where he lives. The problem is that he may be impossible to get at. Lop is gathering as much information about him as he can, and then we'll make a determination," Ava said. "But short-term, if I can get Mo to come to LA, I'll be there waiting for him, and Lop can go on to Beijing by himself."

"How soon will you know about Mo?"

"I have to talk to Hines, and he has to persuade the other side, but none of that can happen until we know for certain that Silvana is with us," said Ava. "Can you call her right now, and then get back to me with her answer?"

"Yes, I'll do it at once."

"I'll be waiting," Ava said, and then hung up.

Ava couldn't have been happier with Fai's reaction to the proposal, and with her calm acceptance that Mo needed to pay for Chen and Lau Lau. They had been through a lot during their short relationship, and each of them had seen the other's dark side. But they were open and honest with each other, and with that came understanding and tolerance. Now, she thought, as she reached for the phone again, she needed May Ling and Amanda to be understanding. She could not imagine they wouldn't be, but like in all her friendships she never took the other person's feelings or reaction for granted.

May Ling was at home in Wuhan when she took Ava's call.

"You, Amanda, and I need to have a talk. Can you put us together for a conference call?" Ava asked.

"Sure, give me a minute," said May Ling.

It took longer than that, but eventually Ava heard May say, "Amanda is with us. What's up?"

"I'm phoning to talk about *Tiananmen*. I'm thinking we should abandon it, and that would mean foregoing any chance to recoup our costs," Ava began. "I know this isn't my decision to make alone, but I do feel really strongly about it and I hope you will go along with me."

"Is this because of what happened to Chen and Lau Lau?" Amanda asked.

"That was the catalyst, but even if that hadn't happened we were facing a rocky road with no clear idea of how or where it all might end," Ava said. "And to be truthful, I've become increasingly concerned about the safety of Fai and Silvana."

"I can't blame you for feeling like that. It should be a worry," said May.

"Lastly, we've been able to stay under the radar as far the Chinese government is concerned. If we want to ensure things stay that way, I think walking away from the film is the prudent thing to do."

"I agree, but how will you manage the process?" May asked.

For the next ten minutes, Ava explained what she and Harold Hines had concocted, and answered her partners' questions.

Amanda's last one was "So all we need now is Silvana's co-operation?"

"Yes," Ava said.

"But you also seem determined to get Mo to Los Angeles," said May.

"I am, but I wouldn't sacrifice the agreement if I couldn't."

"I'm glad to hear that, because I'm completely in favour of what you're proposing. We've been lucky so far not to be directly identified with the film," said May. "Given what happened to Chen and Lau Lau, we shouldn't push our luck any further."

"I am too," Amanda said. "Those two deaths rocked me to the core, and I can't help worrying about Fai and Silvana."

"Thanks for the support. I know that's a lot of money to write off."

"I never thought of it as being our money anyway," Amanda said.

"Me neither," added May. "So now what happens?"

"We'll have to get Silvana to agree, and when we do, Harold Hines can finish negotiating with the other side," Ava said. "This isn't going to be drawn out. The Oscars aren't that far away and I'm sure the Chinese want this finalized as soon as possible."

"Keep us updated," May said, and then paused before asking, "One last thing, if Mo goes to LA, what is going to happen to him?"

"We are going to kill him," Ava said without hesitation. "But we won't do it until he's signed the agreement."

20

MAY'S QUESTION ABOUT KILLING MO HADN'T SUR-
prised Ava. The two women had a long history that involved
several deaths, and May never shied away from condoning
what she thought was necessary, particularly if it was to
protect her family and friends. And Amanda wouldn't have
been shocked by the question either. She knew from personal
experience a lot about Ava's past, including the fact that Ava
had twice saved her father's life and taken other lives to do it.
What did surprise Ava was how this kind of trouble seemed
to follow her. When she'd left the sometimes violent and
always tense debt-collection business, she'd thought her life
would be calmer. It hadn't worked out that way.

She checked the time, and realized she needed to call Lop
to give him a heads-up that he might be going to Beijing
by himself. Would he back out? She thought not, but again
she wasn't taking anything for granted. Before she could
call, though, her phone rang and she saw Fai's name flash
on the screen.

"I hope you have good news," she answered.

"Silvana is onside; in fact she was relieved when she heard

what we wanted her to do," Fai said. "She told me she had been worrying about going back to Hong Kong. The Chinese government has become so aggressive there that no one feels safe. So she welcomes any protection we can negotiate."

"That's excellent. I've just spoken to May and Amanda and they're supporting our position. Now I can tell Harold to go full bore."

"He's good. I'm sure he'll do well."

"I like your optimism."

"What's the other option—be broody? I had enough of that when I was a debt collector."

Ava laughed. "You're handling all of this very well. I'm impressed."

"It's a hundred times easier to cope with challenges when you have someone you trust and love by your side."

"That is so true, and you know it cuts both ways," Ava said. "Now, I should call Harold before it gets any later. He said the other side was willing to keep talking tonight, and I want to give them that chance."

"Go, I love you," Fai said.

"Love you too," Ava said, and hung up.

There was noise in the background when Harold Hines answered the phone.

"Am I disturbing something?" Ava asked.

"I'm at home and we're having dinner, but I told my family I was expecting a call from you, so no one is going to be upset when I go to my office. Give me a minute to get there," he said, and then in less time than that, he spoke again. "I'm ready to listen. How did it go with Fai and the others?"

"It couldn't have gone much better. They're all onside with our proposal."

"Fai and Silvana will turn down their Oscar nominations?"

"Yes, and as Lau Lau's ex-wife Fai will turn down his as well. Silvana will decline the best picture nomination on behalf of BB Productions."

"She can do that?"

"She was Chen's live-in partner, and he had no other family we're aware of, so it seems only logical that she would inherit his stake," Ava said. "If that isn't sufficient, then I can arrange to have her given a proxy from the other shareholders, through the law firm in Hong Kong that set up BB."

"I think her relationship to Chen should be sufficient," he said. "Now, in terms of your demands, have any of those changed?"

"No, we want every possible assurance that Fai and Silvana will be safe no matter where they are. And, Harold, we are counting on you to find the appropriate language to express that—as well as structuring the agreement so there are real consequences if the other side reneges."

"I'll do the best I can, but you know I can't guarantee they won't renege."

"Of course, but can you at least ensure the agreement is to be interpreted by American law, and that any dispute will be settled in an American court?"

"We will insist on that."

"And one more important thing—we want any agreement that's reached to be signed in person, and in Los Angeles," Ava said. "Fai and Silvana will sign for our side. We want Mo Ming, the head of the China Movie Syndicate, and at least one other senior Chinese official who isn't connected to the Syndicate to sign for them. Their Consul General in LA, Wang Ping, would suffice, but we wouldn't object to someone else from Beijing, just as long as they aren't working for the Syndicate."

"They're going to ask why it has to be done in person, and why Mo Ming?"

"Fai wants to look him directly in the eyes. They have history, and she wants him to know this is to be the end of it," said Ava. "Besides, why would Mo object? He's won. He'll have control of the film, and he'll be able to gloat as Fai and Silvana throw away the Oscar nominations. It should get him a gold star in Beijing."

"I'll stress that it is important for him to be part of the process."

"You could phrase it as him being part of the ceremony. That's how the Chinese often refer to signings, particularly when they are on the best side of one."

"Okay, I'll use that term," Hines said. "Now, assuming we do reach an agreement, that leaves the question of how and when Fai and Silvana announce their Oscar decisions, and who prepares the announcement."

"We'll do nothing, of course, unless we have an agreement, but once you're satisfied we've secured one, we don't really care about the how and the when. What's in the announcement is another matter. I know Mo will want them to admit that making *Tiananmen* was a mistake, and that the subject matter was treated in a way that distorted the truth, but we need them to be able to say that in a way that isn't grovelling. Why don't you prepare a draft statement prior to the meeting so we have time to review the wording? You could even approach Patricia Nolan from Make Them Dream for her input. As I remember, she was clever at making the worst situation sound almost palatable."

"Using Patricia is a very good idea."

"Then let's, but there's no point in contacting her until we know there's a deal. So now, what's the plan?"

"I'll call Eli Brand and tell him what we have on offer. He should be able to contact whoever he's speaking to in Beijing," said Hines. "If he can, I'll ask him to get back to me tonight—regardless of the time."

"Then I'm going to stay in Taipei to wait to hear from you. I was thinking about going to Beijing, but I'll postpone it until we know where we stand with Brand and the others. Who knows, with any luck Los Angeles will be my next destination."

"Yes, sit tight. I'll push them as hard as I can from my end for a quick resolution," Hines said.

Ava ended the call, made a coffee, checked the time, and called Lop.

"It's me," she said.

"And it isn't ten yet, are you thinking of leaving earlier for the airport?"

"No, and there might be a substantial change in plans," she said. "I might have found a way to get Mo to come to Los Angeles. If it works, then I want to be there to greet him. I don't know for certain that he'll go, but I'm going to stay here until I find out. That could be later today, or later than that. Either way, I don't want to leave Taipei until that decision is made."

"Do you want me to stay as well?"

"That's up to you, but truthfully I don't think there's much value in both of us hanging around waiting for word about Mo. I was thinking you could go to Beijing as scheduled and start to look for information on Lin," she said. "And if by chance Mo does come to LA—"

"Ava, I should tell you that if Mo goes to LA, I can't join you there," Lop interrupted. "I don't have a US visa, and in fact I've been turned down twice for one."

"I'm glad you told me that now," she said, hiding her disappointment. "But if Mo does go to the US, I'm sure I can make some other arrangement."

"I'll still head to Beijing today. I've already set up a few discreet meetings with people I trust."

"Excellent, then I'll forward your flight and hotel details," she said. "Let's keep in touch."

Ava sighed as she put down the phone. She was comfortable working with Lop, and not having him available for LA was a setback. She considered her other options, came up with two, and then—since both involved asking for favours—opted to wait until she'd heard from Harold Hines. In the meantime, she had time to kill, and an imagination that was going full tilt. A long, hard run, she decided, would help both of those situations, and she went to the window to look outside. It had started to rain, and from the way pedestrians were walking it seemed the wind was strong. Ava didn't really enjoy running indoors, but that seemed to be the best choice.

Twenty minutes later she was on a treadmill in the hotel gym. She set the pace for ten kilometers an hour, which would give her a decent workout without being draining. As she settled into the run, her mind fixed on the possibility of Mo actually going to Los Angeles, and the prospect captured her so completely that she was barely aware that her body was moving.

21

AVA FINISHED A TEN-KILOMETRE RUN WITH EASE,
thought about going a bit further and faster, and decided it
was foolish to risk overdoing it. Instead, she headed for her
suite with her phone in her hand. During her run it had sat
in plain sight and easy to reach, on the seat of an exercise
machine next to her. She was anxious to hear from Harold
Hines, had glanced at it repeatedly, and went back and forth
debating whether not hearing from him yet was a good or
a bad thing.

She checked the hotel phone for messages when she
entered the room, saw there were none, wondered if she
should shower right away or wait for Hines's call, and then
felt annoyed for being so impatient. He would call when he
had something to report, she told herself, and no amount of
impatience was going to make that happen any faster.

So Ava showered, taking her time doing it, and then lei-
surely dried her hair. It was lunchtime when she finished,
and her stomach reminded her that she hadn't eaten breakfast. She scanned the room service menu and was preparing
to place an order when her phone rang. She picked it up

without looking at the incoming number and was disappointed to hear Lop's voice.

"I'm at the airport and we're getting ready to board," he said. "I couldn't help wondering if you've heard anything more concerning Mo."

"I'm still waiting to hear from our lawyer," she said. "I promise I'll send you a text as soon as I know something."

"I hope it's good news, and by that I mean that Mo will be going to Los Angeles. The more I think about it, the better an idea it seems. For one thing, it will be tough enough getting to one guy in Beijing, let alone two—and for another, there's no way Mo will have the same level of security in LA that's available to him in China."

"If he does come, my hope is that he sees no reason to have any security at all, unless of course the deaths of Song and Bai have set off alarm bells."

"We don't know that they've found Song yet, and even if they have, they'll need to figure out who killed him and Bai and why they did it. As far as I can figure out, there's no obvious tie to Chen and Lau Lau's deaths, and there is certainly nothing to connect us to Bai and Song, so I'm not worried about alarm bells."

"There is Tsai."

"It would take someone in the MSS with phenomenal intuition and imagination to finger Tsai as a possible source of information. And even if someone did, he's not going to say anything."

"I think you're ..." Ava began, and then stopped when she saw Hines's name appear on her phone screen. "Lop I have to go. I'll text you later." She switched lines. "Harold, what's the news?"

"We're making progress," he said.

"That sounds like we're not there yet."

"We're close."

"What don't we have?"

"According to Brand, Mo doesn't see any need to travel to Los Angeles. For the rest of it, they're prepared to give us what we want: guarantees of personal safety; the agreement subject to American laws and courts; and the Consul General as a signatory."

"I want Mo," she said.

"I understand that, Ava, but the other side isn't buying into it. They kept reiterating that the Consul General is the official representative of the People's Republic of China in southern California, and that his signature should be sufficient."

"He doesn't represent the Chinese movie industry, and what is this about if not a Chinese movie? And it was a representative of the Syndicate that signed the original deal with Top of the Road. It only makes sense that they'd sign off on the one that gives them what they've wanted all along."

"I hear you, but I can only repeat what they told me."

Ava sensed she was starting to go in circles and switched gears. "Did they raise any objections to an in-person signing?"

"They actually like the idea, and in fact they asked if Fai and Silvana would make themselves available to the local media after announcing they were refusing the Oscar nominations."

"Why would Fai and Silvana ever say yes to that kind of public humiliation?"

"It isn't a demand."

"Good, but Mo coming to Los Angeles to sign the agreement is."

"I've made our case. They've said no. I don't know what else can be done. I know you feel strongly about this, but I'm still not completely sure why."

"My reasons don't matter. If there's no Mo, then I'm prepared to take the deal off the table," Ava said, deciding to test those waters.

"That is rather drastic," said Hines.

"I know, but I don't think he will let it get to that point. Let's start with the fact that he wants this deal," she said slowly. "In fact, he's probably doing cartwheels at the thought of it. If he gets it, he's going to make a lot of senior people in the Communist Party very happy, and whatever criticism he was facing for letting the film be made and released in the first place is going to fade away. Does that seem logical to you?"

"It does."

"And Mo's reluctance to come to Los Angeles to sign it is based on what—an aversion to long flights, the fact he doesn't want to have to confront Fai and Silvana, or something else as stupid?"

"I don't know. I did ask, but no one cared to answer."

"Well, I actually don't need an answer, because all that matters is that we get his bum on a plane." She hesitated, then continued. "And I've just decided that if threatening to withdraw our offer is what it takes, then that's what we should do."

"What if they don't change their position?"

"Then we take the deal off the table, and we wait for them to come back to us," Ava said. "The way I see things is that they have a lot more to lose than we do. We'd get the burst of publicity that comes with the Oscars, and we would still have legal challenges we can pursue. Why would Mo want to put himself through any of that when a solution to his problems is on the table, and all he has to do is sign it?"

"I agree with your assessment, but do you really want to risk the chance that they'll walk away?"

"They won't," Ava said.

"You seem very sure of that."

"Mo is a survivor. I don't know what crazy reason he has for not coming to LA, but threatening to take the deal off the table will be a wake-up call, and his survival instincts will kick in. There is no way he'll want to go to his superiors and tell them the deal is dead because he didn't want to get on a plane."

"Assuming they know about it."

"If the Consul General has been consulted—and I'm assuming he has been, because they're telling us he'll sign—then Beijing knows."

"Well, let's find out if you are correct," Hines said. "Brand is waiting for me to get back to him. I'll put it to him as directly as possible."

"Then do it now, please. I'm anxious to hear what their answer is." As she put down the phone, she muttered, "Shit." Mo's refusal to come to LA mystified her. Was something going on in Beijing that was keeping him there, or wouldn't allow him to leave? The most logical possibility was that someone had connected them to the deaths of Bai and Song, but then she thought about what Lop had said and knew that was so unlikely that it was almost impossible to believe. Well, she figured, they should know soon enough why Mo was reluctant. In the meantime, her hunger had returned with a vengeance.

She called room service on the hotel phone, ordered a

bacon cheeseburger made from Wagyu beef, French fries with gravy, and an additional side of creamy coleslaw. She knew it was probably too much food, but in her current mood too much was better than too little.

As she waited, she opened the notebook, circled Mo's name, and wrote: *How do I get to him when he comes to LA?* She knew she was being optimistic making the assumption that he would come, but planning for the possibility encouraged her. In case it happened, how could she get to him? She needed to isolate him, so it couldn't be in a crowd or a public place. The most logical locale would be his hotel room, but she had no idea where he would be staying and what kind of security the hotel might have in place. She wrote HOTEL? and then stared at the word, realizing how difficult what she wanted to do might be. A knock on the door broke her concentration. She went over to it and saw room service had arrived.

Ava ate slowly, enjoying the cheeseburger but relishing the French fries. Fries with gravy had been one of her teenage favourites—much to the disgust of her mother—and she had even tried poutine, which involved adding globs of white cheese curds to the dish, before deciding that was too much. She had finished the burger and was still working her way through her fries when Hines called.

"Harold, what are they saying?"

"Mo will come to Los Angeles."

"Yes!"

"He evidently hasn't been feeling well and that was the reason for the initial reluctance. I'm not sure I believe that, but what does it matter? He'll be here."

"When?"

"They're proposing to meet three days from now. Obviously, the sooner Fai and Silvana reject the nominations and put out a statement, the better it will be for the Chinese. Does that timeframe work for you?"

"Our team can be in LA faster than that, but my concern is if it gives you enough time to prepare the agreement, and for us to come up with a statement."

"We'll just have to make it work, but we'll need your input," Hines said. "How quickly can you get here?"

"Within twenty-four hours. I'll send you my itinerary as soon as it's in place."

"Good, we'll start drafting something right away, and I'll leave my calendar open for you."

"And I'll contact Fai and Silvana and tell them to book flights."

"Well, it sounds as if we have a plan."

"Thank you for your efforts. I apologize if I didn't sound grateful earlier."

"I know you've been under a lot of stress. Just be assured that we're here to do whatever we can to help."

"Thank you again. I'll be in touch," said Ava.

Yes, we have a plan, she thought when Hines rang off, but only part of one—now she had to create the rest of it. Before focusing on that, though, she needed to organize getting herself, Fai, and Silvana to Los Angeles.

She went online, found an EVA flight that left Taipei at seven that evening, and would arrive in LA around four thirty in the afternoon. She booked seats for her and Silvana in business class, and then despite the late hour in Toronto she phoned Fai.

"Hey," Fai answered in a sleepy voice.

"Sorry for calling so late, but things are heating up. The Chinese have agreed to our proposal, and we've tentatively scheduled a meeting with them three days from now in LA to sign off on it," Ava said. "I'm leaving Taipei tonight for LA. I need you and Silvana to join me there. Will you call her and let her know? Tell her I've reserved a seat for her on the EVA flight to LA that leaves Taipei at seven tonight. If she doesn't want to go or wants another flight, she should let me know. Otherwise I'll see her at the airport."

"That's terrific news, and of course I'll call her," Fai said. "When should I get there?"

"Leave tomorrow—or, given the time difference, I should say today."

"Where are we going to stay?"

"We were at the Peninsula with Chen and Lau Lau so I don't want to stay there again. The Four Seasons is nearby and is close to the lawyers' offices. I'll see if I can get us suites."

"I don't care where we are as long as I'm with you."

"Me neither, but there's nothing wrong with being comfortable. Now, please call Silvana while I book the hotel."

Thirty minutes later, Fai confirmed that Silvana would join Ava on that evening's flight, and that she had booked her own flight into LA. Ava told her she had reserved two suites at the Four Seasons. With everyone's itinerary settled, that left her with only a few other things to do before she could focus solely on Mo. She texted Lop first to tell him her plans and that she'd be in touch. Next she called Sonny Kwok in Hong Kong.

"Hi boss, great to hear from you, are you calling to say you're heading this way?"

"No, I'm afraid I'm not. What I wanted to ask is if you have a visa for the US."

"I don't, but I could apply for one."

"It would take too long to process, and I'd need you to get there in a day or two," she said, hiding yet another disappointment.

"I could always see if I can buy a fake," he said.

"No, that's too risky."

"Sorry, boss."

"*Momentai*, but maybe you should apply for a real one when you have the chance. You never know when we might need you to have it."

"I'll do that," he said. "Is there any chance I'll be seeing you soon?"

"I hope so," she said, not wanting to voice her reluctance about going to Hong Kong. "Let me know when you get that visa."

"I will, boss."

Ava sighed. She couldn't get Lop or Sonny to LA and she didn't want to use strangers, and right now that included the local triads who had helped her the year before. What she wanted to do was too delicate and too dangerous to take any chances. She needed someone who had suitable skills and who she could trust absolutely. There was only other person she thought fitted the description, and that was Derek Liang. But since he'd married Mimi, Ava had used only his computer talents. Even if he had maintained his bak mei, and Mo didn't represent any physical threat, could she really ask him to put himself in harm's way? No, she decided quickly. Her friendship with him and Mimi was too important, and he meant too much to Mimi and their baby for Ava to put him at risk.

So, what to do? Well, she thought, she had a twelve-hour plane ride to come up with something.

22

AVA SAT TWO ROWS IN FRONT OF SILVANA DURING THE EVA flight to Los Angeles. That wasn't by choice, more that those had been the last two seats available in business class. It worked out well for both of them. Silvana had looked exhausted and hadn't been talkative when she arrived at the airport. As soon as she boarded the plane, she downed two glasses of champagne, then two glasses of white wine with dinner, and slept for most of the trip. It wasn't hard to tell that she hadn't had much rest since the shootings. For her part, Ava watched two films, napped off and on, but couldn't get Mo out of her thoughts. Frustratingly, it wasn't a matter of weighing her options on how to handle him; it was finding even one option that might work. And she still didn't have one when they landed on time in LA.

They cleared immigration and customs in good order, and as they headed for the exit, Silvana asked, "Where are we staying?"

"I booked suites for us at the Four Seasons in Beverly Hills."

"Good, I was hoping it wouldn't be the Peninsula again. There are too many memories there from our last visit."

Ava nodded. "That's why I didn't choose it. I'd see Chen and Lau Lau around every corner."

"Oh my god," Silvana gasped.

"What?" Ava said, wondering if she had somehow upset her.

"There's Fai."

Ava looked at the crowd waiting for arriving passengers, and saw Fai standing in the middle waving at them. She and Silvana walked quickly towards her. Fai stepped forward with her arms extended. When the three women came together they had had brief group hug.

"What a great surprise," Ava said.

"I didn't want to wait to see the two of you," said Fai.

"I'm glad you didn't," Ava said.

They left the terminal, joined a line for limousines, and ten minutes later they were on Interstate 405 sitting in stop-and-go traffic. Given the time of day, the situation wasn't unexpected, and it gave Ava the chance to report on her conversations with Hines.

"Do we really have to put out a statement explaining why we're turning down the nominations?" Fai asked when Ava finished.

"It's something they feel strongly about, but we won't agree to anything that either of you find too distasteful," Ava said. "They also wanted you to hold a press conference. We told them that wasn't going to happen."

"I bet that was Mo's idea. He would like nothing more than humiliating us in public."

"There's no chance of that, and if things fall into place he'll never humiliate anyone again."

Silvana's head spun towards Ava. "Are you saying that

in reference to making Chen's killers pay? I know you said you would, but ..."

"Accounts are being settled. That's all I want to tell you for now."

Silvana trembled.

"Are you okay? Did I frighten you?" Ava asked.

"No, you excited me."

"I'm glad. I just hope I don't disappoint you."

"That's impossible. You are—" Silvana began, but was interrupted when Ava's phone rang.

"Yes?" answered Ava.

"This is Harold Hines. I saw that your plane landed on time and thought we could chat."

"Has anything untoward happened?"

"No, things are progressing as we expected, but there are things we need to review."

"I'm in a limo with Fai and Silvana, and I'd like to plug them into the conversation, but I don't think the driver should be part of it."

"Where are you staying?"

"The Four Seasons."

"Do you want to come to me or shall I come to you?"

"Just one second," Ava said, and then covered the phone with her hand. "Fai, have you eaten?"

"No."

"Harold, we'd appreciate it if you could come to the hotel. We can have our conversation over a drink, and maybe a snack or two."

"That sounds fine, and I would like my assistant to join us. She's been communicating with Patricia Nolan and can report on that."

"The more the merrier, but I don't expect we'll get to the hotel much before six."

"Then we'll plan on being there around seven."

"Great, see you then," said Ava.

Ava's estimate of when they would arrive at the hotel was a quarter of an hour too optimistic, but they still had time to check in and freshen up before gathering in Ava's suite at ten to seven. Fai and Silvana were nervous, which at first surprised Ava, but when she thought about what they were about to do and what was at stake, she realized it was understandable.

"We should check the room service and order something before Harold gets here," she said as the actresses settled side by side on a sofa.

"You look after it. We trust your taste," Fai said.

The menu had a nice selection of Italian appetizers, and without any hesitation Ava ordered a board of cured meats and cheese, two orders of mussels cooked with garlic and white wine in a chili fish broth, and two portions of spot prawns drizzled with a sauce made from olive oil, lemon, garlic, and oregano. She ordered two bottles of Chardonnay to go with the food.

Within a minute of her hanging up, the suite phone rang.

"It's Harold. We're in the lobby."

Ava gave him the number of their corner suite, and then said to Fai and Silvana, "They're on their way up."

Fai took a deep breath and Ava thought she looked worried.

"Are you having doubts?" she asked.

"No, I'm just a little nervous. And in fact, rather than having doubts I feel just the opposite. I've done a lot of thinking about Chen and Lau Lau's legacy over the last little while.

When you told me the plan, I was a bit worried that what we're going to do could damage it, but the more I think about it, the more I believe that actually we can elevate it in a way that even winning the Oscars couldn't."

"What do you mean?" Silvana asked.

"Well, how many of the last ten films that won an Oscar, or how many of the directors who won, can you name?"

Silvana frowned. "I can think of *Parasite*, but only because it was Korean."

"Exactly, but *Tiananmen* is going to be one of a kind. It will be the masterpiece that the Chinese government wanted no one to see; and then the masterpiece that won the Palme d'Or; and then the masterpiece that only a select few others saw; and then the masterpiece that rejected Oscar recognition," Fai said, her emotions showing. "I think our film has a chance to be remembered forever as one of the best films ever made. It may not be, but the fact it can't be seen will create an aura, a mystery, that will keep it in people's minds, and make it part of any discussion about great films."

"I hadn't thought of it that way, but now that I do, I think you are absolutely right. In their own perverse way, the Chinese government is giving the film a life beyond what could be expected of even a massive hit," said Silvana.

Ava listened in amazement as they took the same simple notion she had expressed to Hines and expanded on it. But then that was what great actresses did, she thought. They transformed words on paper into living beings. Now Fai had taken her idea and infused it with meaning that made it somehow grander than just an attempt to secure a safe future for her and Silvana. It also, she realized, made it easier for them to rationalize what they were going to do.

A knock at the door drew Ava's attention. She opened it to find Harold Hines and a stunning young woman. Ava had expected to see the young man who had been Hines's assistant previously, and was caught off guard. "It's good to see you, come in," she said finally.

Ava stood to one side and then followed them into the living area.

Hines held out his hand to Fai and Silvana. "We meet again," he said. They shook, and then he continued. "Let me introduce Maxine Latner. She is currently articling at the firm, but that's a status that shouldn't last for much longer because we are very impressed with her, as I'm sure you will be."

Ava saw the young woman blush. She was tall, lean, fine-featured, fair-skinned, and had ash blonde hair that hung to her shoulders. She was dressed plainly in black slacks and a powder blue cotton blouse that was buttoned to the neck. Her conservative appearance, in Ava's mind, only added to her attractiveness. She was, in fact, exactly the kind of woman that Ava would have pursued in her earlier years. "It's a pleasure to meet you, Maxine," Ava said.

"And I'm thrilled to be here," she said, glancing at Fai and Silvana. "I'm a huge fan of these two ladies."

"Then come and meet them."

There was a round of handshaking and then everyone sat—the lawyers in chairs across from the sofa.

"I've ordered some food and wine. Do you want to start to work now, or wait until we've eaten?" Ava asked.

"Let's start now, and then we can chat as we eat," Hines said, reaching into his briefcase. He extracted a thick pile of paper and put it on the coffee table that separated them. "I brought copies of the agreement that we want the Chinese to sign, and the statement that Patricia Nolan has drafted for Fai and Silvana. Where do you want to start?"

"There will be no statement without an agreement, so let's begin with that," Ava said. "And for clarity's sake, why don't you explain it to us."

"Yes, please, I'm hopeless when it comes to legal jargon," Silvana said.

"I understand. I'll try to keep it as direct and concise as I can." Hines took what looked like a five- or six-page document from the top of the pile and opened it. "There are two basic parts. The first addresses the matter of the safety and security of Fai and Silvana. The second describes the actions that would be invoked if the first part isn't honoured.

"In terms of your safety, we have tried to cover every eventuality. For example, the agreement would be breached if either lady goes missing or is even detained. We have also tried to mitigate any chance of you being charged with a crime. We don't quite request total blanket immunity, but we come close enough. In fact, just about the only crime the Chinese or Hong Kong governments could charge you with is one of a capital nature, like murder, and even then the agreement calls for you to have access to the lawyer of your choice within twenty-four hours, and a public trial."

"Murder?" Silvana said with a smile.

"I know it's far-fetched, but as I said, we have tried to be thorough," Hines added. "And now, in case of any breach—and it would be a US court determining if one occurred—the forfeiture of the film rights is almost instantaneous. In addition we have specified financial penalties aimed squarely at Top of the Road—including its principals—and they are large enough to put the company out of business and ruin the owners."

"I take it the focus on Top of the Road is deliberate," Ava said.

"It is. If the Chinese government reneges, there is no legal vehicle to hold them accountable. So we have to make Top of the Road a party to the agreement and then pound the hell out of them in an American court if something goes wrong."

"Excuse me, are you saying that even if we go ahead with this you still don't think we'll be safe?" Silvana asked softly.

"No, I'm not saying that, but we can't ignore the fact the Chinese government has a record of not honouring agreements. That aside, we all know how they don't want the film released, and we have to hope that may override any animosity they feel about the people involved in making it."

"And turning down the Oscar nominations should help to lessen those that feeling," Ava said, and then looked towards the door. "Excuse me, but I think our food has arrived."

23

THERE WAS NOT MUCH CONVERSATION AS THEY ATE AT the round table near the window that looked out onto a garden. Ava sensed that Harold Hines's reluctance to say the agreement was an iron-clad guarantee of their safety had made Fai and Silvana even more acutely aware of the perils they faced. She completely understood their emotional state but could only respect Hines's honesty. When the last of the mussels were eaten, and after refilling everyone's glasses, she said: "I don't think there is any value in talking about the agreement anymore. I'll read it tonight, and if I have questions I'll discuss them with Fai and Silvana, and then talk to Harold. Is everyone okay with that?"

"I am," Fai said.

Silvana nodded.

"That is your call," said Hines.

"Okay, so that leaves the statement about why the Oscar nominations are being turned down. What do you have?" Ava asked him.

"I spoke to Patricia at length. She was surprised at first about the decision to turn down the nominations, but after

I explained the reasons behind it, she understood. She and Maxine talked before we left the office to come here," Hines said, turning to Latner. "Why don't you tell the ladies what she's advising."

"Something short—in fact very short," Maxine said. "After speaking to Mr. Hines, she and her team worked on various approaches, but found it difficult not to be convoluted. Some of the draft statements ran to almost two pages. The problem—as she sees it—is the moment you start mentioning the Chinese government's sensitivity towards the film, it's like entering a maze with a never-ending number of twists and turns. So she and the team decided to keep it as simple and personal as possible, and to avoid any mention of the politics and history that are involved."

"Read it, please, Maxine," Hines said.

The intern stood, walked to the coffee table, and picked up a single sheet of paper. She rejoined them, pursed her lips, and then said almost melodramatically, "To our dear colleagues, from Pang Fai and Silvana Foo. We cannot adequately describe the depth of grief and sense of loss we feel at the passing of the producer Chen Jie and director Lau Lau. They were more than our collaborators. At various times they were mentors, agents, a partner, and a husband, and at all times they were cherished friends. While we are grateful to the Academy for the nominations it bestowed on our and their work, under the present circumstances we respectfully request that they be withdrawn. We do not believe we could cope with the display of emotion that such a public ceremony would generate, and we believe that Chen and Lau Lau would sympathize with our position."

There was an awkward silence, and then Silvana said,

"That is rather beautiful, but it doesn't even make any mention of the film."

"That is deliberate. Patricia felt if it did, that would compel the Chinese government to demand that their opinions on what happened in Tiananmen Square be part of the narrative. By ignoring it, she's hoping they'll let it slide," Maxine said.

"I told her we needed something that didn't diminish the film or the people who made it," Hines said. "I understand the statement is vague, but I think it permits Fai and Silvana to maintain their dignity, and there is nothing in it that is disrespectful to the Chinese government."

"Do you think the other side will accept it?" Ava asked.

"I don't know, but they might like the idea of exiting quietly, and the statement certainly allows them to do that. If we start including references to *Tiananmen* and the controversy surrounding it, it could look like the Chinese government is strong-arming Fai and Silvana—at least that's the pitch I would make to Eli Brand."

"What do you think?" Ava asked Fai.

"I like it," she said without hesitation.

"How about you, Silvana?"

"Yes, I like it too. I think it humanizes an otherwise inhumane situation."

Ava looked at Hines. "You have a green light for the statement, and assuming we okay the agreement later tonight, what are your plans?"

"I'll call Eli Brand and ask him to meet with me tomorrow—just the lawyers, no principals. I'll take him through the documents and see if I can get him onside. If I can, and if he is as persuasive with Christensen and his partners as

I've heard he is, then the meeting two days from now could be a formality."

"I have trouble believing that Top of the Road won't resist being at financial risk if things go badly," said Ava.

"The Chinese may not give them any choice, and remember they are being paid very well right now."

"Still, I would like you to make it clear to Brand that if there is resistance, we are prepared to walk away from the deal. There has to be a serious level of accountability if this is going to work," Ava said.

"If it is necessary to make that point, rest assured I will."

"One more thing—when I met Brand as Jennie Kwong, I paid him a lot of money to get a copy of the agreement between Top of the Road and the Syndicate. So he is buyable, and we'll pay if that is what it takes to get him working as an advocate."

"I wish you hadn't told me that," Hines said, smiling wryly. "But now that I know, I'll keep it in mind."

"I apologize if you think I'm telling you how to do your job."

"That's not necessary; I prefer clients who provide clear direction."

Ava nodded. "Thank you, Harold, and I think that concludes an excellent meeting. I'll get back to you later this evening if we have any issues with the agreement. If you don't hear from me, you can assume it's a go."

The two lawyers stood. Maxine gathered their papers, and a moment later they left the suite.

"I like him," Silvana said.

"He's very capable," Ava said. "Now, do you want to go over the agreement with me?"

"No, you know that I trust you to do what's best for all of us. Besides, that wine did me in. I'm ready for bed."

"Then we'll touch base in the morning."

"Before I go, though, there is one last thing," Silvana said. "Are you sure Mo is going to be at the meeting?"

"That's what we've been told, and they know if he's not it's a major problem."

"I'm glad he'll be there, but I'm not sure I'm going to be able to restrain myself from hitting him or throwing something at him."

"Me neither," Fai said. "C'mon, Sils, I'll walk you back to your room. Maybe you can treat me to a night cap from your bar."

"Why not," Silvana said.

Fai leaned forward and kissed Ava. "With me gone, you can go over the agreement in peace and quiet."

"I'll do that, so take your time."

When the suite door closed behind the two women, Ava picked up the copy of the agreement from the coffee table and took it to the desk. She started to read the first page before quickly realizing that her mind was elsewhere. Silvana's question about Mo had started her thinking about him again. It was one thing to get him to come to LA, but quite another to safely get her hands on him. She needed to find a way—but how? She opened her notebook in a search for an idea: any idea that had a chance to work.

There were several major problems that had to be solved, beginning with how to get to him, and ending with getting rid of him without being seen. Several things made those formidable tasks. Mo was unlikely to be alone at any given time unless he was in a hotel room. And every high-end hotel in LA had extensive CCTV in the lobby, in elevators, in stairwells, and on each floor. In fact, she doubted there was a square foot anywhere in any of the hotels—outside of a guest's room—that wasn't being observed and taped. So she had to accept that getting into his room without being seen wasn't likely, and even if she managed it, there was the not insubstantial question of being able to leave the same way without being identified. On top of that, she thought, it was safer for all concerned if Mo's body wasn't found. A missing Mo would create confusion and buy time—both of which worked in her favour. *But if I want Mo to go missing, I can't do this alone*, she suddenly decided, and without Lop, Sonny, or Derek, there was only one other option. She had discounted it before, but now she couldn't. She reached for her phone to call Shanghai.

"*Wei*," Auntie Grace answered.

"It's Ava again. Is Xu available?"

"I can't remember a time when you called so often. I like it."

"Thank you, Auntie, I only wish I wasn't bothering Xu so much with my problems."

"He's happy whenever he hears from you. It doesn't matter if it's because you have a problem or not. Now, let me go and get him."

"Hey, *mei mei*," Xu said a minute later. "How is Los Angeles?"

Ava didn't think she had told him she was going. "How did you know I was here?"

"I spoke to Lop last night. He explained what was going on."

"Of course, I should have known that he would. So he also told you about the possibility of Mo coming here?"

"Yes, he said you were working on it."

"It is now a fact, and that's why I'm calling. I need some help here. Neither Lop nor Sonny has a US visa, and I can't do this job by myself, so I'm wondering if you would reach out to Johnny Lam?" she asked, referring to the Mountain Master of the Los Angeles triads.

"I'll do it gladly. What is it you want from him?"

"I need to grab and isolate Mo." She hesitated before adding, "And once he's dead, I would like Johnny's men to dispose of the body. I want Mo to disappear off the face of the earth."

"Do you have a plan for getting to Mo?" Xu asked calmly.

She hesitated again, and then said, "No, but I'm working on it."

"That may make my conversation with Johnny a little awkward."

"I'm sorry, but you know I'll come up with something. And you can tell Johnny that it won't be anything crazy. I won't suggest anything that would put him or his people in harm's way."

"Okay, I'll make the call."

"One more thing—I'll pay him for his help. I can't keep asking you to cash in favours on my behalf. I'll feel a lot better if I pay him, so please let me."

"You know it isn't normally necessary, but this time it might make sense since I can't think of any favours he owes me," Xu said with a chuckle.

"I'll pay whatever he thinks is fair."

"Don't worry—if he agrees to take on the job, I'll work it out with him."

"Do you have doubts that he'll take it on?"

"Not really, but as Uncle taught us both there are some things we shouldn't take for granted."

Ava sighed. "You do know that I don't take you for granted."

"I do, and the same is true from this end. Now, by my calculation it's still rather early in the evening in LA, so I should be able to get hold of Johnny. Be on standby."

"Count on it," Ava said.

24

WHILE SHE WAITED FOR XU TO GET BACK TO HER, AVA returned to the agreement Hines had drafted. She read slowly, trying to parse every phrase. When she finished, the only thought she had was that she couldn't imagine anyone having done any better. If the Chinese government honoured it, Fai and Silvana were completely secure; and if they didn't, well, the film would be theirs, and Top of the Road—and Christensen and his partners—would be financially crippled. What were the odds that the Chinese would renege, she wondered? Short- to medium-term, and that spanned at least five years in her mind. She couldn't imagine the current leadership doing anything that would revive *Tiananmen*. If there was a leadership change, attitudes could shift—to Fai's benefit or against it. But that was nothing they could control. The priority was securing Fai and Silvana's safety right now, and Ava believed the agreement made that possible.

She had made a few notes on a fresh page in her notebook as she read, and now she flipped back to earlier entries. When she did, the name *David Mo* appeared in the middle of a page. Under it were the home address and cellphone number Derek had provided. She stared at it, and then cursed under her breath for not having realized David Mo could be her answer—but how to use him?

Ava opened her laptop, accessed Google Earth, and entered the address. Seconds later she was looking at a bungalow in Brentwood—a middle-class community close to UCLA—that had a neatly trimmed lawn and a Lexus SUV parked in the driveway. She had no doubt about who had bought the car. She was equally sure the neighbourhood wasn't rife with CCTV.

The door to the suite opened and Fai walked in.

"Come and look at this," Ava said.

Fai came to stand behind her and wrapped her arms around Ava's shoulders. "What am I looking at?" she asked.

"David Mo's home—and what is the one thing that Mo Ming values almost as much as his life?"

"David."

"Yes, David."

"Are you going to use him to get to Mo?"

"It's the only thing I can think of."

"You wouldn't let him get hurt though, would you?"

"There's no reason to hurt him."

"Good ..." Fai said, then paused.

"Is everything okay?"

"Yes, but Sils really wore on me. She started to grill me as soon as we got to her room. She's desperate to know if you're going to do something to Mo while he's here. I told her you are very superstitious, and you never discuss the specifics of a plan with me or anyone else for fear of jinxing yourself."

"That's true enough," Ava said, and then wanting to

change the subject she placed her right hand on the draft agreement. "I read this carefully. I think it is as good as we're going to get. If the Chinese accept it, you and Sils should be safe."

"Well, if nothing else it will give her some peace of mind."

Ava's cell rang, and she saw a number with a 310 area code. "Yes?" she answered.

"This is Johnny Lam. Is this Ava?"

"Yes, and thank you so much for calling me. I wasn't sure if I would hear from you or Xu. So you obviously spoke to him?"

"I did, and I told him I would phone you, but that's all I committed to do. He told me roughly what you have in mind. Truthfully, I need more information before I make a decision about helping you."

"Did he mention the name Mo Ming?"

"Yes, and I remember he was the guy you thought ordered the demonstration outside the theatre where your film was showing—the demonstration we broke up for you."

"He's the one, but this time we're dealing with something far more serious than a demonstration," said Ava. "We have certain proof that last week Mo ordered, or at the least instigated, the murders of two of the people associated with the film. Two people who were very dear friends of mine. Two people that I am quite determined to avenge."

"Xu told me that, and I said I had heard stories about you that I hadn't quite believed. Now I am starting to."

"I have no idea what you've heard, and it doesn't really matter. What I can tell you is that Mo deserves whatever he gets."

Lam was silent for several seconds, and then asked, "You aren't concerned about blowback from the Chinese government? I can't imagine they'll take kindly to the killing of a senior official."

"We will do everything we can to ensure the Chinese never find out who did what to whom. That starts with getting Mo to a place that's secure and private, and it ends with getting rid of his body in a place where it can't be found."

"Are you saying you want us to kill him?"

"No, I'll handle that myself," said Ava. "What I'll need, though, is a gun, a private place, help in getting him there, and someone to dispose of the body."

"And when is all of this supposed to happen?" Lam asked matter-of-factly.

"The day after tomorrow seems to be our target."

"That's short notice."

"It's also the only day I'm sure Mo will be in LA."

"Assuming we can make the timing work, have you figured out how we get our hands on him?"

Ava looked at her notebook, picked up a pen, and circled David Mo's name. "His only child, a son named David, lives in a bungalow in Brentwood. Mo adores him. I'm thinking that we could use David as bait."

"You want us to grab the son?"

"Yes, and then we'll have to convince Mo to do what's necessary to free him."

"Do we pretend it's a kidnapping for ransom, or something like that?"

"That's a bit too obvious. We need a story that is more subtle, and won't send Mo running to the police."

"I'm not much good at inventing stories."

"We need something that will scare but not terrify Mo," Ava said as she doodled. "We could keep it work-related."

"I don't know what you're talking about."

"We could pretend to be film distributors who have been trying to get a deal in China but can't get a response from the Syndicate—which Mo runs. We could say we know he's in LA, and all we want is half an hour of his time and a fair hearing. We could apologize for taking David, but say it was the only way we could think of to get his attention. We would have to add, of course, that we hoped we wouldn't have to harm David."

"I kind of like that. It gives us cover, and why would he call the cops if all we want to do is talk?"

"Exactly, and one more thing that might prevent him from doing anything silly is the fact David is gay, and at times quite flamboyantly so. Mo wouldn't want the publicity that calling the cops in might generate."

Lam became quiet again, and then said, "If we get the son, we would insist that Mo comes alone in a taxi to meet with us. And of course we wouldn't tell him where we are holding the son. We would arrange to pick him up partway."

"It sounds as if you have done something like this before."

"We have some practice at it."

"Holding people for ransom?"

"More often stashing away people who owe money in a safe house, until someone pays their debt—as is done in Hong Kong."

"Yes, that is a time-honoured tradition," Ava said. "Are you telling me you have a safe house?"

"We do have one."

"And am I getting ahead of myself by assuming that you are prepared to help?"

"No. I told Xu that I would provide help if your plan made sense. I think it does."

"Then all that's left is to settle on the amount I'm going to pay you."

"I don't want your money," Lam said. "If I give you the help you want, Xu has already agreed to grant a favour I requested. That's good enough."

"I didn't want him to do that."

"Well he has, and you'd do me a favour by not trying to change that understanding."

"Okay, I'll let it go."

"Thank you. Now, I'm going to need whatever information you have on David Mo. You can text it to me at this number."

"I'll do it as soon as I hang up."

"Unless I hear otherwise, we'll plan to pick him up the day after tomorrow, and we'll use tomorrow to scope the place out," Lam said.

"That sounds perfect."

"And do you know where Mo Ming will be staying, or where he'll be when you contact him to tell him about his son?"

"He's going to be at a meeting in Beverly Hills. I can have someone alert me as soon as the meeting ends. But, Johnny, I can't be the one who calls Mo. He knows my voice. You or one of your men should do it."

"Sure, we can make that work, but I'll need his phone number."

"I'll get it for you by tomorrow morning."

"And when do you want to get to the safe house?"

"I'll go once you've confirmed you have David," Ava said. "And by the way, keep him blindfolded. We don't want him to see me or any of you. We need to keep a very tight lid on this."

"That sits well with me. And now, unless there's anything else to go over, let's call it a night."

"Yes. I'll touch base with you tomorrow to confirm we're still on schedule."

Ava felt a surge of adrenalin as she put down the phone. Somehow, almost out of nowhere, there was now a plan—and what was more, it was one that struck her as being entirely workable.

"You look very happy," Fai said.

Ava hadn't noticed her standing in the bedroom doorway. "How much of that conversation did you hear?"

"The beginning and the end; in between, I brushed my teeth."

"I was speaking to Johnny Lam. He runs the triads in LA. The day after tomorrow they are going to be our accomplices when it comes to getting to Mo."

"I wish there was something I could do to help," Fai said.

Ava smiled. "There is. We can talk about it in bed."

25

AVA SLEPT WELL AND WOKE JUST AFTER EIGHT FEELING energized and full of purpose. She could still hardly believe that Johnny Lam had been so accommodating, but assumed that whatever favour he had wrung from Xu wasn't something minor. Whatever it was, she thought as she got out of an empty bed, she would have to find a way to repay her *ge ge*.

After a quick trip to the bathroom, she went into the living room expecting to see Fai, but there was no sign of her. Ava went to the terrace door, looked outside, and saw her leaning back on a chair with her feet resting on a coffee table. "Is that coffee still warm?" she asked as she opened the door.

"Hey babe," Fai said, turning towards her with a smile. "It should be. It got here about fifteen minutes ago."

Ava poured a cupful and sipped. "Not too bad. How long have you been up?"

"An hour or so. That three-hour time difference really affected my sleep. Besides, I wanted to make the phone calls to Beijing that you asked me to do."

"And what did you find out?"

"Mo still has the same cellphone number, and he usually

stays at the Beverly Hilton when he's in LA. I called the hotel. He hasn't checked in but he has a two-night reservation starting today."

"That's really useful info. Did you have any difficulty getting it?"

"No—Mo has been seeing an actress who's a friend of mine. She confirmed the phone number, and knew about the Hilton because Mo has taken her there twice. And speaking of phones, yours that you left in the living room started ringing around six. You obviously didn't hear it, and I didn't answer. I think you might have a message or two on it."

"Let me check," Ava said.

A moment later she returned to the terrace with her phone. She accessed her voicemail, listened intently, then said, "Yes!"

"What's that about?" Fai asked.

"It was Lop who called. He has some news he thinks I might like."

"What news?"

"I don't know yet. I have to phone him," Ava said, and then she did exactly that.

"How is LA?" he answered.

"Going well, and with any luck we might wrap things up tomorrow, but right now I'm interested in what you have to tell me."

"Well ..." he said slowly. "I spent the entire day bouncing around Beijing, meeting people in places where they thought they wouldn't be seen. There is definitely a lot of paranoia when it comes to discussing the MSS and Mr. Lin Chao. This is a man who inspires a great deal of fear."

"But not so much, I gather, that it kept you from finding out something of interest."

"Definitely of interest, and maybe offering a glimmer of an opportunity to get at him."

"I'm all ears," Ava said, feeling a touch of excitement.

"It happened in my last meeting," Lop said deliberately. "My contact confirmed that Lin does work and live in an armed compound in Xiyuan, next to the Summer Palace. He rarely leaves it, and when he does it's usually on official business and he's heavily guarded. But then the contact mentioned Lin Ai, his daughter and only child. She is a talented ballerina and dances with the Central Ballet Troupe, which is the top dance company in China. Evidently, Lin is extraordinarily proud of her."

"I'm not sure where you're going with this," Ava said. "We're using Mo's son David to lure him into the open here. Surely you aren't suggesting we could do something like that in Beijing?"

"I'm not—and by the way, thank goodness for the one-child policy that bonds parents here so tightly to their kids."

"Yes, the policy certainly makes them precious," said Ava. "But I still have no idea how this relates to Lin."

"The Central Ballet Troupe starts a new season four days from now. The opening night program is *The Rite of Spring*, and I was told the principal female dancer will be Lin Ai."

"And if she is?"

"Then there's a strong chance that Lin Chao will be at the theatre that night. I'm informed he seldom misses one of her premieres."

"But if he does attend, he'll be one of how many people—a thousand, two thousand? How could we get close to him? And even if it were possible, how could we get away from there without being seen and probably caught?"

"It would have to be done from long range."

"I don't mean to sound negative, Lop, but what makes you think there's a chance that might work?"

"Earlier tonight I went to the theatre in Xicheng where the troupe dances. Cars dropping off people can't get within a hundred metres of its entrance, and people have to walk across open ground for at least eighty of those metres, and then up more than twenty steps to get to the front doors. Ava, it's a broad expanse, so even if there's a crowd I can't imagine people will be jammed together. If we could pick Lin out, we might be able to take him out."

"With a sniper?"

"Exactly."

Ava hesitated as she processed this information. "Assuming there is even a slight chance to do what you're describing, do you have a sniper in mind?"

"Yes, the one you used in Hong Kong the night that you and Suen attacked Carter Wing's men, who were holding our men hostage," said Lop. "As you know, I wasn't there, but I heard about the sniper from Suen. He was particularly impressed with him."

"Jimmy Li."

"I didn't know his name."

"Jimmy is very capable and very reliable, but truthfully, I'm not sure he'd be up for this. This is a long way from Hong Kong, and we aren't asking him to shoot at triads who are holding hostages. If he isn't game, do you have anyone else in mind you could hire?"

"Not off hand, and it would be rather dangerous to start asking around town if someone could recommend a sniper I could use."

"True enough," Ava said, feeling slightly foolish that she'd asked that question. "Well, I guess it won't hurt to ask Jimmy if he's willing to do it. I usually deal with him through Sonny, and I don't want to change that relationship, so I'll call Sonny when we're finished."

"Okay, and if he is, we'll probably have to equip him here. If that's the case I'll need a list of what he needs."

"You don't think buying that equipment in Beijing might raise questions?"

"I'll have my men in Shanghai buy it there, so it won't be connected to Beijing."

"Yes, of course, that makes sense."

"Also, if Jimmy is interested, I'd like him to get here as soon as possible. We'll need to scout the entire area around the theatre to find the best spot for him to set up. I also need to get my hands on some photos of Lin."

"Are you saying you still don't know what he looks like?" Ava said, her surprise evident.

"I have a couple of old photos—official party shots. I'm waiting for some that are more recent. It would be ridiculous to go to all this trouble and end up shooting the wrong person."

"If that happened, 'ridiculous' would be a mild description."

Lop gave a little laugh. "Don't worry, I'm getting those photos."

"So now it comes down to Jimmy," Ava said. "I'll call Sonny right away."

"Before you do, tell me how sure you are that you can take care of Mo tomorrow."

"Tomorrow is the only window of opportunity we have. He's scheduled to attend a meeting sometime during the day.

The time and place haven't been determined yet, but they don't actually matter because as long as he actually shows up, we can put our plan in motion. We'll handle things as discreetly as you and I did in Taipei, but when we're done, Mo Ming won't be seen again. All that will be left are a lot of questions without any answers."

"And if you are successful—which I don't doubt you will be—would you plan to join us in Beijing?"

"You can count on it. But first things first, and that's getting Jimmy on board."

"Call me once you know. I don't care what the time is."

"Okay, until later," she said.

Ava put down the phone to find Fai staring at her with a bemused look on her face. She had been so engrossed talking to Lop that she had almost forgotten she was sitting next to her. "What do you find so amusing?" she asked.

"You have no idea how bizarre it is listening to just your side of a conversation like that," said Fai.

Ava poured a second cup of coffee. "Lop thinks he's found a way to get at Lin Chao, but I need to get Sonny to convince Jimmy Li to help."

"Has Jimmy ever said no to one of your requests?"

"Not yet, but there's always a first time. When I'm finished with my calls we should go downstairs for breakfast. Then I should contact Harold Hines to find out where things stand with him and Eli Brand. I suspect I'll be spending the day here in the room. There will probably be a lot of going back and forth, so I want to be not far from my phone and someplace secure. You don't have to hang around here if you don't want to."

"But I will. Who knows—you might need me again."

Ava leaned towards Fai and kissed her gently on the lips. "Why don't you get dressed for breakfast while I call Sonny?"

Fai nodded, lifted herself out of her chair, and left.

Ava waited until the terrace door closed to call Hong Kong.

"Hey boss," Sonny answered loudly, with the sound of traffic in the background.

"Are you in a place where we can speak?"

"I'm outside the noodle shop in Central where you and Uncle used to go. Give me a minute to get to my car."

As she waited, memories of her and Uncle at the shop crept into her mind. There had been some events there that she'd never forget, including seeing for the first time how ill he was.

"Okay, I can talk now," Sonny said. "Did you make it to the States, and did you get the help you needed?"

"Yes, and yes. But I need more help, this time in Beijing."

"Tell me what you want me to do," he said quickly.

"We need a sniper, and Jimmy Li obviously came to mind. Could you speak to him on my behalf?"

"You need a sniper in Beijing?" Sonny asked incredulously, as if he couldn't believe what he was hearing.

"That's our plan," Ava said. "Let me explain it all to you in detail."

26

THE BREAKFAST RUSH SEEMED TO BE OVER BY THE TIME they walked into THEBlvd restaurant, and they managed to secure a table on the patio overlooking Rodeo Drive. After a quick glance at the menu, Ava ordered a crab and egg-white frittata that came with smoked cheddar cheese, and then for good measure ordered a side of Canadian back bacon. Fai opted for THEBlvd Benedict, which had the traditional poached eggs and hollandaise sauce as well as not-so-traditional sautéed mushrooms, spinach, and potato latkes.

When the server left the table, Ava nodded in the direction of the Drive. "My mother would think it was criminal to be staying here and not go shopping."

"The two of you are so different," Fai said.

"Not as much as you might think. It's true I don't like to gamble or shop, but at our very core she and I share a lot of traits. For example, she is totally loyal to her family and friends, and I've never known her to abandon anyone regardless of what kind of trouble they encountered. I like to think that's part of my DNA as well."

Fai reached for Ava's hand. "I know it is, and it's one of the reasons I love you so much."

They took their time over breakfast, but Ava couldn't stop looking at her phone every few minutes. Sonny had promised to call as soon as he had spoken to Jimmy Li, and as minutes became an hour she became increasingly concerned that either Jimmy couldn't be reached or he wanted to think carefully before making a decision. Either way, it was making her nervous because without Jimmy she had no idea what they could do in Beijing.

Her phone finally rang as she and Fai were leaving the restaurant. She answered without looking at the incoming number and was mildly disappointed to hear Harold Hines's voice.

"I just spoke to Eli Brand, and I thought I would update you," he said.

"You sound as if you have bad news," Ava said, stopping in the lobby.

"Not really. He's meeting his clients this afternoon and will review our draft agreement and the ladies' statement with them. If there are no major issues, we have agreed to meet tomorrow at one in my firm's boardroom."

"Will Mo be part of the meeting today?"

"He wasn't specific about who would be attending, but if Mo isn't there today, he'll be here tomorrow."

"How can you be sure about that?"

"I asked Eli specifically."

"Good—and did you discuss the drafts at all?"

"I did, and while he didn't have any big issue with the agreement, he did think we were laying it on a bit thick when it came to possible penalties Top of the Road could face, but he also said he understands why we think it is necessary," said Hines. "As for Fai and Silvana's statement, his only comment was that it wasn't his call, but he thought that his clients would probably want to rework it. I told him we'd be pleased to look at whatever they came up with, but that our objective was to keep politics out of it."

"I hope they're reasonable."

"If they want a quick resolution I told them they had better be."

"Exactly," Ava said. "One last thing, will Brand be calling you after his meeting today?"

"He will, and after he does I'll call you."

"Thank you, Harold."

"Until then."

Ava ended the call and looked at Fai. "Harold said that Mo will be at the meeting tomorrow at the Hines and Ford offices, but I still want you to text me to confirm he's there. And, assuming a deal is reached and Mo puts his signature to paper, you have to text me again."

"What if we can't reach an agreement tomorrow?"

"Depending on what happens with Sonny and Jimmy, I could stay here another day."

"And if that still isn't enough time?"

"Then you and Silvana have to decide what is most important—getting Mo or trying to get a deal," Ava said. "Maybe you should put that question to her this afternoon. If we get into that situation, I will do whatever the two of decide."

"That will mean telling her what you want to do to Mo."

"It's time she knew."

They started towards the elevators, and minutes later

entered the suite. Before Ava could get to the desk, her phone rang again, and this time she looked at the screen.

"Sonny, I've been waiting to hear from you," she answered.

"It took me a while to reach Jimmy."

"But you did?"

"Yeah, and I went over in detail everything you told me. I thought he sounded reluctant at first, but as it turned out that was only because he was worried about making last-minute arrangements for someone to look after his granddaughters. Once he was able to sort that out, he couldn't have been more eager to join the team," Sonny said. "He hates that the Chinese seem intent on eliminating free speech and crushing any pretence of democracy here. He said killing Lin would be a blow on behalf of Hong Kong."

"Well, we don't all have to have the same reason for wanting Lin dead," said Ava. "Did you decide on a fee with him?"

"He didn't want to take any money, but when I told him he'd be insulting you if he refused your offer he backed down. We settled on twenty-five thousand Hong Kong dollars."

"And did he give you a list of the equipment he needs?" she asked, sitting at the desk and opening her notebook.

"His first preference for a rifle is the Barrett MRAD, and he thinks Lop shouldn't have any trouble getting his hands on one. If there's a problem I'll pass along his second and third choices, but for now he'd like us to focus on the Barrett."

"Okay, what else?" Ava asked as she wrote that down.

"He wants a night vision clip-on, and either .338 Lapua Magnum or .300 Winchester Magnum ammo ."

"I'll tell Lop," she said. "On your end, can you book flights to Beijing tomorrow for yourself and Jimmy, and then send the details to me and Lop?"

"Sure."

"I'll ask him to make hotel arrangements for you, and from now on to communicate directly with you. Tomorrow could be a crazy day for me, so I'm not sure what my availability will be."

"*Momentai*, you know Lop and I get on well," Sonny said. "But when do you expect to get to Beijing?"

"Ideally the day after tomorrow, but even if I'm a day later it still fits the schedule we have."

Sonny paused. "I have to say, boss, that I'm really pleased I can help this time."

"Sonny, you are never not a help. I'll see you in Beijing."

After ending the call, Ava immediately phoned Lop. As usual, he answered on the first ring and said, "Do you have good news?"

"Jimmy is in. He and Sonny will fly to Beijing tomorrow. Sonny will forward you their flight details."

"Excellent, and what equipment do I have to get for Jimmy?"

Ava read out the short list.

"I don't think any of those will be a problem," said Lop. "And I'm glad he wants a Barrett. They have a terrific reputation for accuracy."

"From how far?"

"As I remember, from at least fifteen hundred metres. And obviously the further away we are, the more options we'll have in terms of setting up. I was going to scout the area again tomorrow morning, but now I think I'll wait for Jimmy to arrive. He should choose where he wants to shoot from."

"That makes sense, but are there that many options?"

"There are quite a few buildings—offices, hotels, apartments—near the theatre."

"And speaking of hotels, the guys will need one. I told them you'd book it."

"I'll put them in the Grand Hyatt with me. It's large enough that no one pays you any attention."

"Well, it's nice to see things coming together."

"I know, except I can't stop wondering what we're going to do if Lin decides to skip the premiere, or goes into the theatre through a back door. I don't have a backup plan."

"Even the best of plans can't avoid the element of luck," Ava said. "I think I also have a good plan, but I know things can always go sideways, and like you I don't have another option."

"Well, we've been lucky so far. Let's hope it holds," Lop said. "Now, I should go. I have to get my guy in Shanghai looking for the rifle and ammo."

"Let Sonny know if there's any problem."

"Will do."

Ava sat back in her chair. Lop was one of the least pessimistic and most pragmatic people she knew, and it wasn't like him to have doubts—at least, not doubts he would express.

"Are you all right?" Fai asked from the sofa. "You look worried."

"No, I'm fine. I'm just gathering my thoughts before I phone Lam."

"Is everything still on track?"

"Absolutely," Ava said as she reached for her phone again.

"Good morning," Johnny Lam answered.

"I have just been told that Mo will be arriving in LA today, and that he will be attending a meeting tomorrow at one in the law offices of Hines and Ford in Beverly Hills. I have no idea when the meeting will end, but I have someone inside who will text me to confirm Mo is physically there, and then text me when the meeting is over. I intend to be at the safe house when that happens, so you and I will know at the exact same time."

"That sounds very efficient," Lam said. "On our end, I have two men staking out young Mo's house. The guy he lives with left an hour ago, but David is still there. We could pick him up now if you wanted, and hold him overnight."

"No, we'd better not. What if his father tries to contact him today and can't? It might disrupt Mo's plans to attend the meeting. I can't have that happen, so anytime tomorrow before one works best."

"No problem."

"How will the men transport him to the safe house?"

"In the trunk of their car."

"They'll blindfold him?"

"They will, and when they drive away from his house they'll do some loops so he'll have no idea of the direction they're actually going."

"And I need the address of the safe house."

"Forty-two Lynnwood Drive in Rancho Park."

"When you get him there, call me and I'll come directly," she said. "And, Lam, not only don't I want him to see me, I don't want him to hear me."

"We'll take care of it."

"Lastly, I think we should take David out of the house as soon as his father gets there."

"I agree with that," Lam said. "One thing, though, have

you given any thought to what to do if Mo won't come to the house?"

First Lop, and now Lam raising doubts, she thought. "No, I haven't, because he will come," Ava said confidently.

27

AFTER HER CONVERSATION WITH LAM, AVA SAT QUIETLY at the desk in the hotel suite and reviewed the morning's activity. Things were in motion, and for the first time in what felt like an eternity there was nothing immediate she could think of to do. Now it was all about waiting, and that was something she disliked, especially when there were so many ifs, ands, and buts surrounding a job. She needed a distraction, she decided, and went out to the terrace where Fai was sitting down once more.

"I have absolutely nothing to do until Harold Hines calls this afternoon. Why don't we get out of here? I know I said I didn't like shopping, but I think I'd like to buy some gifts for my mother, Mimi, Marian, and my nieces."

"Sure, that could be fun, and why don't we ask Silvana to join us? I have to talk to her anyway about the question you raised about Mo."

"That sounds fine."

Half an hour later, the three women met in the lobby. Ava was dressed casually in a light Adidas jacket, training pants, and running shoes. Fai wore a dark blue cotton summer dress and sandals, while Silvana had on black linen slacks and a powder blue and pink Chanel jacket.

"I feel underdressed," Ava said to Silvana.

"And I'm probably overdressed, but I'm a Hong Kong woman. I can't go into a store and have the sales staff look down on me," Silvana said.

"That's my mother's attitude."

"She's not wrong."

They left the hotel and made their way onto Wilshire Boulevard. Ava was no stranger to high-end shopping, and her condo in Toronto was in the middle of Canada's finest array of stores, but Rodeo Drive was something else entirely. Store after store after store was emblazoned with names known worldwide—Tom Ford, Prada, Gucci, Hermès, MaxMara, Alexander McQueen, Saint Laurent, Jimmy Choo, Versace, Fendi, Celine, Carolina Herrera, and on and on it went. Silvana and Fai didn't go into every store, but didn't miss many, taking their time. Ava contained her occasional impatience, enjoyed a lunch break at Gucci Osteria, bought Hermès scarves for her mother, Mimi, and Marian, and charm bracelets for her nieces. By four, though, she was tired, bored, and starting to become anxious to hear from Harold Hines.

"I think I'll head back to the hotel," she said. "I'm shopped out, and getting frustrated that I haven't heard from Hines."

"Is that a problem?" Fai asked.

"No, I'm sure it isn't, but I'm on edge."

"Then head back. I'm actually surprised you lasted this long," Fai said with a smile.

"I did enjoy being with you and Silvana."

Fai turned to Silvana. "I'm going to go with Ava."

Silvana looked slightly disappointed, but said, "Then I will as well."

As they starting walking in the direction of the hotel, Silvana moved close to Ava and said, "While you were busy in Hermès, Fai spoke to me about the choice we might have to face. She was very direct."

"And what option did you prefer?" Ava asked.

"I didn't say, but I've been thinking about it ever since."

"And have you made a decision?"

"I have." Silvana stopped walking. She stretched out her arms and took both Fai and Ava by the hand. "As much as I care about being safe, the strongest emotion I have is hatred for Mo for what he did to Chen and Lau Lau. So if it comes down to it—I would rather have a dead Mo than a piece of paper full of promises we can't be sure the Chinese government will keep."

"I'm hopeful it's a choice that will never be realized," said Ava.

"Me too," Silvana said, pulling the other women towards her for a hug.

It was an intense moment, and Ava felt slightly self-conscious standing in the middle of the sidewalk on Rodeo Drive. What was more, Silvana didn't seem to want to let go, and as Ava thought about how to ease out of her embrace delicately, her phone rang.

"It's Harold Hines. I have to talk to him," she said, and Silvana released her. "Harold, have you heard from Eli Brand?"

"We just finished speaking for the third time today. His group was meeting this afternoon. They want some minor changes to the agreement that I don't find objectionable, but what they want to do to the statement from Fai and Silvana is another matter."

"Hold on, I have Silvana and Fai with me, and we're standing in the middle of the street. They should hear this, so let me call you back when we get to the hotel. It shouldn't be much longer than ten minutes."

"That's fine, and there's no need to rush. I'm not going anywhere."

"What should we hear?" Fai asked as Ava ended the call.

"The Chinese are okay with the agreement, but they want to make changes to your statement."

"I'm not going to humiliate myself or disrespect Lau Lau and Chen," said Fai.

"Don't jump to conclusions. We don't know what they told Harold."

They hurried towards the hotel, and once they were back in her suite Ava called Hines. "We're here and the phone is on speaker," she said when he answered. "What is it they want to change?"

"Before I start, let me ask you not to overreact," he said.

"Is it that bad?"

"It isn't all bad. For example, they're okay with what we submitted, but they want to add the following: 'We also want to acknowledge that despite the fact *Tiananmen* is presented as a work of fiction, we have come to realize that the film twists historical facts to knowingly distort a chapter of Chinese history. We understand that this has proven to be offensive to many Chinese people, and as such, we want to apologize for having contributed to the film's making.'"

Ava saw Silvana glare at the phone, but before she could speak, Fai said loudly, "They will never get an apology from me."

"Or from me," Silvana said.

"I understand how you feel, and I think I can work our way around that request, but I believe we have to give them a bit more—a little something at least—when it comes to the other main complaint. Maxine has been working with Patricia on something that I think fits the bill."

"Then please read it to me," Ava said.

"What if we agreed to something like: 'As for our nominated film, we understand that not everyone is pleased with how it depicts the events of June 4, 1989, but we would like to stress that *Tiananmen* is a work of fiction and was not intended to be regarded as a fact-based documentary.'"

"That is actually quite good," Ava said. "It doesn't criticize the film, but does acknowledge that not everyone was pleased with it—and that's true enough."

"But it is an odd thing to say. How could you make it mesh with what you wrote previously without making it sound like some kind of awkward tack-on?" asked Silvana.

"We would work with Patricia on that."

Ava looked at the two women. "What do you think? Is it worth the effort?"

Silvana frowned. "I guess so."

"Yes, but there won't be any apology, and I won't allow them to crap all over Lau Lau's work," said Fai.

"You've heard our decision, Harold, so now it is up to you," said Ava. "When will you speak to Brand next?"

"He's waiting for my call."

"One last thing: has Mo arrived?"

"He participated in my last conversation with the other side. They had driven him directly from the airport to Brand's office, which I think indicates how seriously they are taking this."

"As they should be," she said. "Call us after you talk to them again."

"Now I'm especially glad we had that discussion about what mattered more—Mo or the agreement," Silvana said as soon as Hines left the call. "It makes it a lot easier to tell them to go stuff themselves."

"Who knows, they might agree to what Harold is proposing," Ava said.

Fai rose from the sofa and walked towards the mini-bar. "I need a drink, does anyone else?"

"Open a bottle of white wine," Ava said.

"Yes, I'll join you," Silvana agreed.

A few moments later the three women moved to the terrace with their glasses. They sat side by side looking down on the steady streams of pedestrian and vehicular traffic on Rodeo Drive.

"How do you think they'll react to our proposal?" Silvana asked Ava.

"I suspect Mo will be making the decision, and Fai knows him far better than me. She's who you should be asking."

"Fai, what do you think?"

"I imagine he believes we're trying to do a deal because we're scared, and that gives him the upper hand," Fai said. "And anytime I've seen Mo in that position, he couldn't help acting like a bully. So what I expect is that he won't budge from what they've already offered. He'll want us to condemn the film, and he'll want an apology."

"Fuck that," Silvana said.

"We've made it clear that won't work, and I'm sure Harold is relaying that message," said Ava.

"That doesn't mean Mo will relent," Fai said.

"Do you really believe he won't?" Ava asked.

"If he does, he'll be acting completely out of character."

"Hmm," Ava said, and stood. "I'm going to refill my glass."

She went into the living area, poured some more wine, and then sat at the desk to make a phone call.

"Ava," Lam answered.

"Is David Mo still at his house and alone?"

"That was the situation ten minutes ago."

"Then could you put your guys on notice? I think we might need to pick him up today and take him to the safe house."

"That's not a problem."

"I should know shortly whether that's our move. I'll phone as soon as I know."

"I'm here."

Ava went back onto the terrace to find Fai and Silvana talking about the soap opera that had made Silvana famous. She sat and listened as the older actress gossiped about co-stars, many of whom had gone on to make successful feature films—a path that had escaped her until *Tiananmen*. Silvana had a caustic sense of humour, was blunt when it came to talking about sex and body parts, and Ava found herself trying to memorize the stories so she could relay them to her mother, who was a huge fan of the soap.

They had finished the bottle of wine and opened a second when Ava's phone rang.

"Yes, Harold, what news do you have for us?"

"The other side won't bend. They are insistent that the

statement has to point out the historical inaccuracy of the film and has to include an apology."

"Is that the sentiment of everyone on the other side?"

"No, I think that Brand and Christensen would have gone along with our suggestion, but Mo Ming and the Consul General won't. In fact, they were quite vociferous, Mo in particular. I think he's calling those shots."

"Well, that makes things clear."

"What do want me to do?" Hines asked.

"Nothing for now. We'll talk this over among ourselves and get back to you, although it might not be until the morning."

"What about the meeting that's scheduled for tomorrow? Do I cancel? Ask for a postponement?"

"Leave it as it is."

Hines hesitated, and then said, "I feel bad that I haven't been able to find a suitable middle ground."

"Don't blame yourself; when the other party refuses to compromise there can be no middle ground."

"Well, I won't give up entirely. I told Brand I'd let him know tonight what our position was, and even though that won't be possible until tomorrow, I'll make use of the call to work on him. Maybe he can still convince his Chinese clients to meet us halfway."

"I doubt he will, but it's worth a try. Thanks for your efforts. We'll talk in the morning."

"Well?" Fai asked when Ava ended the call.

"You were right. Mo won't budge."

"So now what?"

"The time has come to deal with him."

28

DURING HER YEARS WORKING WITH UNCLE, AVA HAD come to admire competence. Success, she had learned, wasn't the result of people doing spectacular things, but most often the result of people simply doing their jobs properly. And within two hours of telling Johnny Lam that their project was a go, she added him to the list of competent people that she'd worked with, because David Mo was that quickly ensconced in the safe house in Rancho Park.

After getting that news, Ava left the hotel in a taxi for Lynnwood Drive. She felt calm, and was pleased that her emotions were under control. Fai and Silvana hadn't been as restrained when they'd first realized Ava's plan was being put in motion, but to her satisfaction, they had gradually become quieter, and almost sombre, when the gravity of it all sank in.

Ava was accustomed to long car rides in LA, and it was a surprise when the cab came to a stop after only a fifteen-minute drive. Absorbed in thinking about what lay ahead, she hadn't been paying attention to her surroundings, and now that she did, she found herself on a tree-lined street of modest single-family homes. Forty-two Lynnwood was a ranch-style house and had the same neat lawn and general appearance of David Mo's home in Brentwood. One difference was that this house had a double-door garage and there wasn't a car in the driveway.

She went up the brick pathway to a black front door that had no window and rang the doorbell. It was opened by a short, thin, middle-aged man wearing blue jeans and a floral short-sleeved shirt. His face and head were clean-shaven, and he had no tattoos or any other visible sign that he might be a triad. He smiled at Ava and stuck out his hand, "I'm Johnny," he said softly. "And if you're Ava, you aren't quite what I expected."

"Truthfully, neither are you," she said with a smile.

"I like to keep things low-key. There's nothing to be gained by drawing attention to myself."

"That is Xu's philosophy as well."

"I know, and that's one of the reasons he and I see eye to eye on so many subjects," Lam said. "Now come inside."

She went into a house that had uncovered wooden floors, a living room with a single sofa and large-screen television, and no other furnishings. "Where's David?" she whispered.

"He's sitting in the kitchen."

"Did he give you any trouble?"

"My men said he was like a lamb, but he's really frightened."

"Have you said anything to him?"

"Not yet. I thought we'd wait for you."

"Let me see him."

"Follow me," Lam said, walking towards a closed door at the rear of the house. He stopped when he got there, opened the door, and stood aside to let Ava in.

They had taped David Mo's mouth and eyes and secured

his ankles and wrists to a padded kitchen chair. Two of Lam's men were in the kitchen, one leaning against the sink and the other sitting in a chair about six feet from David.

Ava pointed to a towel that was draped over his lap. "What's that for?" she mouthed.

"He peed himself."

She nodded and whispered, "Let's go to the living room to talk." She backed out of the kitchen, and sat on the sofa.

"So, he's seen and heard nothing?" she said.

"Absolutely nothing."

"Good. Now here's how I want us to play it, and if you have any objections or concerns please voice them. I've thought this through as best I can, but I'm always prepared to listen to others."

"Go ahead," Lam said.

It took Ava some time to explain the scenario she had in mind. Lam interrupted her twice with questions to clarify certain things, but otherwise didn't appear to have any problem with the plan. When she finished, she asked, "Do you have someone who can spin that tale for us?"

"You're looking at him," Lam said, and then smiled. "Before I fell into my father's business, I spent a year in the drama department at UCLA."

"How fortunate for me."

"So let's go talk to young Mo."

They returned to the kitchen, Lam announcing his arrival by saying, "I'm ready to speak to you, Mr. Mo."

Ava saw the young man flinch and begin to shake.

"There's nothing to fear. This is about your father, and not about you," Lam said quickly. "We have no intention of hurting you, or for that matter hurting him. Nod if you understand."

David nodded several times.

"Did you know that your father was in LA?"

He nodded again.

"Good. So what we have here, young Mr. Mo, is a situation that your father can easily resolve. I am a film producer here in LA. My latest, an action film, has done well enough in Europe and North America for us to almost recover our investment, but in order to turn a profit we need the Chinese market. We have been trying for months without any success to get the approval to distribute there from the China Movie Syndicate. It isn't that they've said no, it's that they've been ignoring us completely. They won't answer our phone calls or emails, and they refused to meet a local representative we hired to sort of grease the rails. So, as you can understand, it has all been rather frustrating.

"This morning I got a call from our representative to tell me that your father was coming to LA today on business, and I thought I would take advantage of that to try to arrange a meeting. I have your father's phone number, and I called it. He hung up on me. My guess is that he won't hang up on you," said Lam, and then he turned to the man at the sink. "Take the tape from his mouth."

When the tape was removed, David took several deep, gasping breaths, and said, "This is crazy."

"No, this is business. All I want is half an hour of your father's undivided attention to talk about my film. I'm sorry this is what I have to do to get it, but this is Hollywood, and everyone loves drama. So here's what's going to happen. I am going to dial your father's number using your cellphone. If he answers, you tell him that you're with someone who really needs to talk to him. If he doesn't answer or hangs up, you have to leave a voice message telling him you're in trouble, and that he needs to call back. Got that?"

"Yes," said David.

"If he does answer or calls back, then you should be truthful. Tell him that you were taken from your house, put into the trunk of a car, and driven to an unknown location. Stress the fact that you haven't been hurt, but you aren't sure how much longer that situation will remain the same."

David trembled, and Ava thought she saw tears around the edges of the tape on his eyes.

Lam must have seen the reaction as well because he immediately added, "We aren't going to hurt you, of course, but we need to give your father as many reasons as possible to come to your aid."

"This is so crazy," David repeated.

"I admit it is a bit unusual, but it's the only thing I could think of," said Lam. "Now, when you finish describing your situation to your father, I want you to pass the phone to me. I'll take it from there. And I promise you, the second your father walks through our front door, you will be able to leave."

"Are you going to hurt him?" David asked.

"All I want is half an hour of his time so we can talk. That's all, just talk. So, what do you think, can you do this?"

"I don't know."

"Well, I do need you to try."

"I'll do the best I can."

"That's all anyone can ask," said Lam. "Now, I'm going to call his number, put the phone on speaker, and hold it close to your mouth. Just say what I told you to say and everything should go well."

Ava admired the way Lam's manner seemed to calm

David, but still held her breath as the phone call was made. Mo's cell rang four times, then stopped abruptly, and she heard his distinctive raspy voice say in Chinese, "David, I'm in a meeting. I can't talk right now."

"No, you have to talk to me. This can't wait. I'm in terrible trouble and I need your help," David blurted in English.

There was a pause on the other end of the line before Mo said, "Give me a minute to find some place more private."

"That's very good so far," Lam whispered to Ava.

"What is going on?" Mo asked a moment later, in a tone of annoyance and concern.

David rattled off almost word for word what Lam had instructed him to say. When he finished, Lam moved the phone away from his mouth. "This is not a game. We are deadly serious. We have your son, and the only way he's going to be released is if you agree to meet with us."

"How much do you want?" Mo asked.

"You don't understand, we're not holding him for ransom. What we want is the opportunity to meet with you to discuss a film project. I realize this is a strange way to go about getting a meeting, but the way the Syndicate has been treating us has left us with no other choice."

"Is this some kind of prank?" Mo asked in disbelief.

"Mr. Mo, your son is sitting in front of me with his arms and legs taped to a chair. He also has his eyes taped up, and until a minute ago his mouth was as well. We have done nothing to harm him, but if that's what it takes for you to realize how serious we are, then we are prepared to."

"No, that's not necessary," Mo said quickly, sounding alarmed. "I'll meet with you."

"Excellent."

"Where are you?"

"It isn't going to work like that," said Lam. "There's a Ralphs supermarket in Westwood, at the intersection of Westwood and Le Conte. You are to take a taxi there, and when you arrive, phone your son's cell. One of our people will come to get you. He'll be driving a grey BMW. You should stand outside, at the front doors," Lam said. "Where are you now, and how soon can you leave?"

"I'm in an office on Wilshire Boulevard, and I can leave within ten minutes."

"Then we should see you at Ralphs in about thirty to forty-five minutes," said Lam. "What are you wearing?"

"A blue suit."

"One last thing, Mr. Mo. You are to tell no one about this, and you are to come alone. If we see anyone with you, or we think you have been tailed, we'll leave you standing at Ralphs, and we'll deal with your son."

"I won't say a word."

"Then we'll see you shortly."

29

AVA SAT ON THE SOFA TO WAIT FOR MO'S ARRIVAL.
Immediately after his phone conversation, Lam had sent two
cars to Ralphs. One was the grey BMW, and the second was
a Chevrolet that would shadow the Beamer and make sure
it wasn't being followed. When Ava complimented Lam on
the thoroughness of his arrangements, he shrugged and said,
"As I told you, we've done things like this before, although
usually the car is sent to get someone bringing money to us."

Lam had just come from the kitchen, and she asked, "How
is David holding up?"

"He's obviously relieved to know his father is coming. But
that raises the question of how you want things handled
when he gets here."

"I don't want Mo to see me until his son has left the house.
He might blurt out my name, and that wouldn't be good."

"You can wait in one of the bedrooms. It won't take us long
to evacuate the son. He'll go back in the car trunk for the
trip home. We'll drop him off a block or so from his house
with his eyes and hands still taped. He'll be able to yell for
help, but by the time it arrives we'll be long gone."

"I'm pleased he wasn't harmed."

"Me too. It is always unpredictable when innocents get caught in the middle of something like this."

"You should warn him, though, before you let him go, to keep his mouth shut. Tell him he might not hear from his father for twenty-four to forty-eight hours, but he is to say nothing about it to anyone. You should remind him that you know where he lives and that if he gets out of line you will make another house call."

"I'll handle that personally," said Lam. "But coming back to how you want to handle things with someone who isn't quite so innocent, how much assistance do you need with Mo?"

"I would appreciate it if you would tape him to the chair just by the ankles and wrists, because I want him to see me and be able to talk to me. But after he's been secured, I would like to be left alone with him."

"Are you sure you want to take care of him by yourself? I have men who are good at it and wouldn't mind doing it."

"As I told you before, this is very personal."

"In that case, I should get you the weapon Xu said you wanted," Lam said. He disappeared into what she assumed was a bedroom and returned a minute later carrying a brown paper bag. He reached into it and pulled out a handgun. "A Glock 19, lightweight but very effective. My supplier told me it is a favourite among women."

"Thank you," Ava said, taking it and putting it in her LV bag. "Now, where should I wait?"

Lam pointed at the door he had just exited. "That bedroom would be fine. You should be able to hear him arrive. I'll knock on the door when he's secured. When do you think you'll be finished with him?"

"I have no idea. He and I need to talk over some things and I'm not sure how co-operative he'll be," she said.

"There's no rush, so call my cell when you're done and we'll take it from there."

"I will, and thank you," Ava said, and she turned and headed for the bedroom. Its sole furnishing was a single bed covered by a red blanket. She sat on the edge, and then almost without thinking she slid to her knees on the floor, clasped her hands in front of her face, and began to pray. As she had countless times before, she prayed to Saint Jude, the patron saint of lost causes. He was the last remnant of her attachment to the Catholic Church. It had abandoned her with its stand on issues like homosexuality and abortion, but somehow Saint Jude had remained in her life.

"I am going to kill a man today, and I am searching for forgiveness," she began. "I understand that in many eyes I will be committing a mortal sin, but all I am seeking is equal justice. The man I am going to kill caused the death of two beautiful and gentle souls, and there is no government, no law, and no court that will hold him accountable, so it falls to me. And it falls to me because I know what he did, and for me not to do anything would in my eyes be a sin of omission, so I instead I choose to commit a sin of commission. I take no pleasure in it. In fact, I dread the thought, and I'm pray-ing to you to help me find the strength to do what's right, the strength to avenge my friends … Amen."

She stayed on her knees for several minutes, gathering her emotions. Lop had taken care of the two men in Taipei, and now it was her turn, she told herself. Not to do what had to be done would be failing Chen and Lau Lau, and she wasn't sure how she could live with herself if she didn't follow through.

"Ava," Lam's voice said through the door. "We've picked up Mo at Ralphs. He'll be here in less than five minutes."

"Thank you," she said, rising from the floor. She sat back down on the bed. As she waited, she thought about her inter-actions with Mo in Beijing and in Cannes. Fai was right—when he thought he was in control, he was a bully, but how much courage would he have when he was taped to a chair?

The five minutes passed as if they were twenty, until finally Ava heard familiar voices through the door. One was Lam's, the other was Mo's—raspy and angry and demanding to know where his son was. Lam's answer was indistinct, but Ava was certain he was handling the situation well. Several minutes later there was a knock on the bedroom door and then it opened. "He's all yours," Lam said. "The son is gone."

"Thank you," she said. "I'll stay here until you and the others have left as well."

"We're heading out now."

Ava waited until she heard the front door closing before leaving the bedroom. She hovered in the living room and listened to Mo alternately shouting questions and making threats before she walked into the kitchen. Mo, who had broad shoulders and a thick chest, didn't seem as physically intimidating bound to a chair. He stared at her question-ingly, and then in disbelief. "You goddamn bitch," he yelled.

"I don't know what you think swearing at me might accomplish," Ava said.

"What do you think you are doing?" he demanded, his rage undiminished. "Whatever it is, I promise that you won't get away with it."

Ava moved to the kitchen counter and leaned against it, which forced Mo to turn his head to look at her. Foam bubbled at the corners of his lips, and that—combined with eyes that had narrowed into dark slits—gave him the appearance of a man quite out of control.

"Do you want to take a guess at what I'm doing, and why you're here?" she asked.

"No, but you must know this can't end well for you."

"So far it hasn't gone so badly. I have you here tied to a chair, and no one, and I mean *no one*, knows you're here except for your son, and he doesn't have a clue where *here* is, or that I even exist."

Mo turned his face away from her, and she could almost see his mind turning over as he absorbed what she had just said. Seconds later when he looked at her she saw that the rage had started to diminish. "Tell me what this is about."

"Chen and Lau Lau," Ava said softly.

"What!" Mo said, and then lowered his chin to his chest and shook his head. "What do I have to do with those two? I was finished with them when Top of the Road won in court."

"No you weren't. You were responsible for their deaths. Maybe you didn't give the direct order, but you instigated it."

"That's crazy talk," he said quickly.

"You contrived with the Ministry of State Security to get it done."

"How can you believe crap like that? I'm head of the China Movie Syndicate, not the Ministry of State Security."

"But you are familiar with that ministry, are you not?"

"I know of it. Who in the government or anyone in the country with any intelligence doesn't?" he asked, averting his eyes.

"But not everyone has a friend or an associate as senior in the MSS as Lin Chao."

"I have never even heard that name," said Mo. "Why would I? And for God's sake, how would I? The MSS is so secretive that only a handful of people know who runs what there."

"That's odd, because I was told that when Lin made a call a few weeks ago to the MSS office in Taipei, he mentioned your name."

"That's a lie."

Ava shrugged. "I was told by a reliable source."

"Who would know something like that? Someone is just inventing stuff."

"Actually, I understated it. I was told that by an *unimpeachable* reliable source. His name is Bai, the former chief of the MSS's Taipei bureau. Now, tell me, why would he give me your name and relate specific details of his conversation with Lin Chao?"

"You'd have to ask him."

"I did, but unfortunately I can't do it again because he's dead," she said matter-of-factly, but with her attention tightly focused on Mo's reaction.

His face remained impassive, but Ava sensed it was a struggle.

"Are you quite sure you don't remember having a conversation with Lin? The subject would have been how and when to murder Chen and Lau Lau."

"Now I know," he said suddenly.

"You know what?"

"What this performance of yours is about—it's Pang Fai, isn't it? I always suspected you were involved with the film and all the legal manoeuvering, and now I think you could be behind this deal that Fai and Silvana Foo have concocted. What is it you want from me? We have already basically agreed to the deal. The only sticking point is the statement they want to issue. How about I accept the statement as they wrote it?"

"Bravo, that was a very nice pivot on your part, and while some of the points you've made are correct, they have no bearing on why you're in this position. This is about Chen and Lau Lau, and I really want to know why you thought it was necessary to kill them."

"I told you, I didn't have anything to do with it."

"And I don't believe you, so where does that leave us?"

"You're the one in control, so you tell me."

"Well, I choose to believe Bai because he had no reason to lie, and in fact had every reason to tell me the truth because his life was in the balance."

"If that's the case, then how did he die?"

"We shot him anyway."

Mo's face turned red, and she saw beads of sweat on his upper lip. She wasn't sure he believed her, but she wasn't going to elaborate.

"Sure you did," he said in an awkward attempt to treat it as a joke. "But seriously, it isn't too late to fix things between us, between me and you, and Fai, and Silvana. Let me go and I'll forget this ever happened. I won't say a word to anyone, and I'll make sure my son says nothing either. Then tomorrow I'll sign off on the agreement and the statement the way you want it, and we can all get on with our lives."

"Except that isn't possible for Chen and Lau Lau."

"How many times do I have to say it, I had nothing to do with their deaths."

Ava approached Mo. He flinched when she reached into his suit pocket and took out his cell. She unlocked her own phone and found Eli Brand's number. "I'm going to call Brand on your phone. You're going to tell him that you've changed your mind and that you're willing to accept the agreement and statement as submitted by Harold Hines, and then ask him to relay that message to the Consul General. That's all you're going to say. If he asks a question, don't answer it."

"Are you saying that we have a deal?"

"Are you willing to make the call?"

"Yes, sure," he said, after a slight hesitation.

Ava nodded, and then entered Brand's number. When the receptionist answered, she said, "Mr. Mo is calling for Mr. Brand."

"Just one minute," the woman replied.

Seconds later, Brand said, "Ming, I didn't expect to hear from you again today."

Ava moved the phone towards Mo.

He repeated exactly what she had told him to say in a manner that, to Ava's surprise and pleasure, was completely without emotion. When he finished, Ava took the phone back and turned it off.

"So now what, can I get out of here?" Mo asked.

"Not quite yet," she said.

She left the kitchen and went to the bedroom. Her LV bag was on the bed. She opened it and took out the Glock. *Do I have to do this?* The question had barely settled in her mind before the answer was there. Lop had stressed there should be no loose ends, and nothing could be looser than Mo. Despite his protestations, she was certain he had advocated killing Chen and Lau Lau. She drew a deep breath, put the gun back into the bag, and carried it into the kitchen.

Mo looked at her warily, and then gave her a limp smile. "Whenever I have anything to do with you I always seem to come off second best. I hope this is the last time we bump into each other."

"It will be," she said, taking the gun from the bag.

30

AVA STOOD LOOKING OUT OF THE LIVING ROOM WIN-
dow while she waited for Lam. He arrived in the grey BMW
within ten minutes of her calling him. Behind his car was
the Chevrolet with four men in it. The BMW parked on the
street, while the Chevy pulled into the driveway and stopped
at a side door. Four men bundled out, and three of them went
immediately into the house while the other one opened the
car trunk and took out a tarpaulin. Lam exited the BMW
and walked to Ava.

"Are you okay?" he asked.

"I'm fine."

"So it went well, and by that I mean you found out what
you wanted to know?"

"He lied and denied everything. I know if I'd kept at him
I would have eventually got him to confess, but truthfully I
couldn't stand looking at him, let alone talking to him for
the time it would have taken."

Lam nodded. "There are people that turn my stomach
as well."

"I think I would like to get out of here now if you don't mind."

"Sure—where did you leave the gun?"

"On the kitchen counter."

"We'll dispose of it with Mo."

"What will you do with him?"

"He'll be deposited at sea—far out to sea, tightly wrapped in a tarp, and securely weighed down."

Ava sighed. "I'm glad this is over."

"Me too. Now c'mon, I'll drive you back to the hotel," Lam said.

Ava sat quietly during the trip, and Lam let her be. She finally spoke when they reached the Four Seasons. "You know that I can't thank you enough for everything you've done, but one thing I can do is let Xu know how terrific you've been."

"I would appreciate that."

She opened the car door, and then stopped before getting out. "And if there is ever anything I can do for you, all you have to do is ask."

"I'll remember that," Lam said.

As Ava made her way into the hotel she noticed it was dusk. She had been so oblivious to time that it almost surprised her. And for the first time since walking into the house on Lynnwood, thoughts about something other than Mo entered her mind. It would be midday in Beijing. Had Sonny and Jimmy arrived there already, and how soon should she leave LA? The meeting with Hines and the Top of the Road team was scheduled for one tomorrow. She didn't want to go anywhere until she knew what its result was. But would Mo's absence cause the other side to want a delay, or worse a postponement—or worse yet, a complete cancellation? She would have to brief Hines so he would be prepared to deal with those possibilities, and she knew he would have questions that she didn't want to answer. Was he savvy enough to accept that?

She became so engrossed thinking about Hines that she wasn't really prepared to see Fai and Silvana when she opened the door to the suite and found them both there. They were sitting on the sofa, and rose to their feet as soon as they saw her.

"Is it over?" Fai asked.

"Yes, but I'm not ready to talk about it," Ava said. "What I would like is a hug from the two of you."

Fai and Silvana came immediately to her, and as they had earlier on Rodeo Drive, the three women wrapped their arms around each other with Ava and Silvana's heads tucked against the neck of the taller Fai.

"I'm so glad it's done," Silvana said, her voice cracking.

After about a minute, Ava extracted herself. "I need to go to the bathroom, and then I have to speak to Harold Hines. You should listen to that conversation because it has a bearing on tomorrow."

"If there is no Mo, will there still be a meeting?" Fai asked.

"That's why I want you to listen; it will save me from repeating myself. Now let me go freshen up."

Ava went into the bedroom, took a clean Giordano T-shirt from her bag, and went into the bathroom. She took off the shirt she'd worn to Lynnwood, scrubbed her hands and face, and roughly ran a brush through her hair. When she was finished, she stared at herself in the mirror, and rehearsed what she wanted to tell Hines. Once she was satisfied, she muttered, "I'm still the same person and I'm only doing what I think is right."

Fai and Silvana had resumed sitting on the sofa, but this time there was a bottle of wine open on the coffee table.

"I'm about to pour. Will you have some?" Fai asked.

"Sure, and don't be stingy," Ava said.

Carrying a full glass of wine, she went to the desk and called Harold Hines's home phone.

"I didn't expect to hear from you tonight," he said when he answered.

"I had an eventful afternoon, and I have some information that you'll need for tomorrow."

"I'm listening," he said, in a tone of curiosity and expectation.

"The most important thing is that Mo Ming has decided to accept both the deal and Fai and Silvana's statement that you submitted to Eli Brand," she said.

"What! Are you serious?"

"Perfectly."

"But how do you know this?"

"I spoke to Mo. He told me he gave that instruction to Brand, and I believe him. He also told Brand to call Wang Ping and tell him that was his decision."

"What could possibly have caused him to have such a drastic change of mind, especially about the statement?"

"He decided that your argument about making no reference to Tiananmen Square made sense. He said he realized it was better to keep the politics attached to both sides of the issue out of it; what he wanted could create a debate and negative backlash that the Chinese government might not like. I also might have made a contribution to his change of mind when I told him the industry would assume that Fai and Silvana had been coerced to disrespect the film, and that wouldn't be a good look for the Syndicate or his government."

"That is great news in fact so great I can hardly believe it."

"We decided to put our past animosity aside, and once we did that, our conversation was cordial."

"And he actually said he told Brand that he was prepared to accept our draft?"

"He did."

"If that's true—and I have no reason to doubt it—it should make tomorrow's meeting a pleasant formality. I have to add that it's a relief, because I was quite unsure about how it would play out."

"There is one other thing I have to tell you," Ava said, then paused. "Mo said he won't be attending the meeting, so we're going to have to waive our request that he be one of the signatories. We'll have to accept the Consul General's and leave it at that. That isn't an issue for me, Silvana, or Fai."

"This is getting increasingly unusual," Hines said. "Did he give a reason for not being there?"

"His son, who is in a film studies program at UCLA, has some kind of problem that needs Mo's attention. In fact, he told me he could be tied up for a few days. The son is his only child, and Mo dotes on him," said Ava. "I asked him if he wanted us to put off the meeting, and he said that given our understanding there was no reason to delay it."

"How did Brand react to Mo's decision to skip the meeting?"

"I'm not sure he or the Consul General knows," she said. "Harold, Mo's son is gay, and I believe the problem is somehow related to a relationship he's in. Even in this day and age, homosexuality is considered shameful in China, and I don't think Mo wants anyone to know about his son. He might not have wanted to provide an explanation."

Hines became silent, although she could hear him breathing. She guessed he wasn't buying what she was selling, but it was the only story she had to spin, and if he pressed her all she could do was repeat it.

"Ava, I have to say that as pleased as I am with the outcome, I do find it a bit odd."

"The outcome is all that matters to Silvana and Fai."

"Of course, and I wasn't suggesting anything else," he said, although his tone hinted that he was. "So, I guess I'll see the ladies tomorrow at my office."

"You can count on that."

"Then enjoy the rest of your evening," he said.

Ava put down the phone to find Fai and Silvana looking at her. "I don't think he entirely believed me about why Mo would be absent."

"If the issue comes up tomorrow we can reinforce what you told him," Fai said.

"But Ava, is there any way they can find out what happened?" Silvana asked.

"No, all they can do is guess. The one person who could raise an alarm is his son, and I don't believe anyone will hear from him for a couple of days. Still, if the signing goes as planned tomorrow, we shouldn't hang around LA. I know I can get a flight tomorrow night to Beijing, and Fai has a lot of options for Toronto. Sils, do you have any idea where you'll go from here?"

"I'll head back to Taipei for a while. I have things there I need to pack up and ship to Hong Kong," she said. "But why are you going to Beijing?"

"There is one more person who was involved with the deaths of Chen and Lau Lau, and that's where he lives."

"Do you really feel comfortable going there?" Silvana asked, casting a worried look at Fai.

"I won't be alone. I have some very capable associates who are there already."

Silvana hesitated, looked at Fai again, and then said, "Good luck."

"Thank you," said Ava.

"And I'll look into flights to Taipei tonight," Silvana said, looking at her watch. "But right now what I'd like to do is eat. It's past my usual dinnertime. I know I shouldn't feel hungry, but I am. Do you want to join me downstairs for a meal?"

"I'll pass. I have more phone calls to make," Ava said.

"I'll go with you," Fai said. "Ava, can I bring something back for you?"

"No, I'm fine."

Silvana stood and walked towards the door, with Fai following. Ava waited until they had left the suite before reaching for her phone to call Lop in Beijing.

"*Wei*, Ava," he answered.

"I have done what I came to do here. I'm going to catch a flight to Beijing tomorrow night."

"I'm glad to hear it. Were there any complications?"

"No, it went far easier than I'd anticipated, thanks to help from some LA triads. Xu used his influence to get their co-operation."

"I've never known anyone with so much *guanxi*."

"It is remarkable," she said. "And how are things on your end? Have Sonny and Jimmy arrived yet?"

"Their flight arrives in three hours. I'm going to meet them at the airport. The rifle and other equipment Jimmy wanted are scheduled to be delivered this afternoon."

"You were able to get everything?"

"There wasn't a problem."

"Excellent. Did you also get the more recent photos of Lin?"

"I did, and I've been gathering other information that will be helpful. I'll share it with the boys when they get here, and then I'll take them to the Tianqiao Theatre complex on a scouting mission. Hopefully Jimmy can find a setup location to his liking."

"What kind of information?"

"I'm meeting someone who can tell me what kind of vehicle Lin is likely to arrive in, and another person who knows what the transportation protocol is at the theatre."

"Those *are* important things to know," said Ava, impressed with the way Lop was laying the groundwork. "Did you manage to get the boys into the Grand Hyatt?"

"I did."

"I might as well stay there too, so book a room for me—and remember I'll be travelling as Chow Qi."

"I'll do that today. When do you expect to arrive?"

"I'll send you my flight details later by email. Say hello to the boys for me when you meet them."

"Will do," he said, and then hesitated. "This could be an exciting few days, but I have to say I still don't like not having a backup plan. Even if we're lucky enough that he goes to the theatre, we're only going to get one chance at this guy unless we can come up with something else."

"Having a solid plan A is better than having a string of iffy plans, and I think that's what we have," Ava said, and then unexpectedly yawned. "Excuse me, I'm suddenly quite tired. It was an emotional day and it seems to have done me in. So, look, I'm going to book a flight, send you the info, and then get some sleep. You won't hear from me again unless there's a problem."

Ava hadn't misled Lop when she'd said she was tired. In fact, what she felt was sudden bone-sapping exhaustion. The day had exacted a heavy toll, and the conversation with Hines had drained almost her last drop of adrenalin. She had just enough left to book a China Southern flight to Beijing and email the details to Lop. Then she took a sheet of hotel stationary and wrote:

FAI, I HAVE NO ENERGY LEFT AND WENT TO BED. PLEASE DON'T WAKE ME. I'LL SEE YOU IN THE MORNING, LOVE AVA.

She placed the sheet upright against the screen of the laptop so that Fai wouldn't miss it, and then headed directly to the bedroom, where she stripped off her pants and fell into bed in her T-shirt and underwear. She was asleep in minutes.

She didn't choose to dream, but as so often happened when her life was unsettled—even subconsciously—Uncle visited. They sat on a bench in the small Kowloon park that he had often frequented during the last months of his life. He was smoking, which given his illness annoyed her, but she couldn't be critical. The park was busy, the benches taken up by older men and women, and the pathways filled with yayas from the Philippines and their young charges.

"I killed a man today," she said somberly.

"I know. I watched you," Uncle said. "When I was Mountain Master, I had men killed. I never took any joy in it, and I always thought long and hard about whether it was necessary. Sometimes it was. Do you believe that you and Fai would be safe if he was still alive?"

"No."

"Then you have the answer to the question you haven't asked."

"But he didn't confess to his involvement in Chen and Lau Lau's deaths. I wish he had."

"Men lie, and when their lives are at stake, they lie as forcefully as they can."

"After I shot the Red Pole in Macau I hoped that I would never have to do anything like that again."

"I have always carried some guilt about Macau. When I told you he had to die, I should have realized that you would insist on doing it yourself, and I should have made sure Sonny was the one who did it."

"You were right that it had to be done, and ultimately it was my responsibility."

"Just as it was with Mo," Uncle said. "The man was completely untrustworthy. If you had let him live, he would have done everything he could to bring you down. Killing him saved you and Fai and did the world a favour."

She reached for his hand. "I leave tomorrow for Beijing. There is another man there who deserves to die, and God knows how much blood he has on his hands. I suspect that Chen and Lau Lau are the very tip of the iceberg."

"You are using my old friend Jimmy Li?"

"Yes."

"He's a good man, a reliable man."

"And combined with Lop and Sonny we have a great team."

"From what I know about what you are trying to do, you'll need them all."

"What do you mean?" she asked, but then felt his breath—no, a sweeter breath—tickle her senses. She opened her eyes and saw Fai staring down at her.

"Sorry, but I really want you to make love to me," Fai said.

31

AVA WOKE NAKED AND WRAPPED IN FAI'S ARMS. AFTER
falling back to sleep there had been no dreams, and she had
slept soundly. She eased herself from Fai's embrace, slipped
on a T-shirt, underwear, and Adidas training pants, and
went into the living room. She ordered a large pot of coffee
from room service, and then sat at the desk to check her laptop and cellphone. There were emails from her mother, her
sister, Mimi, and several other friends. She answered them
all briefly, ensuring everyone that all was well and she'd be
back in Toronto sooner rather than later.

The only text message was from Lop. He confirmed he'd
received her flight information, would be at the airport to
meet her, and said Sonny and Jimmy had arrived on schedule. That was the extent of it. Ava had hoped for more detail,
but guessed Lop didn't have that much more to pass along.
She considered calling him, but remembered she had said
she wouldn't unless there was a problem. Still, she was curious about their scouting expedition to the Tianqiao Theatre
complex, and was about to pick up her cell when the buzzer
sounded at the suite door. Ava assumed it was room service,

and it was. She had the server place the tray on the table on the terrace, and then sat down there.

Ava leaned her head back so that her face could catch some sun. She stayed like that for some time, her mind turning over as she only opened her eyes to sip coffee or pour a fresh cup. Her thought process had now moved past Los Angeles—where there was nothing more to be done unless Harold Hines had a problem—to Beijing. Lop, Sonny, and Jimmy were all capable, and she wasn't certain what she could contribute to that operation, but she felt she had to be there just in case she was needed. They were, after all, going to try to kill one of the most senior people in the Chinese government, and it would be irresponsible not to expect that there could be glitches—and glitches, if not handled properly, often turned into disasters. A disaster in Beijing would result in what—the four of them receiving a bullet in the head after a ten-minute trial?

Thoughts about Beijing led to questions, some of which—such as what did the Tianqiao Theatre complex look like—could be answered by basic research. She fetched her laptop from inside, placed it on her lap and googled the theatre. There were a large number of photos to look at and she scanned through them. Its exterior rather disappointed her. Aside from a moderately sized gold edifice and high arch above five sets of doors, it lacked any real colour and architectural distinctiveness. In fact, if she hadn't known what it was, she might have guessed it was a large railway station. What did please her, though, was the accuracy of Lop's description of the expansive open plaza that ran from the road to the first of twenty broad steps that led to the doors. The plaza, she figured, looked like it could easily accommodate several thousand people, and unless Lin used a back door, he would have to cross it to get inside.

The theatre was in Beijing's Xicheng district, and now Ava switched to Google Earth to look at it. She zeroed in on the area around the theatre, and while there weren't any structures abutting it, it appeared there were many within a kilometre. What had Lop said was the range of the Barrett MRAD—fifteen hundred metres? It looked like they could set up closer than that.

"What are you looking at?" A voice behind her startled her.

"You are so damn quiet. You move like a cat," Ava said to Fai.

Fai sat in the chair next to her and reached for the coffee. "Did you know it is almost ten o'clock? I can't remember the last time I slept so late."

"A bottle of wine and good sex always seems to relax you."

Fai laughed. "And knowing that I won't have to face Mo, and knowing that we have a deal with the Chinese government also helps."

"I do hope the meeting goes as smoothly as we want," Ava said.

"Do you think it might not?" Fai asked, her alarm evident at the thought.

"No, no, I wasn't suggesting anything of the sort. But you know me. Even if there's only a one per cent chance it could go wrong, I won't stop worrying until things are completely finalized."

"If they are today, what time is your flight?"

"Five, so I'll have to leave the hotel by two. Your meeting should be over by then. Once it is, don't waste any time booking a flight to Toronto."

"And how long do you think you'll be in Beijing?"

"Two or three days at the most; if we haven't done what we're planning by then, it probably won't get done."

"What do you think your chances are?"

"We are firstly completely dependent on the importance our target places on seeing his daughter dance at the premiere of a ballet. And if he does come, we have to hope that he will arrive at the front of the Tianqiao Theatre and attempt to enter through those doors. Lastly, we have to trust that Jimmy Li can get a clear shot and won't miss."

"Those are a lot of ifs," Fai said.

"But they are supported by facts and aren't without logic. This just isn't wishful thinking on our part."

Fai drained the last of the coffee pot. "We should order more.".

"Sure, let me do that," said Ava.

When she returned to the terrace a minute later she noticed a slight change in Fai's attitude. There was a hesitancy, mild but present, when she looked at Ava. "What are you thinking?" Ava asked.

"Nothing in particular."

"Fai, tell me what you're thinking."

Fai pursed her lips, reached for Ava's hand, and said, "Well, since you're going to be in Beijing, do you think you could visit my house? I don't know if I'm ever going to see it again, and we can't discount the possibility that the Chinese government could seize it. You know they do that often enough."

"Why do you want me to visit it?"

"There are things I left there that I don't want to lose— photos, awards, some jewellery, and a couple of cheongsams that I love, including the one I wore the very first night we met. I have a suitcase in my closet there that you could use."

Ava hesitated. Fai's house was in a courtyard that ran off a hutong, and she had neighbours who were familiar with Ava. Was there a risk …?

"And it wouldn't be taking you out of your way," Fai said. "I know you probably didn't realize it, but the theatre is in the same district as my house. You could be in and out in no time. I'd give you a list of what I want and describe exactly where you can find it."

What the hell, Ava thought. "Okay, give me the list before you go to the meeting today. I'll make every effort to get to the house, but if I can't …"

"I'll understand."

Ava leaned over to kiss her. "I remember that cheongsam. It fit you like a second skin. I thought you were most beautiful and exotic woman I'd ever met."

"And now here we are, sliding into middle age together."

"That's not something—" Ava began, only to be interrupted by her phone. She looked at the screen and saw it was Harold Hines.

"Good morning, Harold, I trust everything is going well," she said when she picked up.

"I'm not sure how it's going. Eli Brand called fifteen minutes ago to say he wasn't sure the meeting was going to happen."

"And why not?"

"Well, he confirmed that he had spoken to Mo, and that Mo had changed his mind about the ladies' statement. He also confirmed he had relayed the message to the Consul General, but when Wang reached out to Mo to find out why the change in position, he couldn't get in touch with him. That prompted a call to Beijing, and according to Brand, they haven't been able to contact him either. So, in a nutshell, they are reluctant to do anything until they talk to Mo."

"Did you tell Brand that Mo had personal business to take care of?"

"I did, and he and Wang found that unusual because Mo has a reputation for putting his work ahead of anything else in his life."

"What if Mo believes that his work is concluded and that there is nothing more to be done other than the Consul General signing the agreement? If that's the case, why wouldn't he take some time out to help his son through a difficult situation?"

"Brand also talked to the son," Hines said.

Ava felt a knot the size of a fist form in her stomach. "And what he did have to say?" she asked, struggling to remain calm.

"According to Brand, he was rather emotional, a bit scatter-brained, and evasive," said Hines. "But he did tell them he expected to see his father shortly, and when he did, he'd let him know they wanted to talk to him."

"The young man is in trouble, and Mo is obviously trying to help him through it without making a public fuss. Can't you get Brand to understand that?"

"I can try, but what happens if I'm not successful and they request a postponement until they can talk to Mo?"

"We are prepared to walk away from the deal, and that isn't an idle threat. And if we do, we're willing to spend a ton of money generating negative PR."

"That could be viewed as an unreasonable position."

"It is no more unreasonable than the position Mo took before he came to his senses."

"Well, whether that's true or not, I won't give them that ultimatum unless I really have to. I'd rather stress the positive, which is that all it takes is one signature and *Tiananmen* will be something they never have to worry about again. I'll tell Brand that after all of Mo's bluster he obviously came to that conclusion, and that was why he changed his position. It's up to Brand to convince the Consul General to follow Mo's lead."

"We have tremendous faith in you."

"Be that as it may, I can't guarantee a satisfactory result. All I can do is try. Don't stray too far from your phone."

"That sounded like there's a problem," Fai said once Ava had ended the call.

"The Chinese want to talk to Mo before signing off."

"Shit."

"Harold has to persuade Brand to persuade them that it isn't necessary."

"And if he can't?"

"Then there's no deal and we all get out of town as fast as possible."

The morning passed agonizingly slowly. Ava and Fai packed their bags, and Fai booked an early evening flight to Toronto. Deal or no deal, they were exiting LA.

Silvana called at eleven to ask when they would be leaving for the meeting.

"We're not sure there is going to be one," Ava said.

"Why not?" Silvana asked, her voice full of concern.

Ava related her conversation with Hines, and then said, "Did you book a flight to Taipei?"

"Yes, it leaves around dinnertime."

"Are you packed?"

"Yes."

"Then bring your bags to our room. We might as well wait this out together."

Silvana arrived five minutes later, and the three women gathered on the terrace.

"Do you think the Chinese suspect that something bad has happened to Mo?" Silvana asked Ava.

"If they do it's a guess, because they certainly don't have any proof."

"And do you think they'll end up signing our deal?"

"I have no idea, although it would be stupid of them not to. With or without Mo's signature the deal would be valid, and *Tiananmen* would stop being an irritation. But I'm not much good at predicting how they will react to anything."

"I find all of this nerve-wracking."

"I try not to worry about things I can't control," said Ava. "We've made our decisions and laid the groundwork as best we could. Now it's up to the other side."

"And the worst-case scenario is that by this evening we'll all be on planes heading to places where we're safe," said Fai.

"But Ava is going to Beijing. I can't think of that as safe," said Silvana.

Ava started to respond, but stopped when her phone rang. "Yes, Harold, we've been waiting for you to call. Fai and Silvana are with me. I'm going to put you on speaker."

"I have news, and it is what I'd hoped for," he said. "Wang Ping will be in my offices at one with Eli Brand and several of the officers from Top of the Road to sign the agreement."

"Congratulations," Ava said.

"Eli deserves to hear that more than I do. I did manage to convince him that going ahead was the best option, but he had to sway the Chinese, and obviously he did a great job of it."

"So all those concerns about Mo have been put aside?"

"No, it's more that they've decided to ignore them for now. I have no doubts they'll be revisited."

"That's as much as we can expect, and it's certainly good enough."

"So, I'll be seeing Silvana and Fai here around quarter to one?"

"You will," Fai said.

"And Ava, you and I can talk later?"

"Sure, although I'll be on my way to the airport or already there. I'm leaving LA tonight, and I'll be hard to reach for a few days."

"Where are you going?"

"I'd rather not say."

"Well, safe travels to wherever it is," Hines said after a pause.

Ava put down the phone and smiled. "This couldn't have worked out any better."

32

THE THIRTEEN-HOUR FLIGHT TO BEIJING WAS PLEAS- antly uneventful. Ava watched six episodes of *Ozark*, slept on and off, and tried not to think too much about what lay ahead. She had spoken to Fai before leaving LA, and Fai had reported that things had gone smoothly at the signing. The Consul General, Wang Ping, had asked her and Silvana if they had seen or heard from Mo, and when they said no, he had barely spoken to them again, and left Hines's offices immediately after putting his name to paper. He had acted, Fai said, as if he didn't want to be there.

"He was probably ordered to go by Beijing. I guess burying our film is of more immediate concern to them than finding Mo," Ava said.

"And let's hope it's more important than Silvana and me."

"I don't think you have anything to worry about. The agreement gives us leverage we didn't have before," Ava said as encouragingly as she could. "And what about the statement, when will it be released?"

"Tomorrow, Patricia will look after it and answer the questions it will generate. We spoke to her from Harold's office and she's on top of things. She'll also make it clear that Sils and I won't be commenting any further."

"She will be asked if you were coerced."

"And the answer to that will obviously be no. She'll say our decision was—as we said—based purely on personal, emotional reasons."

"Which in a way it was. But anyway, LA is behind us now. You and Sils can get back to living more normal lives, and in a few days I should be in the same position."

Fai hesitated, and then said, "Please be careful in Beijing. I can't stop thinking that something could go wrong, and if it does I'm afraid I might never see you again."

"I promise that we won't take any unnecessary chances. Besides, I have Lop, Sonny, and Jimmy, and you know they'll do anything to protect me."

Ava didn't expect to see all three of them at Daxing Airport when her plane landed, but they were in the arrivals hall when she exited customs and immigration. At first glance they were a trio of misfits, with the mountainous Sonny in his black suit, black tie, and white shirt looming over the wiry Lop and the even smaller Jimmy Li.

"Hey boss," Sonny said, reaching for her bag.

She gave it to him, and got on her tiptoes to kiss him on the cheek. "It is so good to see you again," she said, and turned to Jimmy. "And you too of course."

"I'm always happy to work with you," he said with a slight nod of his head.

"I guess the new passport worked well," Lop said softly.

"The immigration officer actually looked at it long enough to make me uncomfortable, but obviously it passed inspection," she replied just as quietly. "What's our schedule for the day?"

"We'll go to the hotel, let you check in and get settled. We've arranged for Jimmy to test the rifle at a range; when he's finished, we'll drive to Xicheng. We spent yesterday afternoon there scouting locations and found one that we think works, but we want your opinion," Lop said.

Jimmy's opinion matters a lot more than mine, she thought but didn't say. "That sounds fine."

"Great, let's head for the rental car," said Lop.

It was a long walk to the car through the sprawling airport. On her previous visits to Beijing, Ava had landed at Capital International Airport. Daxing was new, and like most new airports in Asia was built to accommodate decades of growth.

"How far are we from the city?" she asked when they finally reached the parking lot and located a black Honda CR-V.

"About thirty kilometres," Lop said. "It's an easy half-hour drive."

Ava thought Lop would be driving, but to her surprise Sonny climbed into the driver's seat. Lop sat next to him, while Ava and Jimmy occupied the back seat. Minutes later they exited the indoor parking lot in the direction of the highway, which the signs said would lead them to the city centre. Almost as soon as they were outside, Ava noticed how poor the air quality was. "I knew they had a smog problem here, but I didn't think it was this bad."

"This is the worst it's been since I arrived," Lop said. "The smog is always there, but today we have sand to worry about. A storm blew in from the Gobi Desert overnight, and a lot of the city is shrouded in thick brown dust. It can be like that here in March and April, and the storms usually don't end until the summer rains arrive."

"When I spent time here with Fai it rained like hell. She told me winters and springs were worse, but I didn't see how that was possible. Now I do."

"And it isn't going to get any better," Lop said. "The deforestation in Inner Mongolia has accentuated the problem."

Ava turned to Jimmy. "What kind of impact on your visibility might there be if the smog and the dust don't leave?"

"It isn't ideal, but the night vision telescope will help. Also, while the Barrett's range is officially up to fifteen hundred metres, I've used it from two thousand, and the spot we've tentatively identified for setup is only a thousand metres from the front of the theatre."

"Where is this spot?"

"It's the Red Tree Inn, a six-storey hotel directly facing the theatre," Lop said. "Jimmy thinks he can get a clear shot anywhere from the fourth floor up."

"The sixth is obviously best," Jimmy interjected.

"Obviously we'd have to book a room that looks onto the theatre," said Ava.

Lop turned to look at her. "We're holding a reservation for tomorrow night on a fifth-floor room that does exactly that. We paid the desk clerk a thousand yuan to let us look at it, and then an extra thousand for holding it for us. Also, if a room on the sixth floor becomes available, we get first crack."

"What name did you use?" she asked.

He grimaced. "I had to use Chow Qi. I hope you don't mind. Guests can't check in without ID, and yours is the only name that can't be traced. I told the clerk you were my sister arriving from Shanghai," he said. "I also paid extra for early check-in. We can occupy the room at noon instead of three. That is assuming, of course, you agree it's a good place to set up shop."

Ava had to smile. "I can't anticipate thinking otherwise."

Traffic suddenly slowed, and then came to a full stop.

"Shit, I was afraid of this," Lop said. "These dust storms wreak havoc on transportation."

"How far do we have to go to the hotel?" she asked.

"Another ten kilometres at least, but there's no predicting how long it will take."

They crawled, stopped, then inched forward for the next hour. Ava saw it was trying everyone's patience and tried to keep the conversation light, but as an hour turned into another, Jimmy in particular looked increasingly worried.

"Something is bothering you. What is it?" she asked him.

"I was supposed to be at the firing range at four, but if we stay on this highway to go to the hotel, I'm afraid I'm not going to make it," Jimmy said. "The gun and sights are probably okay, but I hate taking the chance that they aren't. It would be a stupid mistake, to say the least."

"How far is the firing range?" she asked Lop.

"Let me check my GPS," he said, taking out his phone. "We're going north, and the range is in the Fangshan district, about fifteen kilometres to the west."

"We just passed an exit sign for a highway that had Fangshan on it," Sonny said.

"Can you get back to it?" Ava asked. "Having Jimmy test the gun is obviously far more important than checking me into the Hyatt."

"I can try," Sonny said.

"Then do that, please."

It took ten minutes to reach the next exit, but only a

few minutes to get back on the highway going in the oppo-site direction. Traffic leaving the city was lighter than that heading towards it, and they quickly reached the exit for Fangshan. Lop continued to give directions to Sonny, and in twenty minutes the car stopped in front of a two-storey red-brick building with a sign saying BAMBOO FURNITURE. Lop got out of the car and disappeared inside. Moments later he reappeared.

"We're a bit early, but they'll let Jimmy shoot," he said. "The place is owned by some former PLA friends of mine. It's officially illegal. Unofficially, all kinds of military and ex-military guys use it to stay sharp. But they're fussy about who they let inside. Ava, do you and Sonny mind staying out here?"

"Not at all," said Ava.

"Then, Sonny, could you pop the trunk for Jimmy?"

Ava watched Jimmy take a golf bag out of the car and enter the building with Lop.

"Whose idea was it to put the rifle in a golf bag?" she asked Sonny.

He shook his head. "I don't know. I think it came from Shanghai that way. Just as well, don't you think, since you can't walk into a hotel with a rifle?"

"No, you can't."

Sonny was quiet for a moment, and then said, "The hotel really is perfect for what we want to do. Jimmy should have a clear sightline."

"I don't have any doubts about that. I trust you—the three of you—completely."

"No one wants to let you down."

"And none of you ever have."

Sonny fell briefly silent again before saying, "How was LA? Did you get your man?"

"Yes, I got him. I didn't get any pleasure out of it, but I don't feel as guilty or as remorseful as I did after we killed the Red Pole in Macau. One difference is that I knew the guy in LA. Over many years he had abused Fai and other women, and that alone was almost reason to kill him. But what he caused with Chen and Lau Lau was unforgiveable, and then in my mind there was always the threat that he might try to do the same to Fai."

"I obviously didn't know anything about him, but I said to Jimmy that if Ava wants him dead, then there's bound to be a really good reason."

"The same holds true for the guy here," she said. "I don't know him on a personal level but he probably has more blood on his hands than anyone we've ever dealt with—and that includes the worst of the worst of the triads we've known."

"Well, if Jimmy can see him, the odds are that he'll shoot him."

Ava shook her head. "When I saw Jimmy at the airport, I had to remind myself what he's capable of doing, but that happens every time I see him. He looks like someone's retired grandfather—which of course he is."

"Jimmy still thinks of himself as an army man. He and Lop are similar that way. They like the clarity that obeying an order brings with it. I'm not ex-military, but I understand how they feel. I had no structure to my life until I decided to do whatever Uncle, and now you, told me to do."

"I'm not that bossy, am I?" Ava asked, trying to hide her surprise at Sonny's thoughtful analysis.

"Sometimes, but then you are the boss, so why shouldn't you be?"

Ava smiled. Months went by when she and Sonny wouldn't speak, and the gaps between them seeing each other were even longer, but she knew in his mind it made no difference—she was always and would forever be the boss. "How are things for you in Hong Kong these days?" she asked.

"Your father and brother keep me busy driving, and I have a new girlfriend who likes to get out and about on weekends. So I'd say things are okay. Sometimes I miss the excitement of the old days when Uncle was Mountain Master, and later when you and he were running the debt collection business."

"Tell me a bit about the girlfriend," Ava said.

Sonny shrugged, but for the next few minutes chatted about Samantha, who managed the coffee shop at the Shangri-La Hotel. She was slightly younger than Sonny, had never married, had no children, and according to Sonny seemed content with having a relationship that wasn't overly demanding. When he finished, Ava began asking questions about Uncle Fong—one of Uncle's closest and oldest friends, who Ava and Sonny had promised to look after. Like Sonny, Fong was a former triad and had never married, but there any comparison stopped. Over the years, Fong had spent his not inconsiderable income on gambling, booze, and women, and when he retired he'd had nothing to fall back on. Ava now sent him money monthly, while Sonny looked in on him every week and often took him out for dinner. Sonny spoke at length about Fong, and expressed some concern that he seemed tempted at times to fall back into bad habits. Ava said she would call him and remind him that his monthly stipend from her was attached to his promise not to use it for gambling. Then the door to the Bamboo Furniture building opened and Lop and Jimmy emerged.

"How was the rifle?" Ava asked after Jimmy put the golf bag in the trunk and slid into the front passenger seat.

"It's perfect, and they had a dark room where I could test the night vision clip. It worked terrifically as well."

"Great, so all we need is to get set up at the Red Tree Inn and for Lin to co-operate."

"Speaking of which, should we head to Xicheng now rather than going to the Hyatt?" Lop asked.

Ava hesitated. "You know what, Lop, I don't think I need to see the inn until I check in tomorrow. So let's skip Xicheng, head for the Hyatt, and go out for a nice dinner. Does Da Dong appeal to you?"

"It's never disappointed me."

"Good. We can review the plans for tomorrow over a great dinner."

33

TRAFFIC WAS STILL VERY HEAVY GOING BACK TOWARDS the city centre, and they didn't reach the hotel until almost six. Ava checked in and went to her suite to freshen up. The group had agreed to reconvene in the lobby at quarter to eight to go to Da Dong, where Lop had made an eight o'clock reservation.

After a shower, Ava sat down at the desk in the suite and opened her laptop. Both Fai and Silvana had emailed to say they had arrived safely in Toronto and Taipei. Ava hadn't expected anything different but was relieved all the same.

Harold Hines had also emailed with a summary of the signing meeting that jibed with everything that Fai had told her, but he'd had another—more problematic—conversation with Eli Brand later in the day. Brand had told him that Mo was still missing and had asked a myriad of questions about Jennie Kwong. Hines wrote that he had sidestepped the Jennie questions as best he could, and had repeated the story about Mo's son having issues that demanded Mo's attention. Brand replied that he had trouble buying that story, but didn't press the matter too hard.

So things are calm for the moment, but I can't imagine them

staying that way for much longer if Mo remains out of touch and out of reach, Hines wrote.

Brand said Wang Ping had been ordered by Beijing to do whatever was necessary to find him, including hiring private investigators. If he does, there can't be any doubt that their first stop will be David Mo's residence, and if he spins a different tale than the one we've been promoting … well, who knows where that will lead? But even without knowing the answer to that question, I think you and the ladies made a wise decision to get out of the city as quickly as you did.

Harold more than just suspects that I've got something to do with Mo's disappearance, Ava thought. That didn't surprise her, since he had made it clear enough that he had found her story about Mo's change of heart rather strange. And he also knew that she had ties with local triads. Had he put two and two together? That didn't actually concern her since she was certain that even if he knew something, he wouldn't share it with anyone. More troubling was the sudden realization that there could be dots for Lin to connect.

He would certainly know about Bai and Song by now, and she had to assume that word about Mo's absence might have reached him. Questions would be raised. After all, the only thing those three men had in common was their connection to the deaths of Chen and Lau Lau. Was it possible he might think they had been targeted, and that maybe he was the next one on the list? It couldn't be discounted. And if he came to believe that, then he could very well be a no-show at his daughter's premiere.

I'm overthinking this, Ava thought. *They don't know where Mo is. And if they hire private investigators, they have to give them at least a day or two to dig into it. All we have to do is get through the next twenty-four hours. Lin won't have the information he needs to put things together before then.*

Her phone ringing broke her concentration. She saw Fai's name on the screen, smiled, and answered. "Hi babe, I was waiting for another hour or so before calling you."

"I had trouble sleeping. How was your flight?"

"Boring—which is exactly how I like it."

"And how are things in Beijing? Is everything as you'd hoped it'd be?"

"It is, and the boys are ready for tomorrow night. All we need now is for our good fortune to last," Ava said. "And if it does, I'll be out of here the day after."

"I can't help feeling anxious."

"Fai, the guys are professional. They know what they're doing, and part of that is exercising the necessary amount of caution. I don't know for certain that we'll be successful, but I'm completely confident that whether we are or not, we'll be able to get safely out of Beijing."

"I believe you. It's just that my nerves are on edge. Patricia will be releasing our statement in a few hours, and I expect I'll be inundated with requests for comments."

"You should turn off your phone and not look at emails," said Ava.

"I intend to, and so does Silvana."

"Things will calm down soon enough. Are you going to school?"

"Yes, and it will be nice returning to a normal routine," said Fai. "Speaking of which, I should start getting myself organized."

"I'll let you go. Have a good day, and please stop worrying. I'll call you tonight," Ava said. "I love you."

"Love you too."

At seven forty Ava left the suite and made her way downstairs to the lobby. Lop, Sonny, and Jimmy were already there, and the four of them piled into a taxi for the short ride to Da Dong.

Ava had eaten at the restaurant with Lop on a previous trip. It was famous for its Peking duck, and although Ava didn't consider herself to be a connoisseur of the dish, she had eaten it often enough to have an opinion about quality. In the case of Da Dong's duck, she believed that it was the best she'd ever eaten. Several things set it apart. One was that the skin had virtually no fat or meat attached to it, was less oily and more crisp than any other she'd tasted, and when dipped in sugar it almost melted in her mouth. Another was that unlike the traditional way of slicing off the skin of a whole duck at the table, and then carving the meat in the kitchen, Da Dong brought a platter of skin and a separate one of meat—accompanied by a plate of hollow buns—to the table at the same time. The buns were meant to be stuffed with the meat, along with choices that included bean paste, julienned cucumbers, radishes, and the white part of scallions.

On that previous visit to Da Dong, she had been impressed enough with the meal to ask the server if she knew how they prepared the duck. The woman had obviously been asked the question before because she didn't hesitate to detail the process. Their chef, she said, pumped air between the skin and fat to separate them, and then marinated the duck in a unique sauce. After that, the skin was air-dried, and the duck roasted in a woodfired oven over fruitwood for longer than it would be in a standard metal roast oven. The result was—to Ava's thinking—heaven.

There wasn't much talking on the cab ride to the restaurant. Ava was comfortable with silence and knew the three men well enough to know they were too. Sonny rarely initiated a conversation, so it wasn't rare for him to be quiet, and she imagined that Lop and Jimmy were preoccupied with thoughts about the following day.

Despite their reservation, they had to wait ten minutes for a table when they arrived at Da Dong. Unlike her mother, Ava didn't get offended when she wasn't promptly seated. None of her companions seemed bothered by the wait either, although as platters of duck skin and meat were brought to a table nearby, Lop said, "I can't believe how hungry that makes me."

When they were finally seated, the men all ordered bottles of Tsingtao, and Ava asked for a glass of Chardonnay. While they waited for their drinks, Lop passed a menu to Ava. "Why don't you order for us?"

"Yes, do that," Sonny said.

Ava nodded. "Does anyone have a preference for anything other than duck?"

"I wouldn't mind a soup," Jimmy said.

She glanced at the menu. "They have a lobster soup."

"That sounds good."

A moment later the server returned with their drinks. After he placed them on the table, Ava said, "We'll order now."

"Go ahead."

"The imperial Peking duck, lobster soup, pan-fried matsutake, scallops with mangos, and the Boston lobster noodles," she said. "Will that be enough food for our group?"

"It should be," the server said.

When he left with their order, Lop raised his beer bottle. "Zhu ni shun ni."

"Indeed, and I'm sure things will go smoothly," Ava said.

They clinked bottle to bottle, bottle to glass, and drank. Then Lop said, "I was fortunate to work with fine people in the PLA, and I'm proud to be part of Xu's organization, but I've never felt more confident with a group than I am with this one."

"That's great to hear, and on that point, is this a good time to discuss the plan for tomorrow?" Ava said.

"It isn't complicated. Like I said, you can check in at the Red Tree any time after twelve. If a room facing the theatre on the sixth floor is available, that's perfect; if it isn't, take the one I've reserved on the fifth. After you check in, call me with the room number and I'll pass it along to the guys. Jimmy will join you at five, and Sonny should arrive around an hour later than that," said Lop. "What we don't want is for the three of you to be easily connected, so arriving separately will help. As well, I don't think Jimmy and Sonny should take the elevator directly to whatever floor you're on. Like we did at Song's apartment building, they should get off a floor or two below and take the stairs."

"That sounds simple enough," Ava said. "What kind of CCTV setup does the place have?"

"I saw cameras in the lobby and none anywhere else. But since the room is in your name, and Jimmy and his golf bag are definitely going to look suspicious if CCTV footage is reviewed, I think both of you should disguise your faces as much as possible."

"I have a hoodie I can use," said Jimmy.

"I'll come up with something," said Ava. "But you haven't mentioned where you'll be while we're at the inn."

"Do you remember me telling you that I was trying to find out what kind of vehicle Lin might be travelling in?"

"Yes."

"Well, I succeeded. I was told he rides in a Red Flag limousine. The car is reserved for bureaucrats and politicians of the highest rank, and there won't be that many other people in the mss who qualify," said Lop. "I thought it would be useful to know when Lin leaves the compound, so that's where I intend to go tomorrow. I've scouted the area and I can park my car within eyesight of the main entrance, in a spot where his car has to pass me to get to the theatre, without drawing attention to myself. When I see the limo leaving, I'll call you with an approximate ETA."

"Assuming he does leave the compound, and assuming he leaves by that entrance."

Lop smiled. "Maybe I should have said *if* he leaves the compound."

"I didn't mean to sound like I doubted your plan," Ava said, smiling in return. "But I've never heard of a Red Flag limousine. How easy will it be to recognize?"

"The car is definitely distinctive. It's a monster with a massive frame, a huge front grille, bug-eyed headlights, and is at least six metres long. The standard colour is black, and it will probably be flying a flag. I've given Jimmy and Sonny a photo of one."

"We'll bring it with us tomorrow," Sonny said.

"Thank you," Ava said to Sonny, and then turned to Lop again. "Will you be able to tell if Lin is in the limo?"

"I was told the car windows are usually tinted so I think that's unlikely. Also, the sun sets around six so it will probably be dark when he leaves. I bought night vision binoculars for each of us, but I doubt they'll be of any use on the windows."

"Do we all need binoculars? From what I saw online, the front of the theatre is very well lit."

"I know, but even in good light I figured three sets of eyes would be better than one when it comes to identifying Lin—even eyes as sharp as Jimmy's."

"That's true enough," said Jimmy.

Ava looked at him. "How long will it take you to get set up?"

"We're lucky that the room window opens so we don't have to cut a hole in it. Given that's the case, I won't need that much time, but by getting there at five I can get accustomed to my surroundings and as familiar as possible with the sightlines."

Their server approaching the table carrying a tray laden with food brought discussion about the Red Tree Inn to a halt.

"I like the look of that," Sonny said.

"Here's hoping it eats as well as it looks," added Ava.

It did, and half an hour later, every platter was empty, and three more bottles of beer and another glass of wine had been downed.

"That was absolutely a great meal, and when you read military history, many armies had one on the eve of an epic battle," Lop said. "And that's sort of how I think of tomorrow—this just isn't about one man, this is a battle within a war because taking Lin out is going to have an impact that far exceeds him."

"That's how I see it too, and I feel like I'm doing it for Hong Kong," Jimmy said. "Bit by bit our rights—like freedom of speech or peaceful demonstrations—are being obliterated by the communists. There's nothing I can do about it there, so I'll make a stand here ... Sonny, you must feel the same."

"You know that I'm not into politics. I'm here because of Ava."

"But surely you have an opinion about what's happening to Hong Kong?" Jimmy pressed.

Sonny shook his head and looked mournful. "Jimmy, in my life I've always had to struggle to stay out of trouble and not disappoint the people who were relying on me. I didn't have the time, the energy, or the interest for anything else. Now all I want to do is to keep serving my boss, and from time to time make my girlfriend happy. I'll leave Hong Kong's problems to people who are smarter than I am."

"Not everyone has to worry about the big picture, Jimmy," Ava said. "Sonny will contribute in his own way."

"I wasn't trying to start an argument," said Jimmy, taking Ava's remark as a reprimand.

"I know you weren't. I know how deeply you care about Hong Kong, and I respect you tremendously for it."

There were a few seconds of uncomfortable silence that Lop ended by saying, "We know how we're going to handle matters up to the moment Jimmy takes out Lin, but now I think we need to discuss what we do after it's done."

"You obviously have given this some thought," Ava said.

"I have. I'm assuming that Lin will have a security detail of some kind with him, and I'd like to start by asking Jimmy how easy it will be for them to identify where the shot originated."

Jimmy pursed his lips. "Well, to begin with, we'll be about a thousand metres away from the theatre, and I'll be in the dark, so unless someone has night vision and looks at the window the second I fire, I won't be seen. There will be a sound but it will be slight, and there's a four-lane road in front of the inn which will have noisy traffic, so I doubt they can use the sound to locate us."

"I was thinking the same, but I'm pleased to hear you say it," said Lop. "But is it possible for them to get a sense of the general direction of the shot, by the way it strikes Lin?"

"Most definitely—that is if they're any good, and if they're his security team they will be good, but as far as pinpointing the inn as the shot's origin, that's going to be a lot harder. I counted at least six buildings in the area that could have provided me with a clear shot."

"Surely his security team won't be that big," said Ava. "And after the shot they'll be caught up in taking care of Lin. I can't imagine them immediately charging towards the inn."

"I wasn't suggesting that they would, but the MSS will move quickly, and I would expect they'll have tens if not hundreds of operatives within the general area within a few hours. If that's the case, they'll eventually find their way to the Red Tree Inn, and perhaps to the room that was supposed to be occupied by Chow Qi—except she won't be there."

"Which will make them undoubtedly suspicious," Ava said. "As will the two unknown men, one of them carrying a golf bag, who entered the hotel after she did."

Lop looked at Jimmy. "I know that Sonny and Ava have been fingerprinted, have you?"

Jimmy nodded.

"Lop makes a good point. We don't want to leave a trail of any kind," Ava said. "We should wear gloves at all times in the room. Jimmy, would that interfere with your shooting?"

"Are you thinking of latex gloves?"

"Yes."

"Then no, they won't interfere."

"I'll buy them. There's a pharmacy close to the hotel that should have some."

"Okay, now obviously all of you need to leave the inn as quickly as possible after Jimmy has done his thing, but I'd like to suggest that you leave one at a time, say a couple of minutes apart?"

Ava turned to Jimmy. "I know you said the rifle won't be loud, but could the hotel staff hear it?"

"Only if they're standing at our door and recognize it for what it is."

"I'm taking that as a no," said Ava. "So, Lop, where are you as we leave the inn?"

"There's a parking lot about a hundred metres to the right of the hotel's front door as you exit. I'll be there standing by the car. As soon as I see you I'll pop open the trunk for your luggage and the golf bag."

"What happens to the golf bag?"

"We're only a few minutes away from the North Sea Lake. I thought we could toss the rifle into the water, and then find a different resting place for the bag."

"And head back to the Hyatt?" said Ava.

"I'd rather that we didn't," Lop said.

"What are you suggesting?"

"If I'm right about how quickly the MSS will respond, and if our assumption that they'll eventually find their way to the Red Tree Inn is correct, then I would like all of us to be on planes, or better still already on home territory when that happens. I know we're being careful, and I might be slightly paranoid, but time is not our ally."

"I can't disagree with that, if it is logistically possible to leave tomorrow night," said Ava.

"But what if we aren't successful?" Jimmy asked. "And by that I mean, what if he doesn't come to the theatre?"

"We have a plan and timetable that gives us that one chance to get Lin. If it doesn't work, there's no way we should hang around waiting for a second chance that may never come," said Lop.

"I agree with Lop on that as well," said Ava. "Tomorrow night at the theatre is the endgame. If Lin doesn't show, or if he does and we somehow miss him, then that's it."

34

AFTER DINNER AVA PURCHASED LATEX GLOVES AND returned to her room. She then tried to book a late evening flight for the following day—first to Canada, and then anywhere in North America—but there weren't any. She debated going to Hong Kong or Shanghai before deciding that getting completely out of reach of the Chinese authorities was the priority, and she found a flight to Tokyo that left Beijing at ten thirty. Given that the name Chow Qi was going to be in the hotel register and might draw the attention of the MSS, she booked it under Jennie Kwong. She phoned Sonny to tell him, and was pleased to hear that he and Jimmy had secured seats on a flight to Hong Kong that left an hour after hers.

"It looks like we're set. I'll see you tomorrow afternoon."

After showering, she left a voicemail for Fai, and slid into bed with a glass of Chardonnay. She turned on the television and watched a dull news program for about ten minutes before her eyes started to close.

Ava slept fitfully. She didn't dream, but woke up around two with an urge to pee and a sense of uneasiness. Getting in and out of Beijing so quickly reminded her of her days in debt collection when—once a target had been located—speed was of the essence before the money she was chasing had a chance to disappear. This time it was her and her colleagues who had to do the disappearing.

Sleep eluded her when she returned to her bed after her bathroom visit. She lay on her back, stared up at the dark ceiling, and wondered how the day would go. She and Lop had been fortunate so far, but Lin wouldn't be a sitting duck. He was going to be a thousand metres from them, perhaps surrounded by a security team, and amid a large number of ballet attendees, so there was no guarantee that Jimmy would be able to get a clear shot. *But he has to get one*, she suddenly thought. *Lin is the big prize.* Bai and Song had been incidental, and as much as she despised Mo, he hadn't had the authority to issue a kill order.

When Ava woke again there were slivers of light coming through the bedroom curtains. She slid from the bed, went to the window, and opened the curtains. The sun shone dimly through a haze. Was it smog, or smog and sand? Either way, the air was going to be foul again. That didn't bother her, but it did trigger a worry about the haze combined with darkness affecting Jimmy's ability to see Lin clearly.

She went into the living area, made a coffee, sat at the desk, and opened her laptop to look at her emails. There weren't many of interest, but May Ling had written to say she hoped things were going well and asked when Ava thought she'd be finished with the "project." Ava started to write a reply, then stopped and picked up her phone to call Wuhan.

"Ava, I didn't expect to hear from you so soon. Where are you, and is everything all right?"

"It's as fine as it can be. I'm in Beijing for the rest of today, and then regardless of how things go, I'm heading home tonight."

"What are you doing in Beijing?"

"There's a man here who gave the order to kill Chen and Lau Lau. He's the last leg of our journey."

"What about Mo?"

"He won't be bothering us again."

"And the man in Beijing was connected to Mo?"

"The man in Beijing is connected to a lot of Mos. He's a very senior—if not the *most* senior—official in the Ministry of State Security."

"Ava, you can't be serious about going after a man like that."

"That's why we're here, and we do have a plan."

"What kind of plan do you honestly believe has a chance to work?" May asked, her anxiety audible.

"Hopefully, we're going to shoot him from a long distance as he walks into a theatre. It shouldn't put any of us in harm's way, and we think it's doable."

"Good grief, Ava, who came up with that idea?"

"Lop."

"And who is going to do the shooting?"

"Jimmy Li."

"I remember the name. I thought he was a munitions expert."

"He's also a sniper, and a very good one," Ava said.

"So the team is you, Lop, and Jimmy …"

"Sonny is here as well. They're all good men."

"Maybe they are, but even remembering everything we've gone through together, what you just told me makes me more afraid for you than I've ever been."

"We're being careful."

May sighed. "And you're sure that tonight will be the end of it?"

"Absolutely, and then home to Toronto to pursue the ginseng deal that Amanda wants us to do."

"I don't care about ginseng. All that matters to me is your safety," May said, and then added urgently: "Promise to call me tonight when it's done or not done. I don't care about the time."

"You will hear from me."

I shouldn't have phoned her, Ava thought when she hung up. *All I did was give her something to worry about.* She checked the time and figured that Fai would already have been at home for a few hours. She called Toronto.

"Hey," Fai answered without any enthusiasm.

"Is everything okay? You sound down."

"It's been a rough day. School was fine, but Patricia released our statement as planned and the reaction has been overwhelming. I had my phone off all day—thank goodness—so I didn't have to deal with it minute to minute, but when I turned it on I had more texts than I care to count and my voice mailbox was full again. Patricia has been so busy that she told me she feels like she has a phone growing out of her ear."

"What are people saying?"

"It's a mixed bag. Some people seem to understand while others most certainly don't. Patricia said a couple of journalists accused Sils and I of caving into the Chinese government's pressure and betraying our artistic integrity. They were the minority, though. By and large, people seem to be sympathetic—and that includes some who don't necessarily agree with our decision."

"This will blow over in no time."

"That's what Patricia says too."

"But I hope you aren't reading about this online. You know how unhinged people can be."

"I'm not reading or watching anything. Patricia is my sole pipeline for information about the reaction to our Oscar turndowns."

"That's smart."

"More like self-defence," Fai said, and then paused. "God, I wish you were here."

"I have some good news where that's concerned. I plan on leaving Beijing tonight. I have to fly through Tokyo but I only have to wait a few hours before catching a flight home."

"That's so good to hear, but are you going to be able to do what you went to Beijing for that quickly?"

"We have one chance at it, and everything has to fall into place if we're to succeed. If we don't, we've already agreed there won't be a second try. So, one way or another, I should be flying to Tokyo tonight."

"I'm happy to hear that."

"We'll have our chance between seven and seven thirty tonight," said Ava. "That means most of my day is free, and I've decided to go to your house to get the things you want."

"If that's an inconvenience …"

"It isn't, and in fact it will give me a much-needed distraction. And since I'm going to be in your old neighbourhood, I might even have lunch at the Hai Wan Canteen."

"Now you're making me jealous," said Fai. "But if you do go, say hello to the owners for me, order gong bao, and take a picture of it."

"Too bad I can't bring some back with me."

"I'll be happy enough just to see you alive and well."

"Have no worries on that account," Ava said. "Now, I need to get my day started. I'll call you tomorrow morning to report on how the day and evening went."

"Okay, I'll be waiting anxiously. Love you."

"Love you too."

Ava ended the call, stood, and went into the bedroom where her LV bag sat on a chair. She opened it, unzipped an inner compartment, and confirmed that the key to Fai's house and the list she'd given Ava were still there. She thought about getting ready to leave, and then remembered there was one last detail she hadn't talked over with Lop. She picked up the room phone and dialled his room.

"This is Ava."

"Good morning, how did you sleep?"

"Well enough, and you?"

"It took me a while to nod off. I'm always on edge before a job like this."

"It is stressful," she said. "Luckily, I have a chore to do for Fai that will keep me occupied for part of the day. That's why I'm calling. I'll be leaving the hotel in a few hours, but I'll keep my phone on in case you need to reach me."

"What will you do when the chore is done?"

"I was planning on going directly to the Red Tree Inn."

"Do you want to leave any luggage with me? I'll have mine and the guys' bags in the trunk of the car," he said.

"I don't think it's necessary. I'm travelling light. Besides, I should have some luggage with me when I check in at the inn."

"Yeah, you're right."

"Did you manage to book a flight?"

"I've decided to go to Hong Kong with Sonny and Jimmy. I was going there anyway in a week or two to take care of some business for Xu. This will just move it up a bit. How about you?"

"I couldn't get a direct flight to North America so I'm going to connect through Tokyo."

"Anywhere outside of mainland China is good for you."

"I agree," she said. "Well, that's it then, until I see you tonight."

35

JUST BEFORE ELEVEN, AVA LEFT THE HYATT. SHE HAD on no makeup; her hair was pulled back and secured with an elastic band; and she was wearing running shoes, a black Adidas jacket, and training pants. It was as close to inconspicuous as she could make herself. She got into a taxi at the hotel entrance and handed the driver Fai's address in Xicheng.

"That's not so bad," he said. "We'll be going against traffic."

"The house is in a hutong so you can stop at the entrance."

Going against traffic or not, the taxi rarely went faster than twenty kilometres an hour, but it did make steady progress, and half an hour later Ava arrived at the hutong. It was several hundred years old and had somehow survived the urban development that had demolished tens if not hundreds of other hutongs—small community enclaves within Beijing. Ava had the cab stop at the hutong entrance because the alley that split it in two was less than ten metres across, flanked by twelve-metre-high stone walls, and typically bustling with pedestrian traffic.

Fai's house wasn't visible from the alley. It was about

halfway down, and was accessed through red metal double doors with the words GOOD FORTUNE TO ALL WHO ENTER HERE embossed in gold on the lintel. The door led into a cobblestone courtyard that was surrounded in a semicircle by twelve connected townhouses.

As Ava walked towards the courtyard along the alley past stalls, small stores recessed into the wall, a tea shop, and a public washroom, she was pleased to see nothing had changed since her last visit. Fai said that one of the things she loved about her hutong was its timelessness, and that was something Ava had come to appreciate too. Several of the vendors shouted a welcome to her, and she waved back at them.

She reached the door that led into the courtyard, opened it, and stepped inside. There was no one in the yard, but as Ava approached Fai's distinctive dark blue door, she saw that the curtains on the window of the house on the right were slightly pulled back. A man named Fan lived there. He was a retired writer who had actually worked with Lau Lau and Fai, but now—in Ava's opinion—spent most of his time poking his nose into other people's business and gossiping. Ava had exchanged harsh words with him a few times.

Ava opened her LV bag, took out Fai's key, and unlocked the blue door. The curtains had been drawn in Fai's absence, and the house interior was dark, gloomy, and had a musty smell. Ava put down her bag, pulled back the curtains, and opened the window. Then she looked around and found that things were exactly the way she remembered them.

It was a small house, with a living room and kitchen in the main floor, and one bedroom and the bathroom on the second. In total, Ava didn't think the entire house was more than eight hundred square feet, and would have fit four times into her mother's home in Richmond Hill. In the living room were a sofa, easy chair, coffee table, and a large television that sat on a stand. On a shelf in the stand there was a photo album that Fai wanted, and next to it was a gold statue for best actress that she had won at the Asian Film Awards for her role in Lau Lau's film *Betrayal*. The statue wasn't on Fai's list, but Ava decided she'd take it if there was room for it in the suitcase Fai wanted her to use.

Ava had begun to make her way up the stairs to get the suitcase from Fai's bedroom closet when she heard a knock at the door. She was certain it was Fan, felt immediately annoyed, and stood on a step while deciding what to do. *What the hell*, she finally thought. Knowing him he'd probably keep knocking, so she might as well answer the door.

She went down the stairs, opened the door, and to her surprise saw someone other than Fan. "Superintendent Lam, how nice to see *you*," she said to the tall, broad-chested man.

"I hope I'm not interrupting anything, but I saw you arrive. I wasn't sure how long you were going to be here, and I didn't want to miss the chance to talk to you," he said.

Lam was the neighbour on the other side of Fai's house. He was a retired police officer who had served in the Municipal Public Security Bureau. During Ava's first stay at Fai's, he had come to her aid when she was attacked by some machete-wielding thugs, and on every subsequent visit the women had taken him out for a meal.

"Has something happened?" she asked, detecting uneasiness on his part.

"I'm not sure, but it might be best to speak about it inside."

"Of course," Ava said, stepping aside. "Come in. We can talk in the kitchen."

The kitchen was as compact as the rest of the house, and aside from appliances it only had room for a small round table with two metal folding chairs. Lam waited for Ava to sit before taking the other chair.

"I would offer you coffee or tea," Ava said, pointing to the thermos on the counter. "But I'm not sure we have any."

"There's no need for that," he said. "How long do you intend to stay here?"

"A few hours at most—Fai has some things that she wants me to bring back to Toronto."

"Then I'm glad I caught you."

"What's going on?"

"Despite the government trying to keep it quiet, a lot of people know that Fai has made a movie about Tiananmen Square. It is attracting what I think is some unwanted attention."

"Fai didn't actually make the movie. She acted in it. Her ex-husband Lau Lau wrote the script and directed it," Ava said, wondering where this was leading.

"I knew Lau Lau when he lived here. It was just about the time when he started to go downhill."

"Did you know he died recently?"

"No, I didn't," said Lam with a brisk shake of his head. "Was it an illness, or something to do with drugs?"

"No, he was shot while walking into a restaurant in Taipei, only a short time after finding out that he and his film had been nominated for Oscars."

"I heard nothing about that," Lam said, clearly startled.

"Why would you? You were right when you said the government wants no one to know about the film. And I'm sure they're as determined to prevent people knowing that they killed Lau Lau and his producer, Chen, for making it."

Lam hesitated, and then said, "Did I just hear you correctly? Are you really saying the government murdered Lau Lau?"

It was Ava's turn to pause. Had she already said too much? How much trust could be put in a retired police officer? What did Lam value most—his ties to his neighbours or to his past profession? She looked at him and saw nothing but concern on his face.

"I am, and with good reason. I have been told by people who are in the know that his death was ordered by the Ministry of State Security, and carried out by a couple of their assassins."

"What people?"

"I don't want to get into any details about them other than to say I believe them to be entirely credible."

"And they were that precise when they told you about what happened to Lau Lau?"

"Yes. They said that the government decided that preventing people from seeing the film wasn't enough—that it was also necessary to punish those who made it. Lau Lau and Chen were targeted."

Lam frowned and turned his head to look out of the window.

"Superintendent, has something I said upset or compromised you somehow?"

"No, I'm just putting two and two together," he said. "What I had intended to tell you was that the MSS came here about a month ago looking for Fai."

Ava felt her stomach knot, and the onset of a cold sweat. "How do you know that?" she asked.

"I saw men knocking at her door. When they didn't find

her at home, they came to see me and identified themselves. They knew who I was and what job I'd had. When I told them I didn't know where she was, they went from door to door asking the other residents if they had any idea, and if she'd told anyone when she'd be back."

"How many MSS agents were there?"

"Six. They tend to travel in packs. They saw me again before leaving to tell me to call them the moment she showed her face. Then they said they had instructed the other residents to do the same, but if for some reason they couldn't get through to the MSS, they should tell me. Given my background, they naturally assumed I'd be complicit.

"Did they give you any hint of why they wanted to see her?"

"All they said was that they wanted to talk to her. I think we can take for granted it would have been about the film. The thing that's really worrisome is that I'm sure the talk wouldn't have taken place here."

Ava felt the knot tighten. "Do you really think they would have taken her away?"

"I do. They don't send six men if they want to chat in your living room. If she'd been at home, they would have bundled her off."

"Shit."

"Ava, I'm not someone who overreacts, but what you've told me about Lau Lau and the other guy has made me very concerned about her safety."

"I share your concern."

"Then you need to tell Fai to stay away from here until things cool down—assuming they do."

"That was the plan anyway, but this cements it."

"Good, and now we need to get you out of here as fast as

possible. I'm sure some of the neighbours saw you arrive like I did. The one next door has made it clear a few times that he has an active dislike for you, and I wouldn't put it past him to call the MSS and report that you're in Fai's house."

"Fan would do that?"

Lam shrugged. "Maybe not, but why take the chance?"

"Yes, this is a bad time for me to be pushing my luck. I'll pack up Fai's things as quickly as I can."

"If you like, I'll stay here until you're finished, and then I'll walk you to the cab stand at the hutong entrance."

"I really appreciate that, and I know that Fai will be grateful as well."

"You know I've lived here for more than twenty years, and Fai was always unfailingly kind. The thought that I might not see her again rather saddens me. Please tell her that, but be sure to add that I'd rather be sad than worry about her being at risk."

36

AVA LEFT FAI'S HOUSE HALF AN HOUR LATER PULLING a medium-sized suitcase and toting one of her own bags. Lam walked slightly behind her, carrying Ava's other bag and covering her back. She had tried to stay calm and focused as she worked on Fai's list, but the conversation with Lam had alarmed her, and despite knowing realistically that it was unlikely the MSS would show up at Fai's that quickly, it was with an increasing sense of relief that she left the house, then exited the courtyard, and finally reached the cab stand.

"Say hello to Fai for me," Lam said as the driver put Ava's luggage in the trunk.

"I will, and can you do us a favour?"

"What is it?"

"Could you text or phone me or Fai if the MSS returns. My contact information is on my card," she said, handing one to him.

"Of course."

Ava slid into the back seat of the taxi, waved goodbye to Lam, and said quietly to the driver, "Do you know the location of the Hai Wan Canteen?"

He nodded but looked displeased. "It isn't far from here. You could walk there."

"I know it's close, but I want you to wait for me and then drive me somewhere else," she said. "I also tip very well."

"Okay, lady," the driver said.

Three turns later, the car stopped in front of an unsigned store front that Ava knew housed the canteen. As she got out with her LV bag she said, "I'll be half an hour or so."

"The meter is running, so there's no rush."

It was the beginning of the lunch hour and the canteen was busy. Most of the ten larger round tables in the centre were occupied, but there were several vacant smaller tables against the walls. She went to one furthest from the door, sat, and put her bag on the plastic sheet that covered the table. A moment later a woman who Ava recognized as one of the owners came to the table with a broad smile.

"You are Pang Fai's friend," she said.

"I am."

"We haven't seen Fai in a long time. Is she all right?"

"She's fine. She decided to live in North America for a while so she could learn English."

"Will you be seeing her soon?"

"Yes."

"When you do, tell her we miss her."

Ava smiled. "And she misses your food. I told her I was coming here and going to order gong bao and she was jealous."

"So you want gong bao?" the woman asked, grinning again.

"Yes, and hot and sour soup, and a glass of water."

After the woman left, Ava looked around the restaurant.

There weren't many men wearing suits or women dressed like they were office workers. It was a working-class crowd, but one—as far as she was concerned—being treated to food as good as they would find anywhere in Beijing. Ava didn't know if this was particular to Chinese food, but she had often come across Chinese restaurants like the canteen—no sign, a worn tile floor, faded prints of waterfalls and rice paddies on the wall, tables covered in plastic sheets, and chairs that looked like they'd been taken from a mah-jong parlour—that somehow created magic in the kitchen. And she didn't have to look any further for magic than the large bowl of hot and sour soup that was then placed in front of her.

Her memory of it the last time she ate in the canteen was that it was some of the best she'd ever had, but rating hot and sour soup was tricky because not only did it vary from restaurant to restaurant, but even the same restaurant's recipe could change from day to day. In this case—as she looked down at the maroon surface with chili oil shimmering on top—it looked exactly as she remembered. She took her first spoonful and extracted broth, a sliver of duck meat, fungi, and a small translucent shrimp. She tasted it and smiled. It had an initial sweetness that gave way to a light hint of vinegar, and then the chili kicked in. She ate slowly, her spoon also discovering wood mushrooms, green pepper, scallops, and a slice of chicken.

"How was it?" the owner asked after Ava had emptied the bowl.

"Wonderful—again, one of the best I've ever had, and I've had it in probably hundreds of restaurants."

"It is my husband's favourite dish to prepare, and the one he is proudest of. I know that many of our customers come here for the gong bao, but he is never happier than when someone likes his soup."

"Please tell him that I am a very happy customer indeed."

The woman lowered her head slightly in acknowledgement of the compliment and said, "Your gong bao is ready. Let me get it for you."

In North America, Ava knew gong bao was most often referred to as kung pao, and was a stir-fried chicken often served with peanuts, and various vegetables. Comparing the canteen's gong bao to its North American cousin was— in Ava's opinion—like comparing a Wagyu filet mignon to Grade A American beef. The canteen used sliced chicken thighs that had been marinated in a concoction of soy sauce, sesame oil, black vinegar, rice wine, and hoisin, and then flash stir-fried them with cashews and chili peppers that the owner swore came from a private source in Sichuan. Whether they did or not, they were explosive.

When the food arrived, Ava took a picture and sent it to Fai. Nothing has changed at the Canteen. Same owners. Same great food. We all miss you, love Ava.

She ate slowly, savouring every bite. As she did, her mind kept coming back to the conversation with Superintendent Lam. She didn't doubt anything he'd told her, and that fact was a cause for alarm. Two things were obvious—Fai was at risk, and there was no way she could return to China in the immediate future, or perhaps ever. The question that nagged at Ava was whether she should tell Fai about the MSS visit. Not unless it was necessary, she decided. There was nothing to be gained by doing it, and a lot to lose in terms of Fai's peace of mind.

Ava looked at the people enjoying their lunch. How many

of them knew what their government was prepared to do to maintain control and protect its image? And if they did know, how many of them would actually care? She thought of her mother, whose only concern was the safety and security of her immediate family. As long they weren't threatened, her mother didn't care about the political structure that made that possible, and said that most of her friends felt the same way. Was that equally true in China? Ava was becoming more and more certain that it was for the majority of people. What they wanted was stability in their day-to-day lives and they didn't care what the government had to do to provide it. And after everything the country had gone through over the last sixty to seventy years, maybe that kind of pragmatism was justified. Unless, of course, you were a victim of that government's heavy hand; but then, even if you were, who would know—and if it was known, what difference would it make? *Absolutely none*, she thought, and then chided herself for being so negative. There might be nothing that could be done to impact the system in a major way, but there was always room for small victories, and eliminating Lin would classify as one of those.

As Ava finished her meal, she realized this might be the last time she would eat in the canteen, and decided she wanted more than memories of it. She picked up her phone and began to take pictures of the interior. The owner saw her and came to the table.

"There's nothing worth taking photos of in here," she said good-naturedly.

"I don't know when Fai and I will be able to come back, so we'll have the pictures to look at," Ava said. "And there's one more thing—a favour—I'd like to ask for."

"What's that?"

"Is it possible for me to get the recipes for the hot and sour soup, and gong bao?"

The woman hesitated and Ava expected her to say no. Instead, she said, "I'll have to ask my husband."

"Please tell him they're just for Fai and me. We would never share them with anyone else."

"I'll be right back."

The woman was gone for five minutes, and the more time passed, the more Ava became convinced that the answer was going to be no. But when the woman reappeared she was carrying a paper bag and was smiling.

"Here you are," she said, placing the bag on the table when she reached Ava. "The recipes are inside. They are for much larger quantities than you'd ever make, but you can adjust them. My husband also put in some of our Sichuan chilies."

"That is so kind," said Ava.

"But there are two things my husband wants for you to do for him."

"What are they?"

"After you've made the dishes for the first time, he would like you to email some pictures, and to tell him how they tasted. And he would appreciate it if Pang Fai could send him a signed photo of herself. He will put it on the wall at the entrance."

"You can tell him that we'll do both of those things. Now, I have to get going, so I would like to pay for my lunch."

"Payment isn't necessary."

"Yes it is," Ava said, and she reached into her bag. She put seven hundred yuan onto the table, the equivalent of just over one hundred US dollars.

"That's too much," the woman said.

"Your food is worth it," said Ava as she stood.

The woman walked with her to the door. When they reached it, she lightly touched Ava on the arm. "Please tell Fai to stay safe," she whispered. "Customers talk and we've heard things. It's good that she is in North America. China isn't pleased with her right now."

"I'll tell her," Ava said, surprised that the woman had waited so long to say something, and resisting the urge to ask what she had heard.

The taxi was in the same spot she'd left it. The driver had his eyes closed and his head resting against the back of the seat. Ava opened the back door, slid in, and slammed it shut. He sat up, his right hand rubbing his eyes.

"You can take me to the Red Tree Inn," she said. "It's near the Tiangiao Theatre."

Less than ten minutes later the cab stopped in front of a building that had a modest red plastic sign that read RED TREE INN, above a set of double glass doors. Without the sign, the six-storey brown brick building could have passed for rental apartments or low-cost offices. Ava paid the driver the fee on his meter and then doubled it as a tip. Looking happy, he got out and ran to the trunk to get her bags. She stood on the sidewalk and looked across a four-lane road to the broad expanse that fronted the theatre. There was a clear sightline, but then she had expected nothing less.

The driver offered to carry her bags into the hotel. She declined, waited until he had left, opened her Shanghai Tang Double Happiness bag and took out a plain black baseball cap and sunglasses. She removed the rubber band that was holding her hair so that it could fall around her face. She put on the glasses, pulled the cap down over her eyes, and turned up her jacket collar as far as it would go. It wasn't a perfect disguise, but it was as inconspicuous as she could make herself for CCTV. She pushed open one of the glass doors and made her way into a lobby that was as unremarkable as the inn's exterior. A young female receptionist stood behind a long wooden counter that had a round clock as the only backdrop. On the lobby's left there was a glass coffee table, and a sofa and two chairs that looked like they were made of synthetic leather. On the right there were two elevator doors. There were CCTV cameras on either side of the counter that she figured—given the lobby's small size—could capture the whole area. Ava hoped that Lop was correct that the cameras in the lobby were all there were.

Ava approached the counter and saw the receptionist was wearing blue jeans to go with a black T-shirt. The informality was reassuring when it came to assessing the inn's level of security.

"Hello, my name is Chow Qi and I have a reservation," Ava said, offering her passport.

"Yes, Ms. Chow, I was on duty when your uncle made the booking," the receptionist said as she took the passport and hardly glanced at it before handing it back, then punched some information into her computer. "We were holding a room for you on the fifth floor, but he said that one on the sixth that faced in the same direction would be even better. As it happens, a room on the sixth is available. Do you want it, or would you prefer to stay with his original booking?"

"I think I'll take the room on the sixth floor."

"That's not a problem. Now how will you be paying?"

"Is cash okay?"

"The room rate is eight hundred yuan."

Ava reached into her bag. "I'm only staying one night. So, here's one thousand to cover that and any incidentals."

"That will be fine," the woman said, entering more information.

A moment later, Ava made her way to the elevators, found one immediately available, and headed for the sixth floor. There were no CCTV cameras in the elevator, and none that she could see when she exited it. Room 608 was in the middle of the floor. Ava took a pair of latex gloves from her bag and put them on, then she tapped the door open and walked in to see everything she could have expected in a two- or three-star Chinese hotel. There was a double bed with a brown velour headboard and a mauve woollen blanket; a round table with two chairs by the window; a three-drawer dresser made of some kind of compressed wood; and a desk that was similarly constructed. She tossed her bags onto the bed and went to the window. The Tiangiao Theatre could not have been in clearer view. Ava took out her phone and called Lop.

"Hey, where are you?" he answered.

"I'm in room 608 at the Red Tree Inn."

"It's great you were able to get on that floor. Any problems?"

"None."

"I'll pass your room number to Jimmy and Sonny."

"Tell them to knock hard two times when they come to my door."

"I will," he said. "Now that you guys are set it comes down to Lin."

"I think it is almost sad—no, I think it is ironic that we're using Lin's love of another human being to avenge his cruelty to god knows how many others."

"At the end of the day we all get what we deserve. There's no escaping our final reckoning. I don't know when mine will come, but I hope that if we're successful this will count in my favour."

"Me too—and successful or not, I'll see you later tonight."

Ava carried her bag to the desk and took out her laptop. Instructions on how to connect to the inn's Wi-Fi were on a piece of paper taped to the top of the desk. She opened the computer, got online, and accessed her email. When she saw nothing that needed her attention, she unlocked her phone, found the pictures she had taken in the Canteen, and forwarded them to Fai with a message referring to the recipes that read: I have a nice surprise for you when I get home.

37

DURING HER DEBT COLLECTION DAYS THERE HAD BEEN
times when long waits were part of the job. Given that she
was naturally impatient, it was something she had to learn
to handle. But now, years away from that job, her impatience
had begun to assert itself again, and as she waited for Jimmy
and Sonny to arrive, she found herself bouncing between
watching television, checking her computer and phone, and
rather pointlessly going to the window to look at the theatre.
So it came as a sense of relief when just before five she heard
two hard knocks on the door. She opened it to see Jimmy
standing in the corridor with the golf bag, wearing a hoodie
tied tightly around his face.

"I hardly recognize you. Any problems downstairs?" she
asked, handing him a pair of gloves, then stepping aside to
let him into the room.

"None, they totally ignored me," Jimmy said. He took in
the room and asked, "Have you tried opening the window?"

"No."

"Do you mind if I do it?"

"Of course not."

He slipped the hoodie from his head, and then carried the golf bag across the room to the double-paned window that looked out onto the theatre. He pulled down a handle and swung the window open to one side. "It's the same as the room on the fifth floor. I didn't expect it would be any different, but you can never be completely sure."

"How will you set up?" she asked.

"I'll rest the rifle on the ledge," he said, and then pointed at the chairs by the table. "I'll need something to sit on. Is there anything else besides those?"

"There's a small wooden bench in the bathroom."

"Can I see it?"

"Sure," Ava said, and returned a moment later with the bench.

"That looks like it could be the perfect height," said Jimmy as he took the bench from her. He carried it to the window, set it on the floor, and then sat. He extended his left arm like it was a rifle and squinted down a sightline. "Yes, this will work just fine."

"You don't want to test it with your real rifle?"

"Not until it starts to get dark. Even though I know it would be a one in a million chance that someone would spot the rifle if I did it now, there's no reason to take that risk."

Ava went to sit at the desk, and Jimmy took a seat at the table. They had time to kill before Sonny was due to arrive, and as she had done in similar situations, she tried to change the focus from what lay ahead. "Tell me all about your grand-children," she said.

Jimmy smiled. "They are two beautiful little girls who are so damn smart that they can already run rings around me," he said.

For the next forty-five minutes, Ava asked questions and shared memories with Jimmy. Despite an army career as a munitions expert and sometime sniper, and despite his willingness to snipe in the past for Uncle—and now for her—he came across as a gentle, caring man. His wife had died from cancer in her late thirties, leaving him with a teenage daughter to raise. He had taken early retirement from the military to do just that, and when his daughter had married, divorced, and was left with two children, Jimmy had moved in with her to take care of them.

He had just finished explaining the education fund he had set up to help his granddaughters get through university when there were two knocks on the door. Ava opened it to find Sonny.

"Hi boss," he said.

"How did it go in the lobby?" she asked, again dispensing gloves.

"No one said a word to me," he said as he put them on.

"And you took the stairs from a lower floor."

"I got out of the elevator on the third."

"All good," she said.

Sonny nodded at Jimmy. "Hey, how's the view from there?"

"It couldn't be better," said Jimmy.

Ava returned to her seat at the desk while Sonny joined Jimmy at the table. She checked her watch. "Not that much longer to wait," she said and then looked at Jimmy. "Although I don't think I've ever seen you display even the slightest bit of impatience."

"You can't be a successful sniper without being patient. Sometimes I had to wait seven or eight hours before a target showed his head; and sometimes I waited longer than that and didn't have the chance to get a shot off."

"How frustrating was that when it happened?"

Jimmy shrugged. "It rarely was. I accepted it as just part of the job."

Ava's phone rang and she saw Lop's name. "*Wei*," she answered.

"Are Sonny and Jimmy there?" he asked.

"They are. Where are you?"

"I'm in place near the MSS compound. Did anyone have any problems at the inn?"

"No."

"How's the room? Does Jimmy like the sightline?"

"He does."

"So we're good to go. All we need now is for Lin to co-operate."

"That's out of our control, but we've been fortunate so far."

"Yeah," Lop said, and then he fell silent.

"Are you okay?" Ava asked.

"I'm just nervous. This is a really big fish we're going after. I don't want to screw it up. I keep going over and over the plan in case we've missed something."

"And have you found anything?"

"Not so far."

"Lop, I won't tell you to relax because I know you won't, but don't obsess."

"I'll try," he said and then laughed. "I'll be in touch with you as soon as that Red Flag limo makes an appearance."

Ava ended the call and saw Sonny and Jimmy looking questioningly at her. "Lop is a worrier. It is one of the traits that makes him so effective," she said.

38

AT SIX FORTY, WHEN THE SUN HAD COMPLETELY DISAP-
peared over the horizon, Jimmy reached into the golf bag
and took out the rifle with its telescopic sight and the night
vision attachment. Away from the window, he clipped on
the attachment.

"We should turn off the room lights now," he said to Ava.
She nodded and did as he asked.

At dusk, the theatre's exterior and interior lights—and
those that surrounded the plaza in front—had all come on.
As the darkness intensified, the lights seemed to grow stronger, and when the sun had actually set, the entire area was
bathed in so much light that it looked like it was noon on
a sunny, cloudless day. And luckily, smog and sand weren't
fouling the air.

Jimmy sat on the bench directly in front of the window,
placed the rifle on the ledge, and looked through the scope.

"How's the view?" she asked.

"Perfect. In fact, I'm not going to need the night vision clip.
And look, people are already starting to arrive."

Ava came to his side and looked across the road. The

area in front of the theatre wasn't yet crowded, but some cars and taxis were pulling up at the curb to deliver their passengers, a few of whom made their way inside the theatre, while others remained outside, smoking and chatting. They were almost uniformly well-dressed—most of the men in suits, and the women in dresses that even from a distance looked expensive.

"There are binoculars in the bag for you if you want to use them," Jimmy said.

Ava took two sets from the bag. "Do you want one?" she asked Sonny.

"Yeah, I'll need it later anyway."

Ava pulled a chair over next to Jimmy. Sonny did the same on his other side.

"You'll have to move back when we know Lin is on his way," Jimmy said. "I don't want to feel hemmed in."

"Of course," said Ava, putting the binoculars to her eyes and seeing traffic had picked up. "If the people who have already arrived are any indication, the place is going to be full."

"I'm surprised that so many like ballet. It's hardly a Chinese thing," Sonny said to Ava. "Have you ever been to one?"

"When I was eleven or twelve my mother took my sister and me to see *The Nutcracker.* Putting it on is a Christmas tradition for the National Ballet of Canada in Toronto. It's supposed to be one of the happier and livelier ballets, but it did nothing for me or my mother, and neither of us saw one again. I know Marian has gone a few times in Ottawa, but I don't know if that's because her husband's job obliged her to."

"Why did your mother take you in the first place?" Sonny asked.

"I think she thought it was a cultural event we should experience at least once. She did things like that quite often—dragged us to or enrolled us in things she thought would broaden our horizons, even though she had no real interest in them. Some of them did stick, though. My sister still plays the piano and I have my bak mai."

"Your mother was responsible for you learning that?"

"Not bak mai specifically—when I was ten or so she gave me the choice of playing the violin or learning a martial art. She told me later she was pleased I opted for martial arts because she had always believed a woman should know how to defend herself."

"Then she must be really happy with the way you turned out," Sonny said, turning back to the window and looking through his binoculars at the theatre. "A lot of those people don't seem interested in going inside. They're yakking away as if many of them know each other."

"They probably do. Ballet lovers would be an elite and rather small group in this city."

"Well I wish they'd get a move on and go inside," said Jimmy. "I don't want to have to deal with a last-minute rush."

Ava had her phone in her jacket pocket but had been resisting the temptation to check it. Lop would call when he had something to report, she told herself—and then, as if he'd heard her, the phone rang. She took it from her pocket and saw his name.

"Has he left the compound?" she answered.

"Well, a Red Flag limousine has."

"That's great news."

"It went past me a minute ago. It had a Communist Party flag on a pole on the left front fender. But Ava, I couldn't see inside. I know that doesn't come as a complete surprise, but it's disappointing all the same."

"We have to assume he's in there," she said.

"I know. I'm following the limo now at a safe distance. If it heads in any direction other than the one we expect, I'll call you."

"How long do you think it will take the limo to get to the theatre?"

"It took me twenty minutes to get to the compound from the inn, and traffic right now isn't any heavier."

Ava looked at her watch. "That would put the limo's arrival here at around seven fifteen."

"That's what I figure as well."

"I'll pass the information along to Jimmy."

Lop hesitated, and then said, "Good luck, I'll see you all shortly in the parking lot."

Ava ended the call. "That was Lop. A Red Flag limo has left MSS headquarters. It has a Communist Party flag flying from a pole on the left front fender. We can't be certain that it's coming to the theatre or that Lin is in it, but we'll know soon enough because the ETA is twenty minutes from now. Jimmy, that gives you time to go to the bathroom or take a break if you need one."

He shook his head. "I'm staying here."

Ava moved away from the window and sat at the desk. She knew it was going to be an interminably long twenty minutes, and so, looking for any distraction, she accessed the website of the *China Daily* newspaper. In the arts section there was an article about that evening's premiere of *Rite of Spring* with glowing comments about Lin Ai. The article ended with a quote from the ballet company's managing director saying it could be a night to remember. It could be indeed, Ava thought, but for an entirely different reason. She then turned to the business section and found an interesting story about cryptocurrency. Before she finished it she heard Sonny say, "There are so many goddamn people now."

She returned to the window and looked out at the theatre. There was a long stream of traffic at the curb, and in some spots cars were parked in a double line. The crowd on the plaza was now thick enough that people were forced to shuffle as they headed towards the theatre entrance. "That was sudden," she said. "But we are getting close to the scheduled show time."

"The good news is that most of them are going inside," said Jimmy.

Ava checked the time. "And we haven't heard from Lop, so that's good news as well."

For the next few minutes they watched the crowd as it began to disperse, and then Sonny suddenly said, "I think that's the limo."

Three sets of eyes swung to the right, where a stream of traffic was entering the complex. A large black block of a car sporting the Communist Party flag on its left fender had entered the area. There had to be twenty automobiles in front of it slowly making their way to the point where attendees were being dropped off.

Ava phoned Lop.

"*Wei*," he answered.

"We think the limo has arrived. Can you confirm it was the one you were following?"

"It is. I just watched it turn towards the theatre."

"Then we're on," she said, ending the call and looking down at Jimmy. "That's the limo that left the MSS compound."

"At the rate traffic is moving, I'd say it will be in position to unload its passengers in two or three minutes," he said, reaching into his back pocket and pulling out a photo. He held it close to his face, squinted at it, and then put it back. "Sonny and I looked at that at least fifteen times today. We have the face memorized, but it never hurts to have one last look. Sonny, you'll have your binoculars on that limo?"

"You know I will."

"I don't want to shoot the wrong man," Jimmy muttered.

"The limo is moving closer," Sonny said.

Jimmy rolled his shoulders, pressed his eye tight against the rifle's scope, and took a tighter grip on the weapon. "I'm ready," he said.

Ava lifted her binoculars to her eyes. The limo was idling as it waited for an suv to leave the curb. As soon as it did, the driver eased the Red Flag into that spot. She watched intently, hardly breathing. She expected the driver to open the doors for his passengers, but instead a man who had been riding in the front with him was the first one out of the car. He was a large man, at least six foot three or four, and wore a black suit. He stood on the sidewalk for a few seconds and took in the nearby activity. Ava immediately thought he was security. She watched as he opened the limo's front passenger door and said something to the driver. Seconds later the driver left the car and walked around the front to join his colleague. They chatted briefly, and then the large man nodded and opened the back door of the car.

A woman exited and moved a few feet away. The binoculars were powerful and Ava could see she was wearing what appeared to be black silk pants, a white silk blouse, and a red silk jacket—all of which looked expensive, but would only have cost a fraction of the necklace that alternated balls of green and white jade and was centered by a large diamond. She was middle-aged, impeccably coiffed, and looked distinguished.

"That must be the wife," Sonny muttered. "And here comes the man himself."

The man who got out of the car was wearing a navy blue suit and had a full head of hair that was combed straight back. But that was all Ava could see because he didn't turn to face them, and in fact didn't show any side profile. He held out his arm for the woman, she slipped hers through it, and they began to walk towards the theatre with the driver leading the way and the large man trailing close behind, his body shielding the man in the blue suit. There were people on every side of them, all heading in the same direction towards the doors.

"Is it him?" Jimmy asked.

"I don't know. I haven't seen his face," Sonny said. "But it must be him. Who else could it be?"

"Ava, did you get a look at his face?" asked Jimmy.

"No."

The crowd thickened as it neared the doors, came to a halt, and then started forward again in fits and starts.

"I'm catching glimpses of his back and the back of his head, but only very briefly," Jimmy said, his eye not leaving the scope. "If this was a war zone I might take a chance and shoot, but here it would be risky. And then there's the fact that we haven't actually identified him yet ... Ava, what do you want me to do?"

"We can't afford to shoot and miss, and even if we were to take the chance, there's no point in shooting the guy in the blue suit if we don't know for sure who he is. Let's wait. We may get a better view of him when they reach the doors."

The crowd continued to shuffle forward, and if anything became denser. The security detail pressed closer to their charges, almost forming a human cocoon around them. Ava watched in frustration as the group made their way up the last few steps, reached the doors, and disappeared inside.

"Shit, shit, shit," she said.

39

JIMMY DIDN'T MOVE UNTIL IT WAS OBVIOUS THAT THE man in blue suit was well inside the theatre and wasn't coming out. Then he laid the rifle on the floor next to him, sighed mournfully, looked up at Ava, and said, "I'm sorry."

"There's nothing you could or should have done any differently," she said. "There's no way I wanted you to shoot a man we couldn't identify."

"Ava's right. We had some bad luck, that's all. It isn't on you, Jimmy," Sonny said.

"Now what do we do?" Jimmy asked Ava, in a tone that suggested he was still blaming himself.

"I don't know. I want to talk to Lop, and we should take some time to think. Now please excuse me, I have to go to the bathroom."

Ava closed the door of the bathroom behind her, pulled down the top of the toilet seat, and sat down. Her reason for going in there was to be alone. Despite meaning what she had said to Jimmy, the disappointment of not getting a shot off ate at her. *We were so close, so damn close.*

She had brought her phone with her, and now called Lop.

"What happened?" he answered. "I didn't hear a shot, and everything looks normal in front of the theatre."

"We saw the limo, we saw who we thought was Lin get out, but we couldn't be sure it was him. We never saw his face, not even in profile. On top of that, even if it was him he was being shielded by his security detail and Jimmy never had a clear shot. I can't remember ever being quite so frustrated."

"Fuck," said Lop.

"Are you in the parking lot?"

"Yeah, I am now. How are Jimmy and Sonny reacting to it going off the rails?"

"Badly, and they're wondering what we should do next."

"We have flights booked out of Beijing that leave in a few hours."

Ava hesitated as a thought occurred to her. "What if we didn't take those flights?"

"What are you getting at?"

"Give me a second ..."

She left the bathroom and went directly to the window. Even without binoculars she could see the Red Flag limousine was still parked at the curb. She put the phone back to her ear. "Lin's limo hasn't moved. I'm guessing that it has VIP status and is allowed to wait to take him back to the compound when the show ends. If that's the case it means he'll leave the theatre through the same doors he went in, and he'll have to walk down the steps and across the plaza. If he does, we'll see his face, and Jimmy might be able to get a clean shot. The problem is that I calculate the ballet won't end until about ten o'clock, and if he goes backstage to see his daughter, it could be even later. That would mean we have virtually no chance of getting a flight out of Beijing until tomorrow morning. Would you be comfortable with that situation?"

"No, I wouldn't be, and for all the reasons we talked about earlier," he said immediately.

"Who says we have to fly out of here?" Sonny interrupted.

Ava looked at him. She had been so focused on Lop that she had almost forgotten that he and Jimmy were there and listening to her. "What are you suggesting?" she asked him.

"We could drive."

"Drive to where?"

"Anywhere you want, but if you're going to fly out of China, it should be to a city with an international airport."

"Sonny just suggested that if we stay to take another shot at Lin, we could leave Beijing by car," she told Lop. "He said we could catch flights from another city tomorrow. What do you think of that idea?"

Lop paused and then said carefully, "It might work." Then he paused again before saying, "I hate the thought of not finishing what we started. We've put in a lot of effort to get to this point."

"I feel the same way."

"And if we did manage to shoot Lin, the MSS's initial focus would be here in the city ... and Sonny could be right in thinking they might not immediately extend their reach beyond Beijing."

"So you're okay with Sonny's idea?"

"Yes," Lop said after a slight hesitation.

"Will it be a problem to leave the car in another city?"

"I rented it from a national chain so it shouldn't be."

Ava nodded. "So that leaves us with the decision of where to drive to. How long will it take to get from here to Shanghai?"

"If we take turns driving, and since we're driving at night, I'm guessing about eleven or twelve hours," he said. "But I'd prefer to go somewhere closer—the less time on the road the better. There have to be other options."

"We could go to Yantai. One time, Fai and I drove from Beijing to there to visit her parents. It took about seven hours. If our schedule here plays out as we expect, that would get us there around dawn," she said. "I know it has an international airport. I've flown from it. We could check on early-morning flight availability right now."

"Yes, why don't you do that," Lop said.

"Do you still want to go to Hong Kong with the guys?"

"No, I've changed my mind. I would prefer going to Shanghai."

Ava put her phone on speaker mode, carried it to the desk, and opened her laptop. She chatted with Lop as she began searching for flights from Yantai. Within ten minutes she confirmed there were direct flights to Shanghai for him, to Hong Kong for Jimmy and Sonny, and to Taipei, Seoul, or Osaka for her. "We can all be in the air before ten o'clock tomorrow morning," she said.

"Are you guys okay with all of this?" Lop asked.

"Of course we are," Sonny said loudly.

"Damn right," Jimmy said.

"Then it appears we finally have a Plan B," said Lop. "After I hang up I'll arrange my flight."

"And we'll do the same," Ava said.

"But we should keep our eyes on that limo," said Lop. "If it leaves for any reason without Lin then we're back to square one."

"I won't take my eyes off it," said Jimmy.

"Okay, so let's stay in touch," Ava said to Lop, ending that conversation, and then she turned to Sonny. "That was a really great idea."

"Thanks boss."

"Now let me get your flights booked. I'll need your credit cards and your names as they appear on your passports."

Ava put both men on a direct flight to Hong Kong that left Yantai at eight. She figured they would be leaving Beijing at eleven at the latest, and even allowing for an extra hour for the drive that gave them more than enough time to check in. Organizing her return to Toronto was more complicated. She tried getting there through Taipei and Osaka before settling on Seoul. As Jennie Kwong, she would be leaving Yantai at eight thirty on a ninety-minute Air Seoul flight. She would then have to wait four hours in Seoul for a United Airlines flight to San Francisco, and then there was a three-hour wait for an Air Canada flight to Toronto. It would be an exhausting trip, but the first leg from Yantai to Seoul was all that mattered, and no other flight got her out of China as quickly.

"You are both booked on a direct flight to Hong Kong that leaves at eight. Here is your flight information and reservation numbers," she said as she passed their credit cards and a page from her notebook to Sonny.

"Thanks, and are you set as well?"

"I leave for Seoul half an hour after you."

Sonny nodded, and then pointed to Jimmy, who was staring out of the window at the limousine. "We're thirsty and a little hungry. There's a 7-Eleven around the corner from here. I was going to get some soft drinks and a couple of sandwiches. Is that okay?"

"Sure."

"And do you want anything?"

"A bottle of water would be enough."

Ava watched Sonny leave, and then said to Jimmy. "I have some personal phone calls to make, and I'll do them from the bathroom. If things change in any way, knock on the door."

"Okay boss."

She went into the bathroom and sat on the lowered toilet seat. She had promised May and Fai she'd call when the action was over. It wasn't, but she knew they'd be worrying that they hadn't heard from her already. She phoned Wuhan first.

May answered on the first ring. "How did it go?" she blurted.

"It didn't, but we believe we'll have a second chance in two hours or so," Ava said.

"What went wrong?"

"We couldn't see our target properly so we held back, that's all. We're confident it will go better next time."

"And if you have the same problem?"

"One way or another I'll be leaving China tomorrow."

"I'm glad to hear that," said May. "But stay in touch tonight."

"I will. Talk to you later," Ava said, ending that call and immediately dialing Toronto.

"Hey," Fai answered with the sound of traffic in the background.

"Are you on the way to class?"

"No, I just stepped outside the apartment to get some fresh air. I didn't want to go to school until I'd heard from you."

"Unfortunately I have nothing to tell you, except that our

timetable has been set back by a couple of hours," she said. "There's no reason for you to hang around. Go to school. I'll leave you a voice message as soon as things are settled."

"Will they be?"

"We certainly think so, but whether they are or not, we are driving to Yantai tonight to catch flights. I'll email you my travel schedule later."

"Why Yantai?"

"It's a little complicated to explain, but basically we wanted to leave from any Chinese international airport that wasn't in Beijing. Yantai is the closest."

"Okay," Fai said, sounding doubtful.

"I'll have some time when I get there. Do you want me to call your parents?" Ava asked.

"Sure, they'd love to hear from you."

"Do they know anything about what's been going on with the film and the Oscars?"

"I haven't mentioned a word to them. Even if I did, I'm not sure they'd understand any of it."

"Then I won't say anything. Is Patricia still screening the reaction to your decision to turn down the nomination?"

"She is, so all I've seen are positive comments—and that's just fine with me."

"That was a good decision."

"But a minor one compared to the decisions you've been making. Please don't get careless now."

"So far we haven't put a foot wrong. That's not going to change tonight," Ava said. "Now do me a favour and go to class."

40

THE TIANQIAO THEATRE BEGAN TO EMPTY SHORTLY after nine thirty. There was no couch in the hotel room, and Ava and Sonny were sitting on the edge of the bed watching a Chinese variety show when Jimmy shouted that news at them. He had only left the window once to go to the bathroom during the previous two hours.

They went to join him. The Red Flag limousine was at the curb and was the only vehicle there. As far as they could tell, it was still unoccupied, and Ava assumed the security men were inside the theatre waiting for Lin and his wife. People were initially leaving the theatre in pairs and small groups, but as time passed it became a steady and more disorderly flow. Through her binoculars Ava saw many people making phone calls, and then smaller limos, taxis, and luxury cars began to enter the street to get their riders and customers.

Jimmy sat on the bench with his right eyed glued to the rifle scope that was fixed on the theatre's doors. Sonny stood slightly apart from him with his binoculars focused on the same spot.

"I hope he still has the security detail with him. It will make it easier to pick him out," said Sonny. "Right now I'm having a hard time telling one suit from another."

"The wife is wearing a red silk jacket," Ava said.

As the vehicles pulled away from the curb, they were quickly replaced, but not so quickly as to prevent the plaza from starting to take on the appearance of being occupied by a mob.

"I went to a Jacky Cheung concert once at the Hong Kong Coliseum. When it ended, it was like this—people crushed together trying to get out. I swore I'd never go to another one," Sonny said, without taking the binoculars from his eyes.

Ava glanced at him. It wasn't like him to be this talkative, and she guessed he was feeling stressed.

"So far, no red jacket and no security detail," Jimmy said a moment later. "And I don't think I've missed seeing very many of the people coming through those doors."

"It is possible that Lin and his wife went backstage to congratulate their daughter," Ava said. "It would be a normal thing to do—and if they did, this crowd will be thinned out or maybe even gone by the time they come out."

"Here's hoping," Jimmy said.

The theatre kept emptying and the scene at the curb became more chaotic. It distracted Ava a little but didn't seem to faze Jimmy and Sonny, who kept their eyes locked onto the people exiting through the doors.

By ten to ten the crowd on the plaza had noticeably shrunk, and the steady flow from the doors had been reduced to an occasional departure.

"Where the fuck are they?" Sonny said.

"They have to be still inside," said Ava. "Unless that Red Flag limo is a decoy—and why would it be?—they'll be coming out."

"Yes," Jimmy said suddenly, a hint of excitement in his voice.

"What?" Ava asked.

"I'm looking through the glass doors into the lobby, and I think I see the security guys."

"But not Lin?"

"No, but they could be getting into position to wait for him. He might have given them a time or been told that he's on his way."

"I can't see them," said Sonny.

"My scope is stronger than your binoculars, but look through the far left door. You might be able to see them leaning against a wall."

"Oh, yeah, there they are," Sonny said a few seconds later.

As she had earlier when Lin and his wife were making their way into the theatre, Ava found herself holding her breath. *This has to work—no, this is going to work*, she thought as she turned her binoculars to where Jimmy had indicated. The two security men were definitely there.

At least a minute passed without either of the men moving, and then the larger of the two suddenly straightened. His colleague quickly did the same. "Did you see that?" Ava asked.

"I did," said Jimmy, and then added, "I see them now. It is Lin. There's no mistaking that nose and moustache."

Ava watched as the smaller of the security men rushed to the exit door, opened it, and stood aside to let Lin and his wife pass. For a second Lin was clearly visible. "Jimmy ..." she said.

"I want him to get closer."

The foursome started down the steps to the plaza, the smaller guard in front of Lin and his wife; his partner behind them. Although he wasn't as large as his colleague, the guard in front was big enough to provide a lot of cover for Lin, and Ava began to worry that they had missed their chance when Lin came through the door. But she said nothing.

There weren't many people left on the plaza, and those that remained weren't close to the Red Flag limo. Lin and his wife quickly covered the ground between the theatre and the car, and Ava's fears about the missed opportunity spiked.

Then Jimmy said, "The one in front is going to open the door for Lin and his wife to get into the car. When he does ..."

Ava stared at the man, willing him to do what Jimmy had predicted.

The security guard paused when he reached the limo, put his hands around his eyes to look inside, and then took a step back and opened the door.

Crack.

Ava jumped, the noise from the rifle in their close environment surprising her, and for a second she closed her eyes. When she opened them, she saw Lin lying on the ground further from the car than he'd been. His chest was already bloody, and the colour was spreading.

Crack.

The noise was no longer surprising, but still unnerving. Her hands were sweaty and her grip on the binoculars was less than firm.

"The middle of the forehead. That was a great second shot," said Sonny.

"I wanted to make sure. You can recover from chest wounds," said Jimmy.

Ava surveyed the scene. Lin lay flat on his back, his arms and legs spread in various directions, his chest covered in blood, with more blood running down both sides of his nose. The smaller security guard knelt by the body as if he was still trying to protect it. Behind him, Lin's wife stood bent over, her shoulders crumpled, one hand covering her mouth in shock and disbelief. Some of the people still on the plaza were starting to congregate close to the body.

"He's looking in our direction," Sonny said suddenly.

"Who?" Jimmy asked.

"The other guard. In fact, I feel like he's staring directly at us."

"We're in the dark. He won't be able to see anything," said Jimmy.

"Maybe he saw the second shot."

Jimmy had taken his eye from the scope after shooting Lin in the forehead. Now he put it back.

Ava focused her binoculars on the guard. He did seem to be looking in the direction of the inn. Then he spun around and walked over towards his colleague, who was still kneeling next to Lin. She saw him try to move the onlookers back, and some of them retreated, but as soon as he left them they started to inch forward again. When he reached his colleague, he stood over Lin's body, shook his head in obvious resignation, and then turned and pointed towards the inn.

"He definitely has a sense that the shot came from this direction," she said.

The man went to Lin's wife, said something to her, took her gently by the elbow, and led her towards the car door that his colleague had opened. He helped her get inside, closed the door, and then looked towards the inn again.

Ava thought of Lop's concern that the MSS might quickly figure out where the shot had originated. His worries hadn't been misplaced.

"We need to get moving," she said. "We have a plan to follow, let's do it."

"He's talking on his phone, and he's starting to walk this way," Sonny said abruptly. "I don't know if he's coming to the inn."

Ava saw the guard had crossed the street in front of the theatre, and was about to enter a patch of ground that was poorly lit. "We can't risk that he is."

"No, we can't," said Jimmy, and fired his third shot.

The guard fell back as if he'd been hit by a two-by-four.

"It's quite dark there. The body will be hard to see. Hopefully no one will bother looking for him for a while," Jimmy said.

Sonny left the room first. Five minutes later, when Jimmy—with his hoodie tied around his head again—left, Ava reached for her phone and called Wuhan. When May answered, Ava said, "Everything here went as planned, but I can't talk now. I'll contact you later."

She then phoned Fai, and repeated that message when, as expected, the call went to voice mail.

With those obligations met, she put on her cap and glasses, and stayed at the window waiting for her turn to leave. What looked like two local police cars had arrived at the theatre, and the officers quickly cordoned off the area around Lin's body. The remaining security guard was talking to them, but he wasn't pointing at the inn. Just before Ava left, an ambulance pulled up behind the limo.

She gathered her things and hurried from the room.

When she reached the lobby, even more conscious that she was being captured by CCTV, she slowed her pace and acted as nonchalantly as she could. The desk clerk was busy on her phone and ignored her.

Ava turned right when she left the hotel, and a moment later saw Lop standing by the car in the parking lot. As she approached she saw Sonny was in the driver's seat with Jimmy sitting next to him. When she reached Lop he wordlessly took Fai's suitcase and Ava's Shanghai Tang Double Happiness bag from her and put them in the trunk.

Sonny started the car as soon as Ava and Lop got into the back seat.

"We're going directly to the highway," Lop said to Ava. "We'll ditch the rifle and the golf bag somewhere between here and Yantai."

"Sonny told you about the security guy?"

"He did."

"If he told his partner where he thought the shot might have come from, the MSS will soon be all over the inn," she said. "You were right to insist that we get out of Beijing as fast as possible."

"We still need our luck to hold for another twelve hours or so," he said.

Ava turned and looked behind them at the theatre receding in the distance. Then she gently laid one hand on Jimmy's shoulder, and the other on Sonny's. "I can't thank the two of you enough."

"*Momentai*, boss," said Sonny.

Jimmy simply nodded his head, his eyes fixed on the road.

He looked sad, Ava thought, and she wondered if shooting the guard—however natural his reaction had been—was something he was now starting to regret. That question was on the tip of her tongue when the car began to ascend a ramp onto the highway that would take them southeast to Yantai, but she decided it was better left unasked.

41

DESPITE THE TIME OF NIGHT, TRAFFIC WAS HEAVY UNTIL they reached the outskirts of Beijing, and even then they hit slow patches for another fifty kilometres. Lop repeatedly kept looking behind them as if he was expecting they were going to be pursued, and Ava noticed how everyone tensed when they passed a police patrol car sitting on the side of the highway.

They rode in silence—Sonny focused on the road, the others lost in their thoughts. It wasn't until they were more than one hundred kilometres from Beijing that someone spoke. They had passed a sign that said they were twenty kilometres from the city of Tianjin when Lop said, "Sonny, when we get to Tianjin I would like you to take the exit to the city centre. The Haihe River runs through there, and it is deep and dirty enough to be the perfect final resting place for the rifle."

"How do you know about the river?" Ava asked.

"I was posted in Tianjin for a while."

Ten minutes later, Sonny exited the highway, and a few minutes after that they were driving alongside the Haihe.

They were separated from the river by a swath of grass and a walkway that ran down its side. Traffic wasn't heavy, and there weren't many pedestrians taking a late-night stroll along the dimly lit riverbank, but there wasn't the privacy that would have been ideal.

"How are you going to handle this?" Ava asked Lop.

"I'll hold the rifle tight against my right leg with Sonny walking next to me. If he stays close enough the rifle shouldn't be visible. When we get to the river, I'll wait until we're more or less alone, then slide it quietly into the river."

Sonny stopped the car in a spot where any pedestrians were at least fifty metres away. He and Lop quickly got out, opened the trunk, removed the rifle, and side by side walked to the river. A moment later they were back.

"That river is filthy. No one is going to find that rifle unless they know where to look," Sonny said.

They returned to the highway with the mood in the car considerably lightened. It seemed to Ava that disposing of the rifle had helped put the evening's events behind them.

"What are we going to do with the golf bag?" Jimmy asked.

Lop began to scroll on his phone. "According to this, we're three and a half hours from Weifang. We'll find someplace there to get rid of it."

That someplace turned out to be a dumpster behind the restaurant in a service centre ten kilometres from Weifang.

Ava checked her watch as they pulled away. "It's not quite four. We're making good time. We should get to the airport before six. As I remember it is actually situated about fifty kilometres this side of Yantai, so we won't actually see the city."

"Is there much to see?" asked Lop, sounding more relaxed now that the bag was gone.

"It sits on the coast of the Bohai Sea and has some nice views. It was a major fishing port, and in fact Fai's father fished for scallops and her mother worked in a fish processing plant," said Ava. "But I think fishing now takes a back seat to wine production. Fai claims it is the largest wine-producing area in Asia, and one of the brands—Changyu—has earned a reputation for good quality. Maybe we can pick some up at the airport."

"You know I don't drink wine, but maybe I'll buy some for my girlfriend," said Sonny.

"And me for my daughter, although I've never tasted any wine that is better than a well-brewed beer," Jimmy said.

That started a discussion among the men about the merits of various beers and then liquors. Ava just listened, pleased to hear them banter. It helped pass the time and they were still talking when they saw the first sign for Yantai Penglai International Airport.

"We've made it," Ava said.

The sun was rising on the horizon when minutes later Sonny took the exit for the airport.

"Go to the eHi lot," Lop said.

Sonny followed the signs to the rental car compounds, driving past Hertz and Avis to get to eHi. He parked the car in the area for returns, and Lop got out and went inside the rental office. The others got their bags from the trunk, and then walked to the spot where they could catch a bus to the terminal. Ava could see Lop through a window talking to an agent. It seemed to be an animated discussion, and for the first time since leaving Beijing she felt a touch of disquiet. A bus arrived but Lop was still inside and Ava wasn't about to leave without him.

"What the hell is going on?" Sonny asked.

"I'll find out," said Ava.

She entered the rental office to see another agent had joined the one Lop had been speaking to. "Is there a problem?" she asked.

"They're saying I should have made an arrangement to drop the car off here. They want to charge me an extra fee that's almost as much as the car cost to rent."

"How much is that?"

"More than two thousand yuan."

Ava reached into her bag and took out the credit card she had in Jennie Kwong's name. She passed it to one of the men behind the counter. "Here, charge it to this."

"Why would you argue with them about that?" she asked Lop when they left the office.

"Sorry, I just overreacted to the idea of being ripped off."

"We need to get you on a plane and back to Shanghai. And when you get there, take some time off. Or if you want to, take a holiday. I'll pay for it."

"I'll crash for a few days," Lop said, and then looked at his phone as it rang. He answered. "Chou, this is a strange time to call."

He and Ava walked to the bus area. Lop had the phone pressed to his ear, and as he listened his face became grim. He was still listening when they got on the bus and during the ride to the terminal. It wasn't until they were inside that he ended the call. "Holy shit," he said.

"What was that about?" Ava asked.

"I think we should talk about this alone."

"Guys, excuse us, but Lop and I need to have a word," she said to Sonny and Jimmy. "Why don't you check in? We'll catch up to you inside."

"No problem," Sonny said.

"You're the boss," said Jimmy.

When they left, Lop said softly, "That was a friend—a close friend of mine who works for the MSS. He's the one who told me about Lin's daughter. He said they had more than a hundred men scouring the area near the theatre all night. The Red Tree Inn is at the top of their list of the possible locations the shooter might have used. Among others, they are looking for a woman named Chow Qi, and a guy with a golf bag."

"Among others?"

"Evidently, and luckily, you weren't the only person who was checked in to a room looking out on the theatre and didn't spend the night there."

"Where are they looking?"

"It's local for now; and by local he means Beijing. He suggested that *if I knew* the woman or the guy with the bag, it might be smart to tell them to avoid any public area such as an airport, bus depot, or train station. They are already distributing photos taken from CCTV."

"That was good of him to warn you,"

"We have a bond," Lop said, in a way that suggested Ava not ask if the friend could be totally trusted.

"I don't think they'll ever identify Jimmy from photos. He was wearing a hoodie tied so tightly around his head that I barely recognized him when he came to my room," she said. "I did what I could to disguise my face. I certainly looked different than I normally do."

"That's one less worry, but your photo will still be everywhere. Today it will be Beijing, but tomorrow who knows where—Shanghai, Guangzhou, Wuhan, Hong Kong?"

315 THE FURY OF BEIJING 315

"What are you saying?"

He looked pensive. "I don't think you should plan on coming back to China or Chinese-controlled territories any time soon."

"I wasn't, but I have family in Hong Kong, and friends and businesses in many parts of China."

"Well, we can hope that no one identifies you from the photos the MSS will distribute. I'll stay in touch with my contacts who'll know if a name is ever attached to the photos."

42

NONE OF THEM HAD ANY DIFFICULTY CHECKING IN FOR their flights from Yantai, and after passing through passport control and security without a problem, Ava said goodbye to Lop, and then walked with Sonny and Jimmy to their departure gate. Their flight was already preboarding so there wasn't time for much more than a round of hugs.

"I can't thank both of you enough for everything you've done for me," Ava said, suddenly feeling emotional to the point of having tears in her eyes.

"Anything, anytime, anywhere, boss," Sonny said.

"The same goes for me," said Jimmy.

"Uncle used to tell me that there's nothing more important in life than having friends you can trust, and I've been blessed in that regard," she said, and then spoke directly to Sonny. "Listen, I'm not sure when I'll be coming back to Hong Kong, but we should have a schedule, so if nothing else we can talk regularly by phone."

"Okay, boss, whatever you say."

"And you need to keep in contact with Uncle Fong. I don't want him going off the tracks again."

"I'll keep an eye on him."

She nodded, and raised herself up on tiptoe to kiss Sonny on both cheeks. "See you," she said, then she turned and walked away before he could see her tears.

Her flight boarded on time, sat a bit longer at the gate than she would have liked, but eventually made its way to the runway and took off. As the plane began its initial climb, she felt a sense of relief that was as intense as any she could remember. She was safe, she thought, and the level of her relief was an indication of the feeling of pressure she'd been keeping under control.

The hour and a half flight landed in Seoul on time, which gave her four hours to kill before the next one. She phoned Fai, but her phone was off, and when Ava calculated the time difference she figured she was at language school.

"It's me. I'm in Seoul so there was no problem getting out of China. Time was tight in Yantai so I didn't have the chance to call your parents," she said. "I'll see you soon, but if there's any change in my flight schedules I'll let you know. Love you."

Her next call was to Xu, and as usual it was Auntie Grace who answered the house phone.

"Ava, I'm sorry, he's not here," she said. "He was visiting with a woman last night and he didn't come home. You should try his cellphone."

"That's okay, I don't want to disrupt his love life. But when you do see him tell him I called from Seoul and that I'm heading back to Toronto. I'll phone him when I get there."

May Ling was in her office when Ava reached her, and quickly patched Amanda into the call.

"I'm so glad you're safe," May said.

"There was never any real direct danger, but Lop thinks I should keep a low profile for a while, and that means staying out of Asia."

"I couldn't agree with him more," said May. "We can run the businesses together at a distance."

"Yes, we can," Amanda added. "But what do you want me to tell your father? Michael and I are seeing him and Elizabeth tonight for dinner, and whenever I do he asks me when your next trip to Hong Kong will be. You know I'm not a good liar."

"Just say that I don't have any plans to travel, and that given everything that has happened, I don't want to be apart from Fai—and there is truth in that."

"I'm so happy you two are together," May said. "And listen, you should take a break when you get back to Toronto. Go away with Fai on a holiday somewhere."

"She's attending language school, and I don't want to spend my days doing nothing but waiting for her to come home, so I'd rather keep busy. We've still got that ginseng project to pursue. If neither of you have any objections, I'll meet with the farmer and see if there's a deal to be done."

"Please do that. I think there's a fantastic opportunity for us in ginseng," said Amanda.

It was a twelve-hour flight from Seoul to San Francisco, and Ava slept for about ten. When the plane landed—and even though she was in transit—Ava had to clear US Customs and Immigration, and it turned out to be an arduous, frustratingly long process that didn't leave her that much time to get to the gate for her connecting flight. But she got there, and her flight to Toronto left on schedule.

Rested, stress-free, and with home in her sights, Ava

found herself thinking about the past week. In retrospect, she couldn't have predicted or expected it to have gone as smoothly as it had. It was as if fate had decided that Chen and Lau Lau had to be avenged, and put into place the sequence of events that made that possible. Ava's life had rarely run in such a straight line, and she knew it was something she should assume would never happen again. Uncle had always preached caution, and the week had been anything but cautious. Still, they'd pulled it off, and now she could expect her life to revert to its more usual ups and downs.

But as her thoughts turned to the immediate future, she wondered what being "usual" meant. For more than fifteen years, getting on a plane to go to Hong Kong, China, or other parts of Asia had been as common for her as getting on a GO train was for commuters going into Toronto to work. Now that seemed to be out of bounds indefinitely, as was any physical contact with her friends, partners, and family in Asia, unless they were willing to come to Canada. Maybe some of them would, she thought, and that idea appealed to her. She had been hosted more times than she could count by May, Amanda, and Xu, and she'd love the chance to repay their hospitality. But how could she accommodate them in her rather small condo? Maybe it was time to buy a bigger place. Maybe it was time for her and Fai to buy a place together, a place that could be their home. Doing that would be a very large commitment for both of them, but that thought made her happy rather than scared. How would Fai react to that idea? *I'm getting miles ahead of myself*, she thought, but she still reached for her bag to retrieve a notebook.

Ava wasn't given to daydreaming, but that's what she did

for most of the flight as she filled a page of the notebook with the names of Toronto neighbourhoods that she thought they'd enjoy, and with the things she'd like to have in the ideal house or condo.

As they prepared to land, she looked out of the window and saw the highways were snow-covered. She had hoped that Fai would meet her at the airport, but the weather looked nasty and Fai was a reluctant winter traveller.

International air traffic was light going into Pearson in the early evening, and Ava quickly cleared customs and collected the suitcase that held the possessions Fai had wanted from her house. She exited the arrivals hall, stopped to see if Fai had braved the weather, and when there was no sign of her, walked in the direction of the limousine area.

She turned on her phone as the limo left the airport, and saw she had two messages from Xu and one from Lop. They were brief, and simply asked her to call them when she could. They would have to wait, she thought, as she dialled Fai's number.

"Hey babe, I've landed, and I'm on my way home," she said when Fai answered.

"I know, I've been tracking your flight," Fai said, her voice tinged with excitement. "I wanted to come to the airport to meet you, but I had a Zoom meeting that finished only half an hour ago."

"What kind of meeting?"

"It was with Hal Levine and one of his assistants," she said, her excitement growing.

"Hal Levine, the film director?"

"Yes. We spoke for close to an hour, and it was entirely in English."

"That's fantastic, but what did you speak about?"

"After he complimented me on *Tiananmen*, and said he understood and admired the position that Sils and I had taken, he talked about a lead role in the next film he intends to make—an English-speaking role."

"He offered it to you?"

"Kind of, but he wants his agent to get together with mine to go over some details. The problem is, now that Chen's dead, I don't have an agent. When I told him that he gave me the names of several in LA that he thinks are competent. I'll be making those calls tomorrow."

"Oh, Fai, I couldn't be happier for you."

"It's a start, isn't it—another step towards establishing my life here."

"We'll have to celebrate."

"We will. I bought a bottle of champagne."

Ava saw that traffic was moving steadily, if slowly. "I figure I'll be home in about forty-five minutes."

"I'll put it on ice."

"And decide what you want to have for dinner. We'll order in."

"Okay, see you soon."

Ava hung up, feeling elated. Fai had worked so hard to learn English that she deserved the chance to demonstrate she could act in that language as well as in Chinese. Ava checked the time. It was early morning in Shanghai, but she expected Xu would already be out of bed so she called his number.

"Auntie Grace, it's Ava," she said when the housekeeper answered.

"Wait a minute, dear. I'll get him. He's been waiting for

your call," she said in a tone more sombre than was usual.

What's up? Ava thought, immediately on edge.

"Ava …" he said seconds later.

"Is everything okay? Has something happened to Lop?" she blurted.

"No, he's fine, and he said to tell you that both Sonny and Jimmy had no difficulties when they got to Hong Kong."

"Thank goodness, I was going to call Sonny later. I also have a message from Lop asking me to phone him."

"You needn't bother with that. He told me what he was going to tell you."

"Which is?"

"The MSS have pulled out all the stops in their search for Chow Qi, even though his sources tell them they believe the name is an alias. Your photo, or should I say photos, are posted at every airport and train station in the country, and every media outlet has been featuring them. Auntie Grace and I just saw them on the morning news."

"He warned me that might happen."

"Except, it's more intense that he could have anticipated," Xu said. "They've also doctored a photo of you that was taken from a face-on angle that had you wearing sunglasses, a hat, a raised collar, and your hair hanging around your face."

"Doctored how?"

"They've removed the sunglasses and hat, and then through some kind of facial reconfiguration have posted four versions of what you might look like. One of them is uncannily close to being accurate."

"That's not good. So what can we do about that?"

"I've arranged for some of my men and their wives or girl-friends to contact local authorities to tell them that they've spotted Chow Qi in Shanghai. We'll spread out the calls, and we'll keep changing the locations where you were spotted, but my hope is that it will focus all of their attention on Shanghai. If nothing else it will keep them busy tracking down leads, and if it's necessary we'll do it for weeks—if not months."

"Thank you for that."

"I wish I could do more."

"*Ge ge*, as usual you have done more than enough."

Xu hesitated, and then said, "Lop doesn't think you should come back to China."

"I've already decided that China, Hong Kong, and any other part of Asia where the Chinese government can reach out to grab someone will not be part of any travel plans for the foreseeable future."

"Lop thinks that it might be smart to never set foot in China or Hong Kong again."

"Never is a long time," she said, slightly taken aback by how insistent Xu sounded.

"And this government, and the people, have long memories and a long reach."

"I understand that, and I won't go anywhere near China until you think it's safe."

"That's a relief, but we'll find other ways to stay in touch, yes? We can't lose contact. I don't want us to drift apart."

"Of course, and I was actually thinking on the plane that it would be wonderful if you and Auntie Grace could visit us here."

"I'm not sure I could get her to leave Shanghai and the house, but I like the idea of seeing Canada."

"We would look after you very well. And I hope you don't

mind if I raise the question of when you're coming every time we talk. I'll be a pest."

Xu laughed. "Ava, I love you any way you are."

"And I love you."

(43)

AS OMINOUS AS XU'S WARNING HAD BEEN, IT DIDN'T
affect Ava in any substantial way. She'd already made a
decision, and whether it extended to a year or five years or
longer, she was at peace with it. Living with Fai in Toronto
had made the city more of a home than it had ever been,
and she would be content spending most of the year there.
And if they felt the urge to travel, there was a large world
that existed outside of Asia and the reach of the Chinese
government.

There was one question, though, that niggled at her as the
limo turned into Yorkville and headed towards the condo.
The question was—what if Fai didn't feel the same way? She
had her parents in Yantai; she had the house in the hutong;
she had a host of friends; and Ava couldn't discount the
possibility that she might eventually want to go back. The
thought of Fai leaving knotted her stomach, and Ava took
deep breaths to help her relax.

The limo stopped at the condo building's front door, and
when the concierge saw Ava, he came outside to help her
with her bags and Fai's suitcase.

"I hope you had a good trip," he said as he carried the case and one bag to the elevator.

"It was excellent."

"Everyone in the building is talking about Ms. Pang. They're very proud of her."

"And so they should be," said Ava. "Now, if you don't mind, I'll manage on my own from here."

The door to the apartment opened almost as soon as Ava got to it. She pointed to the suitcase. "I brought your stuff."

"My stuff can wait," Fai said, wrapping her arms around Ava's neck.

They stood pressed against each other for nearly a minute, and when Ava was finally inside and had put the luggage by the door, Fai said, "The champagne is cold. Why don't I pour two glasses, and then I'll bring them and the bottle into the bedroom."

"That's a great idea," said Ava.

They made love, drank champagne, made love again, drank more, and then lay naked with Fai's head resting on Ava's shoulder, an arm and leg draped over her. "I want you to tell me all about Beijing," she said.

"I'd rather hear about Hal Levine."

"No, I want you to go first."

So Ava did, trying not to forget a single detail, including Lop's opinion about the inadvisability of visiting China or any place within its sphere of influence. As she finished, Ava said, "But that doesn't mean you can't travel there. You have the deal we cut in LA. It should protect you."

"Why would I want to go there or anywhere without you?"

"I'm just saying," Ava said, pulling her closer.

"Besides, I think this past week or two has brought closure

to that part of my life. This is my new life. This is where I want to be, and the fact that I may be able to continue my career here makes it all the sweeter. But even if I can't, I wouldn't want to be anywhere else or with anyone else."

"I do love you so much," Ava said.

Fai turned her head and looked into Ava's eyes. "There is one thing I would like to ask though. I've been thinking about it for a while, but I could never find the nerve to follow through."

"What's that?" Ava said, curious and nervous at the same time.

Fai stared at her and pursed her lips, as if she was gathering her courage. "Can we get married?" she asked.

Ava closed her eyes and drew in a short, sharp breath. "Yes, let's," she said.

ACKNOWLEDGEMENTS

GIVEN THAT *FURY* IS PROBABLY THE LAST BOOK IN THE Ava Lee series, I want to take the opportunity to thank the people who helped me on the journey I've been on since that day in July 2009 when the name Ava Lee initially popped into my head, and I wrote the first sentence of what would become *The Water Rat of Wanchai*. At the time, that book was simply titled *Ava Lee 1*, and the next three books were initially titled *Ava Lee 2*, *Ava Lee 3*, and *Ava Lee 4*. What a lack of imagination that displayed.

Before Ava, I had tried writing a novel a couple of times, but the results were in my mind so dismal that the manuscripts simply ended up in a drawer—not read by anyone. When I finished the first Ava I felt different; I felt I had something that worked. So I gave the manuscript to my wife, Lorraine, to read. If she had said, "no good," or words to that affect, another MS would have ended up in the drawer. Instead she was encouraging, and suggested I search for a publisher. I did, only to quickly discover that most publishers prefer to deal with an agent, and so I set out to find one. Through a series of fortunate events I managed to meet with

Bruce Westwood and Carolyn Forde of Westwood Creative Artists, and they took me on. For most of the next thirteen years I dealt mainly with Carolyn, and couldn't have been more pleased with her commitment and efforts. When she left Westwood for other challenges, I dealt with Bruce directly and he was as able. My thanks to both of them.

Getting an agent was one thing, finding a publisher was another. But eventually the books found their way to House of Anansi Press. At the time, Anansi was considered to be mainly a literary and poetry publishing house, and I wasn't sure what they wanted with me. But they offered a four-book deal, which we accepted, and the real work began. My first editor was Janie Yoon. We ended up doing ten books together, and along the way she taught me a lot about writing. When she took on another role at Anansi, Doug Richmond stepped into her role with me, and now we've done ten books together—including *Fury*. I haven't worked with any other editors, but I can't imagine them being better than Janie and Doug. They improved every book I wrote, and I'm grateful for their dedication, patience, and help. So again thanks are in order.

Once the books were written and edited, though, they needed to be promoted, marketed, and distributed. At the start, pushing those efforts was Sarah MacLachlan, the publisher, Matt Williams, executive VP, Barbara Howson, marketing VP, and Laura Meyer, head of publicity. They did a heck of a job. The Ava books won and/or were nominated for several awards, and were consistently on the bestseller lists. I can't tell you how much I appreciated their efforts.

But the publishing industry is fluid, and over the years I worked with a constantly changing cast. Sarah was the longest-serving publisher by far, but she was followed by

Bruce Walsh, Leigh Nash, and now Karen Brochu. Prior to becoming publisher, Karen was VP of sales, marketing, and publicity—having replaced Barbara seven or eight years ago. Laura Meyer was one of seven publicists I worked with in a job that was often quite thankless. I hope it isn't too late to thank all of them now.

In addition to the staff at Anansi, I had support from a wide range of outside sources including first readers (too many to name, and I don't want to offend anyone by omitting them), and fans from all over the world who kept in touch and brightened many a gloomy day. Then there were people in the book business, or leading supporters of the book business, and two of them deserve special recognition—Steele Curry from Calgary, a book collector extraordinaire, and Barbara Peters, the owner of the fabulous Poisoned Pen book store in Phoenix.

Lastly, I want to thank the thousands of readers I spoke to or met at literary festivals and libraries all over North America—Vancouver, Whistler, the Sunshine Coast, Banff, Medicine Hat, Pincher Creek, Edmonton, Calgary, Hay River, Yellowknife, Fort Smith, Cape Breton, Halifax, Saint John, Moncton, Fredericton, Montreal, Quebec City, the Eastern Townships, Ottawa, Kingston, Guelph, Windsor, Sarnia, Kitchener, London, Hamilton, Niagara-on-the-Lake, Albany, Long Beach, New Orleans, New York City, Minneapolis, Phoenix ... and I know there are some I'm missing.

I need to add although this might be the last Ava, I hope it won't be my last book. I intend to keep writing. I'll never match the nineteen books in the Ava/Uncle series, but it will be enough for me to write at least a few more books that are memorable.

Finally, with regard to *Fury*, the book was a joy to write, but, as always, it wasn't without its challenges. Helping me work my way through those was my editor, Doug Richmond, the eagle-eyed copyeditor, Gemma Wain, and on the production side, Jenny McWha. My thanks to each of them.

IAN HAMILTON is the acclaimed author of sixteen books in the Ava Lee series, four in the Lost Decades of Uncle Chow Tung series, and the standalone novel *Bonnie Jack*. National bestsellers, his books have been shortlisted for the Crime Writers of Canada Award (formerly the Arthur Ellis Award), the Barry Award, and the Lambda Literary Prize. BBC Culture named him one of the ten mystery/crime writers who should be on your bookshelf. The Ava Lee series is being adapted for television.

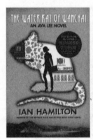  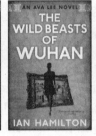  
    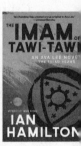
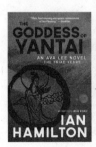 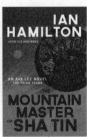   

ALSO AVAILABLE
from House of Anansi Press

The Lost Decades of Uncle Chow Tung

Book 1

Book 2

Book 3

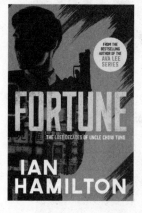

Book 4

houseofanansi.com
ianhamiltonbooks.com

ALSO AVAILABLE
from House of Anansi Press

"Hamilton, author of the Ava Lee mystery series, turns in a stellar performance in this stand-alone…Hamilton pulls us into the story with carefully crafted characters, and keeps us involved by increasing the complexity of the tale: introducing a mystery here, uncorking a shocking revelation there. The book is a departure from the author's more traditional mystery fiction, but his fans will find much here that is familiar: realistic dialogue, characters they can care about, and a gripping story."—*Booklist*

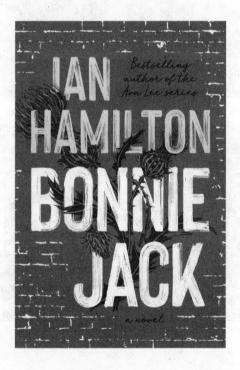

houseofanansi.com
ianhamiltonbooks.com